The Fal...

Vanessa kn... ...ad been in racing
her fiery mou... ...ugh the park—applying
her reins as a ... ...lash to quicken his stride—
when he had reared and thrown her to the ground.

Now she lay in pain, and leaning over her was the
handsome Sir Philip Langhorne.

She knew that he once had been a physician,
indeed practiced that profession still, and she thanked
Providence that he had happened to be here to
come to her aid.

Then she heard his voice. "Sleep, you must sleep,"
he was saying as his eyes caught and held hers.

She remembered something else about him. That
he could bend another to his will with that mesmerizing gaze. That she should be on guard.

But already it was too late. Vanessa was spell-
bound. . . .

The Dangerous Dr. Langhorne

Ellen Fitzgerald

The Dangerous Dr. Langhorne

A SIGNET BOOK

NEW AMERICAN LIBRARY

PUBLISHED BY
THE NEW AMERICAN LIBRARY
OF CANADA LIMITED

NAL BOOKS ARE AVAILABLE AT QUANTITY DISCOUNTS
WHEN USED TO PROMOTE PRODUCTS OR SERVICES.
FOR INFORMATION PLEASE WRITE TO PREMIUM MARKETING DIVISION.
NEW AMERICAN LIBRARY. 1633 BROADWAY.
NEW YORK. NEW YORK 10019.

Copyright © 1985 by Ellen Fitzgerald

First Printing, October, 1985

2   3   4   5   6   7   8   9

SIGNET TRADEMARK REG. U.S. PAT. OFF. AND FOREIGN COUNTRIES
REGISTERED TRADEMARK—MARCA REGISTRADA
HECHO EN WINNIPEG, CANADA

SIGNET, SIGNET CLASSIC, MENTOR. PLUME, MERIDIAN
AND NAL BOOKS are published in Canada by The New American
Library of Canada, Limited. 81 Mack Avenue, Scarborough,
Ontario. Canada M1L 1M8
PRINTED IN CANADA
COVER PRINTED IN U.S.A.

Prologue

Philip Langhorne, dreaming of his native Yorkshire, opened his eyes from a vision of spring, a view of tender green grass and bright wildflowers carpeting the moors. The cerulean-blue skies were dappled with clouds that cast their uneven shadows over the hills. Black-and-yellow butterflies flitted about, larks sang in the trees and, on occasion, young hares bounded out of their holes, their soft nostrils twitching. Fuzzy yellow ducklings floated on the ponds and small, ugly cygnets sailed downstream in the wake of their magnificent parents.

As consciousness reasserted itself, Philip wondered why he should be thinking specifically of May. Then, as he staggered wearily from his cot and stumbled toward the entrance of the tent, he knew why. As he had left for his brief two hours of rest, he had heard one of the young soldiers carried to what passed as a field hospital say in pain-filled but ironic tones, "Heigh-ho for the merry, merry month of May!"

May.

Emerging from the tent and heading for that same hospital, Philip glanced upward at hazy, smoke-filled skies. The pallid sun beat down relentlessly. The stench of gunpowder was in his nostrils, and the sporadic sounds of rifle fire, the deep boom of cannon, as well as distance-diminished cries, shouts, screams, groans, and occasional bursts of mirthless laughter, melded into the amorphous roar that would, he knew, always define war to him.

Jarvis, that wonderfully calm, efficient young man who had been pressed into service as his assistant, raised weary eyes as Philip joined him in the tent housing the wounded and the dying.

"They say we might've 'ad a victory 'ere, sir," he called. "We'll be 'earin' soon."

Their glances locked in wordless communion. Then Philip said the expected "Fine, fine."

He did not need to cite the toll that possible victory had taken, would take before the British pulled out of this small obscure village called Albuera. It was not a time to mourn the dead or pity the maimed. Detachment was required. Fortunately, his years of serving on the Peninsula had conditioned Philip so that he no longer inwardly quailed when he approached the gory table on which he performed so many, many hasty operations.

Nathaniel Davis, a fellow physician, bent over that table. The orderlies had just borne off one patient, and two more lay on bloodstained planks awaiting his ministrations. A third man, his arm in a sling, knelt beside one of the wounded. His battered scarlet regimentals identified him as a captain in the Tenth Foot. As Philip looked at him, he raised his head, turning weary, anxious eyes on him.

With a slight start, Philip recognized John Ventriss, Lord Greysham, who, until they had gone into battle, had appeared to regard war as an entertainment or a game. Probably it had been a game he played often as a lad, he and his wounded companion. They were close friends, the Earl of Greysham and the Marquess of Carlton, two of a kind, a kind Philip did not admire. They were tall, handsome, arrogant, and overly eager for personal glory, often at the expense of the troops they headed. He had actually had words with Carlton on the subject. His remarks had not been well-received. Carlton did not accept criticism from those he considered his social inferiors.

Consequently, it was with some reluctance that Philip moved to the marquess' side. It was a pity that Davis had not yet attended to him. Carlton would have preferred his colleague, he knew, but he could not dwell on such petty considerations at this moment. As he cast a knowing eye over the marquess' battered body, he met Greysham's anguished stare. His friend was badly hurt. Blood seeped from a wound in his shoulder, but his right leg was in worse condition. The limb was badly mangled. There was only one treatment he could prescribe for it.

"Johnny . . ." Carlton opened anguished eyes.

"I am right here, Charlie," Greysham assured him. "And the physician as well." He glanced up at Philip and averted his eyes quickly, but not quickly enough for Philip to miss the sudden sparkle of tears.

He frowned. Greysham had no business being there, as he must know. Carlton did not need his sympathy or his comforting words. He needed only the services of an experienced physician and, afterward, a hopefully quick journey back to England. He looked over his shoulder at Davis. "You can leave us now, Nat," he said.

Visiting a grateful look on his colleague, Davis rose stiffly, his expression revealing what was unnecessary to put into words. It spoke volumes about weariness, helplessness, and anger over the conditions under which they must needs deal with life and, more often, death. Philip himself had been too exhausted to talk when Davis had relieved him. The dream of an English May was fast receding.

He glanced quickly at the other casualty next to Carlton. Clearly the marquess was the more needful. He summoned a pair of waiting orderlies, and pointing to Carlton, said crisply, "Bring him to the table, please."

Greysham came to stand beside Philip as he examined Carlton's leg. He did not remonstrate with the man. His wounded companion needed all Philip's attention. Regretfully, he realized that his findings confirmed his hasty diagnosis. Turning to Jarvis, he said, "I'll need a tourniquet, a knife, and the saw. Hurry."

"No!" The protest exploded from Carlton and was echoed with equal vehemence by his friend.

"There's no help for it," Philip told them quietly and with a regret he could not quite conceal. Amputation was a horror with which he himself was only too familiar, having been similarly threatened. Thanks to the expertise and the prompt ministrations of one Bernard Devlin, he had escaped it with only a limp, but Carlton could not.

His lordship had other ideas. "I'll not give you leave to amputate!" he cried, moving restlessly about.

Receiving the tourniquet from Jarvis, Philip vanquished his burgeoning sympathy. He said crisply, "Please, my lord, we have little time."

"Time!" Greysham exclaimed. "Dammit, man, you cannot make a decision like this in seconds!"

"I know what I'm about, Captain Ventriss," Philip said evenly. "Now I must ask you to leave. You should not be in here at this time."

"Damn your eyes, who are you to tell me where I should and should not be?" Greysham flashed. "This man is my best friend, I'll not stand here and see you butcher him without—"

"Butcher, yes! He's a damned butcher," Carlton cried. "You cannot t-turn me into a c-cripple! I'd rather d-die."

His response roused a host of unwelcome memories. Philip had once said much the same thing, lying beneath the tree from which he, a determined twelve-year-old, had plummeted. He wished that Mr. Devlin, the physician who had attended him, were here to give this patient confidence. Of course, the circumstances were different. Devlin had been able to save his limb. He, Philip Langhorne would not be able to perform a similar service for Carlton. The bone was not merely broken in several places—it was shattered.

"Did you hear me?" Carlton rasped.

"I heard you, my lord," Philip responded, striving for patience and, in spite of himself, feeling very sorry for this man he had never admired. Carlton was known to be intolerant and overimpatient of what he was far too easily inclined to describe as "cowardice." However, he was also known to be as unsparing of himself as he was of his men, leading charge after charge into the very thick of the fighting. Now, if his luck had, at length, deserted him, his courage had not.

"Help that man there." Carlton rolled his eyes toward his fellow patient, who had fainted.

"You must save his leg!" Greysham exhorted.

" 'Tis not possible," Philip responded. "The tourniquet, Jarvis."

"Enough! Let me die, damn you," Carlton half-raised himself and sank back with a groan he had obviously tried to suppress.

Philip stared down at him, hoping he had fainted, but his lordship's anguished gaze was fixed on his face, daring him to commence the hated operation.

Locking stares with him, Philip, foreseeing a continuous contest of wills, said in a soft, dull tone of voice, "You must sleep, my lord. You do want to sleep. Sleep, my lord, sleep."

"I want to die, damn you to hell!" Carlton groaned.

Philip continued to stare into Carlton's angry eyes. He said in that same dull, almost uninflected tone, "You must sleep, sleep peacefully, peacefully . . ."

Carlton blinked. "I do not want to sleep."

"But you will," Philip said softly, insistently. "You know you crave sleep. Sleep, sleep, 'balm to hurt minds, chief nourisher in life's feast.' "

"What are you about?" Greysham demanded edgily.

Ignoring the interruption, Philip continued to stare into Carlton's eyes, repeating his injunction concerning sleep. As he had hoped, Carlton began to relax, and a few minutes later, his eyes, grown wide and blank, closed.

"There." Philip turned to his assistant. "The tourniquet and the knife. We'll need to cauterize the wound before—"

"He *is* asleep!" Greysham said incredulously. He glared at Philip. "You . . . you *sent* him to sleep. I've heard about you, come to think of it. What sort of mumbo jumbo did you practice on him?"

Philip said coldly, "I have told you that I do not have the time to discuss this matter. I must insist that you leave. At once!"

"Damn you to perdition!" Greysham snarled. "I want to know what you did to him."

"You are impeding my work with these questions."

"Your work? To bloody hell with your work. Did you not hear him? He told you he wants to die. Let him die. He's not the sort to drag about with a crutch. He's an athlete, man, a runner, a . . . Christ, Langhorne, is there no way you can save his leg?"

"I have told you that there is not."

"Hear me, Langhorne, if you perform this . . . this operation, he—"

"You are keeping me from my task," Philip said with a patience he was far from feeling. "I have told you that time is of the essence."

"Blast you!" Greysham raised a clenched fist. "I could have you discharged for your bloody insolence!"

"I think not," Philip retorted. "We are woefully under-staffed here. Physicians are at a premium. Captains of the infantry can easily be replaced."

"You . . . you impudent dog!"

"Captain Ventriss! Might I ask you why you are keeping Mr. Langhorne talking when he must needs attend to his patient? Your arm, I note, has been bandaged. Pray take yourself out of this tent."

"I . . ." Lord Greysham turned and paled as he met the cold gaze of his immediate superior, Major Sir William Standbury. He saluted stiffly, but added, "My friend here—"

"Your friend, Captain, is in most capable hands. I hope I will not need to ask you to leave a second time?"

Greysham bit down words that years of discipline had fortunately prevented him from uttering. "Yes, sir," he assented stiffly. Saluting, he strode from the tent.

"Please continue with what you must do, Mr. Langhorne," Standbury said. He added gruffly, "Damned shame. Good soldier."

"Yes, sir." Philip nodded. "Thank you, sir."

"You . . . tell me that I . . . I *slept*? I do not believe you!" The voice, higher in pitch than usual, and uncharacteristically shaky, caused Lord Greysham to wince. Battle-hardened though he was, more tears glistened in his eyes and beaded his long lashes as he stared into his friend's anguished face.

"S'truth, Charlie. You dropped off. 'Tis my guess that Langhorne—"

"Langhorne!" Carlton burst out. "That bloody physician." He paused. "What were you going to say?"

"Just that he's used that treatment on others. He's known for it. He calls it 'mesmerism,' after some doctor who invented it. According to my informant, he's one of the few who know about it. But it can alleviate pain. And at least you did not suffer while he—"

"Relieved me of my leg!" Carlton cried. "Damned sorcerer!" He clutched Greysham's arm. "How could I have slept while he . . . while he. . . ?"

"It's not precisely sleep, Charlie. It's—"

"It's sorcery, I tell you. 'Twas black magic that damned butcher used on me, that . . . that . . ." The words piled in his throat, rendering his speech unintelligible as he sent his anguished gaze over his blanketed body. "My leg, Johnny. God, my leg! I . . . I am a damned cripple! Why could you not have prevented it?"

"I tried, Charlie, believe me . . . but to no avail," Lord Greysham said throatily.

"You could have commanded—"

"I have been told that my command ceases at the entrance to that tent."

"Butcher, bloody butcher. He wanted to maim me. I've tangled him before, you know. He . . . he had the temerity to . . . to accuse me of wantonly sacrificing my men in search of my . . . my own glory."

"Did he?" Greysham frowned.

"Aye, he did. I wanted to send his words down his damned gullet, but . . ." Lord Carlton blinked away tears. He caught at Greysham's hand, holding it tightly. "Kill me now, Johnny, I beg you'll kill me now. I cannot go back to Phoebe like this—she'll not want half a man!"

Tears rolled unchecked down Greysham's sun-browned

cheeks. He shook his head, determinedly freeing his hand from Carlton's feverish grasp. "I could not do it, Charlie."

"Then have the butcher use his knives on the rest of me, I beg you!"

Greysham loosed a tremulous sigh. "I must go, Charlie," he said.

"No, I pray you'll stay . . . kill me, Johnny, kill me, kill me."

Without a backward look, Lord Greysham strode hastily out of the tent, coming to a sudden stop as he saw the tall, slender form of the physician in company with Captain Sir Alastair McLean of the Black Watch. Meeting Langhorne's dark, weary eyes, he said bitterly, accusingly, "Damn you to hell, Langhorne. You had a score to settle with Carlton, did you not? And this was your revenge! Butcher, damned butcher—and sorcerer as well. One day you and I will be even." Turning on his heel, he strode into the gathering dusk.

"Butcher, is it!" McLean said explosively. He ran a hand through a flaming crop of red curls that clustered about but did little to soften a craggy Scottish countenance. He turned a fierce blue stare on Philip. "And you one of the finest surgeons we have. I've a mind to thrust Johnny Ventriss' words back down his gullet—or would, were I not acquainted with his family. By God, if he'd died, he'd be singing another tune."

Philip ignored this anomalous comment. "Carlton's his best friend, and death was what he craved. But 'tis against my principles not to save a life if 'tis possible."

"You'd have been better off abandoning your principles on this occasion. Unless I'm much mistaken, you've made yourself a choice pair of enemies."

Philip shook his head. "Perhaps, but I cannot see that 'twill make much difference in my life. Neither of those two noble lords is like to be consorting with me once we're away from here. Consequently, I'll be spared a duel if that's what you're hinting. Lord Greysham would have shown me the flat of his sword or, more likely, his horsewhip, had circum-

stances been other than they are. You must remember my
. . . er, lowly status.''

"I remember it at all times, and so should you," Sir
Alastair returned cryptically. He added, "I vow, Philip, you
are far too pessimistic. And I know the cause of that and will
tell you that I can think of many worse fates than not to have
won the hand of the fair Maria Ridgeway." His amused eyes
lingered on Philip's face and then his amusement vanished as
he saw the shadow cross his friend's weary features. "Lord,
man, you are done in." He threw a long arm around his
shoulders. "Come, let's have a drink!"

"Lead me beside the waters of Lethe," Philip murmured
wryly.

"I wish I could," McLean said frankly. " 'Tis time and
past that you drank deep of forgetfulness, Philip. But in lieu
of that, I pray you'll settle for some Spanish wine, vile
though it is. Damn the bloody French. If you're going to
occupy a country, shouldn't you share some of your wine-
making skills with it?"

"I miss the black-and-yellow butterflies and . . . the cloud
shadows on the . . . far hills," Philip murmured smilingly.
" 'Tis May, you . . ." He pitched forward suddenly and
would have fallen had not Sir Alastair caught him in his
arms.

"Philip, lad . . . Philip," he cried. Picking him up, he
carried him to the makeshift officers' mess.

The men crowded around him as Sir Alastair deposited
Philip on a settee.

"What? Another corpse?" Greysham, glass in hand, came
to the Scotsman's side. He peered down at Philip's pale face
and started back. "Christ, the physician in a hurry . . . the
butcher. Dead, is he?"

"He's collapsed from weariness," Sir Alastair said sharply.

"Pity," Lord Greysham sighed. " 'Twould have saved me
the trouble of running him through, which I will do one of
these days, Alastair. Mark my words."

"You'll need to deal with me first, Johnny," Sir Alastair

said gruffly. He towered over Greysham, glaring at him menacingly.

"I've no quarrel with you, Alastair. And I charge you, choose your friends more carefully."

"Gentlemen!" The cry, loud and jubilant, caused everyone to turn toward the entrance of the tent. "The day is ours. And there's a victory at Albuera!"

There were shouts, applause, and the clink of glasses, but Philip slept on and Lord Greysham, staring down at him, frowned and repeated, "Butcher. We're not quits yet!"

1

—————◆—————

"Do try to look pleasant," Lady Vanessa Ventriss hissed, pinching her brother's arm to emphasize her injunction. They were walking up the three stone steps that led to the open door and lighted hallway of Lord and Lady Farr's town house. "This is a ball, *not* a state funeral."

Lord Greysham visited an annoyed and unappreciative glance on his sister's lovely face. He glowered even more as he met her sparkling green eyes. "I wish the blasted thing were at an end," he grumbled. "These victory celebrations. There've been too damned many of 'em already."

"Oh, dear, you are a bear tonight," she groaned. "I expect I know the reason for that." She gave him a commiserating look. "I am sorry for it, Johnny, I truly am."

This expression of sympathy caused a burgeoning frown to deepen, to work its way down from forehead to eyes and thence to lips which twisted into a gloomy grimace as he whispered, "I fail to catch your meaning!" Hard on this arrant falsehood, he quickly covered all evidences of a bad mood with a wide false grin as servants came to take his cloak. He added, "I hope you'll not linger in the garderobe gossiping."

"Of course not. I came here to dance," she said, moving away from him and following several other elegantly clad young females into a small chamber pressed into service as a cloakroom. A maid had divested Lady Vanessa of her cloak and now she stood surveying herself in the mirror to see if the

15

wind had done any serious damage to her chestnut locks. She was pressing a vagrant curl into place when someone called delightedly, ''Vanessa!''

''Phoebe!'' Vanessa whirled, holding out both hands as Lady Phoebe Galliard came across the floor to smile up at one whom she had know since they were in long clothes, or very nearly. She was a delicate girl with masses of blond hair and very large blue eyes. She clasped Vanessa's hands, saying, ''Oh, I am glad you came at the same time, and do you not look lovely! Green is most certainly your color.''

''Thank you, my dear, and white is yours. You do resemble an angel!''

''I beg you'll not tell me that.'' Phoebe grimaced. ''Angels are so insipid. I'd much rather be dashing like you . . . and you are so divinely tall!''

''A beanpole, in fact.'' Vanessa grinned. ''That is how I was known at Miss Prichard's, if you'll remember.''

''I do, but if *you*'ll remember, I never called you by that horrid nickname.''

''No, you are a dear.'' Vanessa suddenly frowned. ''I expect you're here with Charlie?''

There was an immediate dimming of Phoebe's bright countenance. ''Yes, he decided to escort me. I expect he'll repair to the card room, at least I hope he will.''

She received a commiserating and understanding look from her friend. Lord Carlton usually did seek the card room immediately upon escorting his fiancée to those routs and balls he deigned to grace. However, there were times when he propped himself against the wall, and upon urging Phoebe to dance with one or another of the gallants who met with his approval, he would proceed to watch her with smoldering eyes in a downcast countenance.

''I expect that Johnny will engage him in a game of piquet,'' she said comfortingly.

''Johnny is a dear,'' Phoebe replied in a low, unhappy tone of voice. She glanced into the mirror and then, turning back to Vanessa, added with determined vivacity, ''There, I expect I am ready.''

"And I? Am I?"

"My love"—Phoebe brightened—"I know you'll have yet another of your triumphs this evening . . . and you may find your true love upon the floor!"

"My true love?" Vanessa looked soulful. "How can you be so cruel, Phoebe? You know full well that my heart is buried with poor Rothmore."

"I know nothing of the kind," Phoebe retorted. " 'Twas an arranged marriage and no one chafed more than you at those bonds. You're not wearing the willow for him. You enjoy being free. I know you. But I pray you'll not wait too long, Vanessa."

"Or I'll become a gray and withered spinster—as my Aunt Elizabeth constantly prophesies?"

"Does she?" Phoebe demanded. "Well, I would never say that, but you cannot keep depending on Johnny for an escort. He'll probably marry soon and—"

"Not he," Vanessa said meaningfully.

"No?" Phoebe's eyes narrowed. She scanned Vanessa's face. "You'll be telling me he found no one in Brighton?"

"In order to find, one must look," Vanessa said. "He does not look. But come, let us go in." She spoke hastily, aware of a lightening of her friend's countenance and then an instant darkening. Vanessa sighed, glad that she suffered none of the complications that seemed to accompany that dangerous emotion called love.

Coming out of the cloakroom, she saw her brother, impatience written large upon his face. With him, leaning on his ivory-headed cane, was Charles, Lord Carlton, grim of countenance, dark eyes deeply circled. Lines of pain were etched deep into his forehead and streaks of white were to be found among his luxuriant black locks.

Oddly enough, none of these outward indications of his suffering detracted from his appearance. In fact, what Johnny and his fellow officers were wont to call his "tragedy" had imparted an extra dimension of character to his face, making him appear more attractive than ever. If only he were not so bitter! Vanessa had once believed he wanted to hold his friends responsible for the cessation of all those activities that had once brightened his life. There had been a time when he could not bear to appear in public, when he had scorned to wear the wooden leg he was now able to use with such ease. Lying on his couch, he had lived on laudanum and brandy, alternately falling into fits of deep depression or into terrible rages. Since many of these had been directed at his fiancée or at Johnny, it was only natural that her brother and Phoebe had drawn together for mutual comfort.

It was hard to say when comfort had become love, but it was there, sticking thorns into both their sides as they continued to cosset the stricken marquess. Vanessa bit her lip. It was a pity no one could tell Charles the truth, but there was none would tax him with so cruel a revelation. Consequently, two people continued to be desperately unhappy. It was at such times that Vanessa was doubly glad that she had never fallen in love. In fact, on recalling Phoebe's remark, she could not understand why her friend would wish her to find her "true" love at the ball, unless she were under the impression that misery loves company.

Coming up to the marquess, she had a smile for him. "Good evening, Charles," she said brightly. "You are looking very well."

"Good evening, Vanessa. You are kind to say so." With a grimace that, she supposed, passed for a smile, he bowed over her hand, and stepping back, said to Phoebe, "You'd best go on up the stairs with Vanessa and Johnny. No need to linger behind with me."

"Oh, do not talk nonsense, Charles." Phoebe spoke with an unaccustomed tartness. "I am in no hurry to get to the top of the stairs."

Vanessa, clutching her brother's arm, felt it stiffen, and stifled a sigh, realizing that the marquess was in one of his moods. That Phoebe was equally aware of it was obvious. No doubt, the reason for the ball was at fault, and as she mounted the stairs, she had begun to agree with Johnny that there were far too many victory celebrations.

* * *

The ballroom at the Farr town house was large, built, its owners were wont to explain, at the time when the minuet was in fashion and the space diminished by the volumnious gowns of the period. Consequently, there was a larger expanse of shining floor than was seen in most private houses and the orchestra was housed in the musicians' gallery, near the ceiling. The walls were golden in hue, and mirrors, inserted on either side of the room, reflected the dancers and also three huge crystal chandeliers into infinity. Tall French doors faced a wide balcony that overlooked an expanse of garden below, complete with Grecian statues and a center fountain, a pretty sight, especially under the full moon which, on this evening in late October, was to be seen intermittently riding through the clouds—or at least it gave that illusion.

In honor of the occasion, the Union Jack was draped over the central doorway along with the flags of Britain's allies in the late conflict. These were couched in silk and fringed with gold. Around the room, there were huge baskets of hothouse roses. In all, it was a sufficiently magnificent spectacle— even without the presence of the very cream of the *ton*. Consequently, when Sir Philip Langhorne, turning to Sir Alastair McLean, said, "I cannot understand why you insisted we come," he received a reproachful stare and an immediate reprimand.

"For shame, Philip, 'tis time you were taking your rightful place in your world."

"My world." Philip firmed his lips and gazed at the noble company, now going through the paces of a country dance. "My world is not here and nor is it at Watier's, where you were so kind as to get me admitted. They stare at me as if I were some *rara avis*."

"Would you," Sir Alastair said sarcastically, "prefer to be back with your pills and potions, paying respectful attention to some fat dowager who believes she is dying, when all she has is the dyspepsia rising from too-frequent meals and not enough exercise? Or perhaps your preference is for that comfortable barracks at Madrid?"

"Oddly enough, either would be more to my taste than

wasting my time amidst this empty grandeur. I was not cut out to be a man of fashion.'' Philip cast a disparaging look at his new suit of well-cut evening clothes.

"I disagree," Sir Alastair replied. "You wear your garments with an air. And that is only natural. Whether you care to admit it or not, you were born to a position which you must fill. You are the last of a noble line. Your title goes back six hundred years. It is your duty to perpetuate it and administer your lands to the best of your ability. You need a wife, Philip, and you'll not meet her in the places you've been wont to wander. Once you are married and settled down, there's nothing to keep you from practicing medicine or, better yet, pursuing your medical research.''

"Very well, Alastair," Sir Philip sighed. "You need not continue to lecture me. I have heard it all from Joliffe, my late great-uncle's solicitor." His gaze ranged over the floor. "I do not know anyone here. Of course"—a smile twitched the corners of his lips—"I could follow the reprehensible example of a Young Lochinvar and throw one of these demoiselles across my saddle bow, but perhaps 'tis only Scottish knights who act in so untoward a manner? I cannot think that the Beau would approve.''

"If you will talk nonsense—" Sir Alastair began.

"Since I find myself in a nonsensical position, how else might I talk?" Sir Philip demanded.

"I refuse to humor you," Sir Alastair snapped. "As to your not knowing anyone here, that need not prevent you from inscribing your name on a ball card or on the spokes of a fan. I am quite sure that any one of the young ladies present would be delighted to dance with you.''

"I am not much of a dancer," Philip deprecated. "My foot—''

Sir Alastair rolled his eyes. "We agreed before we came that you'd not use that ancient injury as an excuse. You were graceful enough during your lessons to please your dancing master, and that should be encouragement enough for you. I charge you, however, to keep away from the chairs.''

"The . . . chairs?" Philip gave him a puzzled glance. "What might you mean by that?"

"I am referring to your natural kindness, a commendable part of your nature, to be sure, but which should not induce you to gravitate toward those females sitting with their chaperons and assorted maiden aunts over there." He waved a hand at a group of women seated in spindly chairs well off the dance floor. "There is," he continued, "a reason for their presence in that vicinity and it does not always lie in their personal appearance or lack of dowry. Generally, they are dead bores. And . . ." He paused, noticing that his audience's attention had been diverted. He saw that Philip was watching a tall young woman in a green satin gown only a shade darker than a pair of large, slightly tilted green eyes under slanting brows. For the rest, her hair was chestnut and he rather thought that her short curls were natural. Her oval face was further enhanced by a mouth which, though not the small rosebud extolled by poets, was similarly beautiful. If part of Sir Alastair's heart were not the property of one Flora MacDonald, distantly related to the glamorous rescuer of Bonnie Prince Charlie, and if another portion of that expansive organ were not allotted to Perdita López, whom he had met in Madrid and whose dark, sultry attractions still haunted his dreams, he might easily have been drawn toward the girl in green, who, now that he looked at her more closely, seemed vaguely familiar. He could certainly understand Philip's interest and, he decided happily, she never could have been banished to a chair in any ballroom throughout the breadth and length of the kingdom!

In his mind's eye, he could see Philip dancing with her. They would make a splendid couple. Jealously he shot a glance at her partner. He was an innocuous young man, certainly not her match in either appearance or grace, but on the other hand, it was extremely doubtful that so lovely a creature were not already bespoken. Sir Alastair's airy castles, wrecked by that lightning bolt of common sense, were blown out of existence by his windy sigh.

Philip, as it happened, was experiencing a most unusual

sensation in the region of his heart. As a doctor, he had always been amused by the fables attached to that particular organ and also by the symptoms cited by poets and female novelists. These generally went by such names as "heart-sick," "heartache," and "heartbreak." Still, at that moment it did seem to him that the sight of the girl in green was causing his heart to beat faster and to continue these unexpected palpitations in his throat. She was so beautiful. As the patterns of the dance brought her closer, he gazed at her with an admiration he had never entertained before. Then she whirled away and he felt actually bereft!

As Philip searched in vain for the young woman who had caught his eye, he felt his arm seized and, at the same time, a voice he had not heard in several years spoke his name. "Philip Langhorne! It is, oh, it is. I thought I could not be mistaken. Oh, Philip, dear!"

Thus so warmly addressed, Philip stared down bemusedly into a delicate little face set with large pale blue eyes. Everything about the girl who looked up at him in such surprise was pale. Her hair was white blond, her complexion very fair, and her gown, though pink, was the hue of an angelskin coral pin his late mother had once owned. It was only a second before he recognized her, but in that period her face fell and she put a small hand to her bosom.

"You do not know me!" she said tragically. "Have I changed so very much, then, Philip?"

"Maria," he said, recovering quickly from his surprise. "But of course you have not changed, not an iota. It is just that I did not expect to see you."

"And you were shocked at the sight of me!" she exclaimed. "Nor did I expect to see you, Philip." Pain edged her tones and her great eyes were suddenly drowned in tears.

Tears, Philip recalled uncomfortably, came easily to Maria. He also recollected that she could faint with equal ease. He hoped that their sudden encounter would not bring on one of her spells, and as this wish arose, a part of him seemed to detach itself and stand aside, surveying Maria—or Lady Glazebrook, as he must remember to address her. That detached self regarded her dispassionately and without so much as a trace of the emotion she had once kindled in his breast— again, a mistaken analogy.

Maria had enough emotion for them both as she said tremulously, "Philip, I'd not heard you'd returned from the wars. You took no hurt?"

"None. I was most fortunate."

"Indeed you were." She looked about her in some alarm. "I hope that no one has been taken ill. The room is so very warm. A few moments ago, I thought I might need my vinaigrette. You remember silly me, always swooning, and you so alarmed."

"Yes." He nodded. "I do remember."

"Oh, I am so glad to see you again," she breathed.

"And I you, Maria," he said politely.

"But why *are* you here?" She regarded him quizzically. "Are you, perhaps, retained by Lord and Lady Farr?"

"Retained by them? No, I am not."

"Sir Philip is a guest, Lady Glazebrook," Sir Alastair said dryly.

She seemed to become aware of him for the first time. "Sir Alastair, I . . . I was not aware . . . I did not see you," she murmured, and held out her hand. As he bowed over it, she stared at Philip. "A guest?" She regarded him confusedly. "Sir . . ." she added. "He called you *Sir* Philip?" As he would have answered, she rushed on. "Sir Philip . . . you *have* come into the title! Oh, I knew you would. I told them . . . Mama and Papa, I told them you would, and they'd not credit it. I said it was quite, quite possible, and it has happened!"

"Maria!" A chunky young man with his dark hair in a short Brutus crop, a style not particularly becoming to his full and, at this moment, red face, came hurrying up.

"Oh, Thomas." Lady Maria, evidently deep in her own thoughts, blinked at him. It was with an almost palpable effort that she added, "But of course, you know Phil . . . er, *Sir* Philip Langhorne?"

Sir Thomas Glazebrook regarded Philip blankly. "No," he

said bluntly after a second's pause. "I do not believe I have had the pleasure."

"But you must have heard me speak of him," Lady Maria insisted. "We have known each other since we were in the cradle."

"Oh, have you?" Sir Thomas, who had been looking definitely out of sorts, said, "Maria knows a great many people I do not know, Sir Philip." He grew a shade redder. "I take it you're also from Yorkshire?"

"Yes," Philip acknowledged. He held out his hand. "I am delighted to make your acquaintance, Sir Thomas."

"Are you?" Sir Thomas blurted, and then added gruffly, "Well, I am glad to meet you too." He shook hands with him.

"And this is my friend Sir Alastair McLean," Philip added.

"Sir Alastair," Sir Thomas acknowledged.

"Sir Thomas," Sir Alastair returned. There was another exchange of handshakes before Sir Thomas said, "Well, Maria, I think we're due for the next cotillion, which is already forming. Shall we join them?"

"Oh, yes, but first do give Sir Philip your card, my love. We would like you to call." Lady Maria fixed her pale eyes on Philip's face. She added urgently, "We do have so much to discuss after so many years. You are staying in town, Philip?"

"Yes, at Grillons until the house is readied."

"The house?" Lady Maria looked puzzled and then added, "Oh, yes, the London house. 'Tis on Charles Street, I seem to recall."

"I must commend you on your memory, Lady Maria." Philip smiled. "Charles Street it is. And I do hope you and Sir Thomas will call on me once I have moved in—which should be in the near future."

"When . . . exactly?" Lady Maria shot the question at him.

"I'd say within the fortnight," Philip replied.

"Oh,"—she clutched her husband's arm—"we must, Tom, dear."

"Yes, yes, my love." Sir Thomas cast a quick look across the floor. "I believe they are waiting for us," he added. "Come now."

After a few more words, mainly from Lady Maria, the couple moved away.

Sir Alastair directed a frown toward the lady's back. "Well, there is Lady Maria," he said thoughtfully.

"There she is." Philip nodded.

"She is in good looks." Sir Alastair regarded Philip narrowly.

"Indeed, she is."

"I wonder how long she intends to remain in London. I understand she has a son."

"Has she?"

"Born a year ago. Motherhood's taken nothing from her looks, though."

"I agree. She has not changed. But I do not expect one changes radically in three or four years. She is some four years younger than myself—which would make her twenty-four."

" 'Tis a dangerous situation," Sir Alastair muttered.

"Dangerous? Why?"

"She's married, Philip, and to a jealous spouse, unless I miss my guess."

"I am sure you do not. That same notion crossed my mind." Philip's eyes twinkled. "I take it you are giving me a warning?"

"I am pleased that you recognize it as such," Sir Alastair responded.

Philip laughed merrily. "I should be a dunce, if I did not. My dear friend"—he clapped Sir Alastair on the shoulder—"my very dear friend, let me assure you that the scab has formed long since and the scar is only faintly visible. It has long ceased to give pain."

Sir Alastair said pointedly, "I hope so."

"Pray believe me."

"I would say that I believe *you*, but as for the lady . . ."

"Maria always was a romantic creature." Philip shrugged.

"However, I do not imagine that she was an unwilling bride. In common with her parents, she has a very practical side."

"I know that." Sir Alastair grinned. "I am glad that you do too. And are you not going to seek a dance with some unattached beauty?"

"I think I would prefer to get a breath of fresh air." Philip looked in the direction of the balcony. "Would you care to join me?"

"No," Sir Alastair replied. He added meaningfully, "Since I am at a ball, I feel that it is my *duty* to tread a measure."

"I have been keeping you from enjoying the dance," Philip said repentantly. "I am truly sorry."

"You need not be. I have been vastly entertained."

"Entertained?"

"By Lady Maria."

"Oh," Philip sighed. "Alas."

"Alas?" Sir Alastair pounced. "You cannot mean that you have yet a soft spot beneath that scab?"

"No, my dear friend." Philip's dark eyes gleamed with humor. "I have not, more's the pity."

"I fail to understand you," Sir Alastair complained. "Can you mean that you wish you were still in love with the lady?"

"I do not—but I do remember my agonies of the past and I fear I am growing old, else I could not take my lost love so lightly."

" 'Tis the only way to take that particular loss—and to be glad of it, as well."

"I am," Philip sighed. "Entirely."

"Ah, good, good, then you stand no danger of entering into a dangerous situation."

"I have told you there is no danger in that situation," Philip assured him. "Even as I speak, all trace of that afore-mentioned scar is vanishing, quite." Sir Philip gave him a friendly clap on the shoulder, and then, keeping to the edge of the dance floor, went toward the double doors opening on the balcony.

As he walked, Philip was chuckling over Alastair's warn-ing. It seemed very hard to believe that he had ever been cast into the depths of despair by Lady Maria's tearful rejection of his impassioned pleas that they run away together. Had he actually proposed such folly? He had.

She had gazed at him affrighted. "But I . . . I could not, Philip. Papa would be so angry." Maria's pale eyes had brimmed with tears. "And though I love you madly . . ."

"Madly." Philip had difficulty suppressing a laugh. Seeing Maria's pink-and-white china-doll charms, he was positive that she and "mad" love were strangers. She had rejected him in favor of Sir Thomas' title and worldly goods, diamond evidences of which had gleamed on her fingers and around her neck when she had accosted him just now. She had, he also recalled, ended her faltering speech of renunciation with a swoon. How painfully that trick had wrought upon his younger self. He had actually gone home to weep over the destruction of what he had considered to be his fondest hopes, and then he had rushed off to join the corps of young physicians bound for the Peninsula.

"Oh, goodness gracious!"

The exclamation, uttered in deep accents of exasperation, brought Philip out of his uncomfortable reverie. He looked around and his eyes widened as he saw the girl in green standing near one of the immense baskets of roses. In another second he noticed that she was tugging futilely at the skirt of her gown, which was higher in back, giving him a glimpse of white silk petticoats and part of a pink thigh.

Philip hurried to her side. "You are caught, I see," he observed.

"I am," she responded crossly. "And I cannot seem to extricate myself."

"Let me," he offered.

"I do not think . . ." She blushed. "I mean . . . my skirt . . ."

Philip said soothingly, " 'Twill take but an instant." He moved behind her, and catching the material, he carefully eased it away from between two wicker twigs. "There," he added, hastily loosening his hold on the skirt.

Half-turning, she smoothed it down and then smiled at him. "I do thank you for your timely rescue."

"Alas, 'twas not a real rescue," he replied. "Rather than being imprisoned by a basket, you should have been in an impregnable castle, guarded by fierce dragons."

Her eyes twinkled. "Unfortunately, Sir Knight, the supply of London dragons has long been exhausted, but still I am most grateful for your efforts."

"Ah, here you are, Lady Vanessa!" A tall young man bore down on them. "I have been searching for you," he added censoriously. "It is time for our waltz."

"Oh, is it?" Lady Vanessa looked almost regretful. "Well, here I am, Lord Mayberry." She smiled at Philip. "I do thank you, Sir Knight."

"I was glad to be of assistance, fair lady," Philip said on a note of regret as he watched the couple move away.

"Philip!"

He turned and found Lady Maria at his side again. "Yes, milady," he said punctiliously.

"I beg you will continue to call me Maria." She stared up at him, her pale eyes glistening with more unshed tears. "We are old friends, after all. Or are you still angry with me?"

"I am not in the least angry with you, Maria."

"You have learned to dissemble, have you not?" she sighed. "I wish I were so adept at hiding my feelings. And Tom is fearfully jealous. A regular Iago . . . or is it Othello?"

"Othello," Philip supplied.

"And Desdemona strangled in the sheets." Lady Maria accomplished an elaborate shudder. "But no matter," she added briskly. "You were speaking with Lady Vanessa Ventriss. Do you know her?"

"Not really," Philip replied, glad that Maria had supplied a further identification of the lady.

"She is so very brave, poor creature," Maria commented.

"Brave?" Philip questioned.

"She has sustained a great sorrow, and even though she hides it very well, I do not believe she will ever recover from his death."

"Whose death?" Philip demanded.

"That of her fiancé, Lord Rothmore, a quite divinely handsome young man who was killed at . . . at Ba . . . Ba . . . somewhere in Spain, or possibly Portugal, a month before they were to be married. She was deeply in love with him, very deeply. It has been four years since he perished and still she has not wed. She wore black for an age! I have it on very good authority that she counts herself his widow."

Remembering their brief exchange and especially the lady's lighthearted smile, Philip said mildly, "Well, one cannot grieve forever."

"Can one not?" Lady Maria lifted her brimming eyes. "Oh, Philip, how I wish that were true. Were I to tell you how very much I have regretted *everything*—"

"Maria!" Sir Thomas hurried toward them. "This is where you are." He glowered at Philip. "Did you not hear me say that I intended to leave directly after the last country dance?"

"Of course I heard you, Thomas. I was just saying my farewells to Philip here." Lady Maria put her little hand on her husband's arm. "Do let us go. We will say good night to you, Philip, and please, you must call. I will send you our direction. Grillons, you said?"

"Yes, that is correct," Philip responded.

After another flurry of farewells, Lady Maria and Sir Thomas, much to Philip's relief, departed. Left alone, he fastened his eyes on the dancers and was soon rewarded by the sight of Lady Vanessa waltzing with Lord Mayberry. As they whirled around, she faced him and smiled. It was a lovely smile, but all her smiles were lovely, he thought, and aware again of the pounding of his heart, he was utterly unable to dismiss the feeling as superstition. In fact, he was forced to conclude, albeit most reluctantly, that it might very well be symptomatic of love at first sight.

2

"But I hardly saw you last night!" Lady Felicia Farr's wide brown eyes were reproachful and her arched brows were drawn together in a brief frown.

"How could you see me, my dear?" Vanessa demanded, visiting an affectionate smile upon her hostess's piquant face. She took a turn around the chintz-hung sitting room where Lady Felicia entertained only her closest friends. "Half of London appeared to be in your ballroom."

"That was Frederick's doing. You know he's so deeply involved in politics that we have the ambassador of this and the grand potentate of that and their entourages . . . I vow my face is quite numb from smiling and if I sound hoarse, 'tis from acknowledging so many introductions *and* passing them along!"

Vanessa laughed and, at the same time, wondered how she might introduce a subject that intrigued her, namely the identity of the man who had freed her gown from the flower basket. That was one reason she had accepted her friend's invitation that morning, but she was currently entertaining second thoughts. To appear interested in the stranger would both intrigue Felicia and provide her with information she might not scruple to confide to their mutual friends. Not only did she enjoy gossip, she had the instincts of a town crier. Consequently, it was better to remain silent on this subject, Vanessa reluctantly decided.

"I did see you," Lady Felicia continued. "Beyond greeting you as you came in . . . Poor Charles, he did look miserable, did he not? 'Tis a shame he does not write poetry.''

"Poetry!" Vanessa exclaimed, completely confused by this digression.

"He reminds me of Byron, that moody look, folded arms and his leg, poor dear. Of course, with Byron 'tis his foot. I almost believe it better to be born with an infirmity. One learns to cope. Poor Phoebe, she is so unhappy, and Johnny too.''

"Was it so obvious?" Vanessa questioned. Before Felicia could reply, she added nervously, "I hope you'll not say anything to anyone about that, my dear. It would be horrid if such speculations were to reach the ears of poor Charles.''

Lady Felicia's eyebrows shot up. She turned an affronted gaze upon Vanessa. "Give me credit for some common sense," she begged. "I would never, never breathe a word of that to anyone save yourself. There are some things that do not bear repeating—though I say, and again, for your ears alone, my love, 'twould be a mercy if Charles did know which way the winds were blowing.''

"It would not," Vanessa said in some alarm. "It would only hurt both Johnny and Charlie. They've been friends forever and 'twas bad enough for them when Will died.''

"Will? Oh, yes, the late Lord Rothmore. The triumvirate, as we used to call them. 'Twas a pity, and so soon after he was sent abroad—which brings me to Sir Philip, the mysterious Sir Philip. And did you probe the mystery, my dear? Mind you, I am speaking figuratively, not literally. Though, if we speak of probes, I imagine he would be the prober.''

"Sir Philip?" Vanessa was used to her friend's wild shifts of subject, but this was completely confusing. "Who, pray, is Sir Philip?''

"Do you not know?" It was Lady Felicia's turn to be confused. "I saw you with him last night and you were laughing. I took that to mean that you were acquainted.''

Vanessa felt a strange little throb in the vicinity of her heart. The subject she had feared to introduce had, inadvertently, made its appearance, at least she hoped it had. She said carefully, "I am not sure I follow your meaning, Felicia. I met so many gentlemen last night. What does this Sir Philip look like?"

"He is quite divinely handsome," Lady Felicia breathed. "I did not expect he'd be so very striking in appearance. It really is a most interesting story—and here I was hoping you could shed some new light on it!"

"No, I am afraid you will need to do the shedding," Vanessa said, curbing her impatience with an effort.

"Well, Sir Alastair McLean brought him. That was why I was sure you knew him. You do know Sir Alastair, after all."

"Sir Alastair . . ." Vanessa shook her head.

"But you *do*," Felicia insisted. "He is a friend of your Aunt Elizabeth's. I saw them together at the opera only recently. Fancy, I think he liked that tenor she was sponsoring. Where does she find them, love? I do dislike a high catlike howl, myself."

"He is tall . . . with red hair?" Vanessa asked.

"Oh, no, he is short and plump. Anything but heroic-looking. I wonder why 'tis always the tenor who wins fame, glory, and the heroine, when he or she does not die? And tenors seem equally popular offstage. Females mass around them. I prefer a baritone."

"Oh, yes, Sir Alastair," Vanessa persisted. "Yes, now I place him. He is a friend of my aunt's, but we've not seen him in some time."

"Nor have we. He is by way of being a connection of Frederick's, you know. A Highlander, but he does not prate forever of the '45 which is a mercy. To my best knowledge, their romantic Bonnie Prince Charlie died a drunkard, though perhaps one cannot blame him for that. It must have been most disappointing to have been routed out of Scotland and to lose the throne."

"You have not described Sir Philip's appearance, not specifically, at least," Vanessa reminded her.

"And you do not know?"

"There was one man to whom I was not introduced. I

seem to recall that he was tall and . . . possibly blond. I am not sure. We did exchange a few words.''

"Did he have brown eyes?'' Felicia pursued.

"Um . . .'' Vanessa wrinkled her forehead. "I believe he might have.''

"It is an unusual combination, is it not?'' Felicia observed.

"Very.''

"I thought you might know him. You were talking very animatedly with him, at least so it seemed to me.''

"Because he was kind enough to free me . . .'' Vanessa explained her predicament.

"Oh, dear, those baskets!'' Felicia rolled her eyes. "They can be hazards, but the roses do lend such an air, do you not agree? I adore roses. My mother, if you'll remember, helped to breed the Barwick Beauty, such a lovely shade of pink and with a gold center. We had a whole bed of them.''

"They were lovely,'' Vanessa said perfunctorily. She made another stab at being casual. "I was very grateful to this Sir Philip. Who is he? He must be new to London.''

"He is. And I found him quite unexceptional. Of course, we did not exchange more than two words. There were such multitudes present. Did you see Lady Caroline? I did not want to invite her. She has made such a cake of herself over Byron, but dear Frederick insisted. He's very fond of William Lamb.''

"The which tells me absolutely nothing about Sir Philip,'' Vanessa burst out.

"Well, the whole tale does remind me of Cinderella. You see, he is a physician, or at least he was. I doubt that he will practice now. It does read like something from the Minerva Press, my dear, which reminds me, did you buy their *Circassian Romance?* 'Twas by a Lady Unknown. It is tremendously exciting, all about this girl who was captured by the Turks. It sold out on its first day of publication and I secured one of the very last copies. I have not been able to put it down.''

"Felicia,'' Vanessa said between her teeth, "you were telling me about Sir Philip . . .''

"Oh." Felicia regarded her intently. "You are really interested in him, I see."

" 'Tis you who have whetted my curiosity," Vanessa said carefully. "Do you know anything else about him?"

"Have I not told you that I do?"

"That is *all* you have told me!"

"Well, my dear, Sir Philip comes from an old Yorkshire family. Have you ever been to Yorkshire? 'Tis miserable at this time of the year, though I am told that the moors are quite lovely in the spring. Frederick says we will go . . . but no matter, I was telling you about Sir Philip. He is the younger son of a younger son of the Langhorne family, which, I understand, is a very old one, dating back to the Edwards—first or second, I cannot recall. Or perhaps it was one of the Williams . . . there was William Rufus . . . No matter. I am not at all certain about his genealogy, but they were barons and then one of their number did something wrong and they were in disgrace for two or three centuries. Then, in Elizabeth's time, they became baronets and so they have remained. Sir Philip's older brother would have inherited the title but he was killed fighting at Oporto, Sir Alastair told me. Then, there were his great-uncle and his first cousin. They both died, and so he has inherited the title. He is very wealthy, I understand. There's the house on Charles Street and also there is a considerable estate up north. I had that from two sources. Lady Maria Glazebrook knows him too. She tells me that the Langhornes have vast holdings in the North. She was considerably surprised to discover that Sir Philip had inherited the title, surprised and a little miffed, I should think."

"Miffed? Why would she not rejoice in his good fortune?"

"I do not presume to understand the workings of her mind," Felicia said somewhat disdainfully. "She can be the most tiresome creature, but never mind that. Sir Alastair tells me that Sir Philip is quite dazed by his good fortune."

"And well he might be."

"Did you like him?"

"We did not speak long enough for me to form any

impression other than that I found him very pleasant," Vanessa said somewhat self-consciously. "It was an unusual situation. My gown was hiked up in the back . . ." She paused as Felicia giggled, then added, "I liked the fact that he did not exhibit any levity, which he might have done."

"Probably because he *is* a physician and not unacquainted with patients in various stages of undress," Felicia said sagely.

"Very likely," Vanessa agreed.

"I did love your gown, by the way. A really divine shade of green. I hope it did not sustain any lasting damage from our basket."

"Not in the least. The gown you were wearing, by the way, was magnificent."

"Oh, dear." Felicia grimaced. "I pray you'll not call it to mind. I loved it too. I was quite prepared to wear it again, but alas, it is quite ruined. Lady Jarrold spilled the whole of her brandy glass on it and it took the color out, clumsy witch!"

Vanessa commiserated with her friend, and in half an hour was able to leave. Upon entering her house, she found her brother just ahead of her on the stairs. "Johnny," she called. She received a gloomy look.

"You're home, are you?"

"As you see." She ran up the rest of the way, joining him on the second floor and looking at him searchingly. "You do seem out of sorts. What's amiss?"

"I've been to see Charles," he explained. "He's in a damnable mood, not that I blame him, but . . ." He sighed. "Poor Phoebe's in for a difficult session, I fear. He was on his way to her when I left him."

"And when is Charles not in a damnable mood?" Vanessa inquired tartly. "It seems to me that he is forever in the dismals."

"He has reason enough," Lord Greysham said moodily. "I'll not deny that. God!" He glared at her, though actually he was not looking at her, but through her at some middle distance.

"What is the matter, John, dear?"

Brother and sister turned to find their aunt, the dowager

Countess of Combe, coming down the hall from the music room. A tall woman clad in the black she had donned for the death of her husband some twenty years earlier, she was in her late sixties. Her hair had retained some of its original brown and on her good days, which usually followed nights when one or another of the singers or instrumentalists she sponsored did justice to her taste, she looked far younger than her years. Evidently Signor Mariani, the young tenor just over from Milan, had performed satisfactorily in the course of a morning musicale, for her hazel eyes were bright and it was easy to see traces of the beauty for which she had been so justly famous.

"Good afternoon, dear Aunt Elizabeth." Vanessa gave her an affectionate smile. "And how did Signor Mariani sing?"

"Like an angel—for all he complained at performing so early in the day," Lady Elizabeth said with a touch of triumph in the smile she quickly smoothed away in deference to her nephew's lowering mood. She had always been extremely fond of him, seeing him as the son she never had. "You've not told me what's amiss. It seems to me I heard you mention Charles." She sighed. "Damn, it's a shame to see the poor lad in such straits, but he *is* managing better with that horrid leg. And it had seemed to me that, of late, he was more himself."

"He has been," Lord Greysham said bitterly. "But last night, he had a rude shock. Both of us did. Can you imagine, that damned butcher was at the ball!"

"That er . . . damned butcher?" Lady Elizabeth repeated. "Lady Felicia does not usually invite tradesmen to her festivities, though once I believe she did have a rather amusing ape. At least he was amusing until he broke free and pulled down the portieres, as well as committing several other unmentionable indiscretions."

Vanessa's burgeoning smile vanished as Lord Greysham said passionately, "I am not speaking of a tradesman, Aunt Elizabeth! I am speaking of the . . . the physician that removed his leg. 'Twas unnecessary, you know. He could have saved it, but he did not even make the effort, even though I told him, as did poor Charles, that he would rather die than suffer that amputation. And now, if you please, he expects to take his place in the *ton*, damn his eyes!''

Vanessa found that her hand had, almost without volition, crept toward her heart. ''A physician in the *ton*?'' she questioned a trifle breathlessly. ''Is that not a little unusual?''

Her brother's eyes were hot with anger and resentment as he responded, ''It is *most* unusual. He owes his fortune to the demise of three men far more worthy than himself—his brother, his cousin, and his great-uncle . . . four, if you count his uncle, who died some years back . . . and five, if you include his father. I had some acquaintance with his elder brother, though I failed to realize that they were related. I am speaking about Sir Desmond Langhorne, who died at Oporto. He was three times the man this Philip is.''

''Philip Langhorne? That's the scoundrel's name?'' Lady Elizabeth questioned.

''Yes. *Sir* Philip Langhorne, if you please. 'Tis hard to understand the workings of the Almighty in allowing this butcher to survive when those more worthy have gone to their death, but of course, he did not join a regiment. He was behind the lines where 'twas reasonably safe.''

''Are you saying that you believe him to be cowardly, John?'' Lady Elizabeth inquired.

''I am telling you that he is a butcher!'' Lord Greysham said bitterly. ''I am also telling you that while he could have followed the example of his brother, he chose to become a surgeon or something approaching it.''

''I suppose it was that or entering the church,'' Lady Elizabeth commented. ''Younger sons are so often at a disadvantage.''

'' 'Tis mighty unfortunate that he chose to save bodies instead of souls! Well, at least he has no more need to turn his clumsy hands to that calling. Many lives and limbs will be saved.''

''Shocking!'' Lady Elizabeth commented.

''Yes,'' Vanessa agreed. She added, ''Are you sure that he had another alternative, this physician, I mean? I cannot imagine that if Charles's leg could have been saved, he would wantonly remove it.''

"I tell you that he did not hesitate a minute. He asked for a knife and a saw—after the most cursory glance. He was in a hurry, you see. There were others awaiting his so-called ministrations!''

"Oh, dear.'' Vanessa shuddered.

"The creature must be a veritable monster!'' Lady Elizabeth exclaimed.

"A monster, yes—and sinister.''

"Sinister? Surely . . .'' Vanessa began, but paused as she met her brother's hot gaze. She looked away quickly, realizing that she had been on the point of denying this particular allegation, thereby suggesting that she had met Sir Philip. She did not feel in the mood to cite the circumstances attendant on that particular meeting. Such an admission would only incite Johnny to greater wrath. Enough had been said already. She wanted to go to her bedchamber. She was feeling weary and her day was not yet at an end. Consequently, she said placatingly, "Surely the army would not employ a sinister surgeon.''

"They did!'' Lord Greysham exclaimed. "He used some form of hocus-pocus to put poor Charles out.''

"Hocus-pocus?'' Lady Elizabeth repeated. "He's a magician, your physician?''

"Something very like it.'' Lord Greysham frowned. "When Charles protested his intentions, he put him to sleep.''

"Sure you are funning me!'' his aunt exclaimed.

"I swear to you that I am not. I saw it done. 'Twas uncanny.'' Lord Greysham actually shuddered.

"And such a man seeks entrance to our ranks?'' Lady Elizabeth demanded incredulously.

"He does. God, I wish I'd known of his arrival earlier. I'd have seen he was blackballed at Watier's. Well, he'll not make any further incursions in this city. I mean to see to that!''

"Evidently he's not without friends.'' Vanessa spoke over a throbbing in her throat. It was very hard for her to connect the well-spoken, pleasant young man of the previous evening with her brother's furious denunciation. However, she had never known Johnny to exaggerate or to wantonly libel anyone. Consequently, she had, albeit most reluctantly, to believe him.

"No, he is not without friends," Lord Greysham agreed. He fastened an accusing stare on his aunt. "Sir Alastair McLean, Aunt Elizabeth, is by way of being his sponsor. He championed him at Albuera, too."

"Sir Alastair!" Lady Elizabeth exclaimed. "He is a remarkably intelligent young man and his father before him. Both are exceptionally fond of music. At least Sir Angus was before he died, and Sir Alastair is a charter member of the Philharmonic Society!"

"That might do justice to his taste in music. He seems to be considerably less intelligent about whom he chooses to befriend," Lord Greysham snapped. "This Langhorne does have a pleasant manner, at least if you do not know him as Charles and I do. He has an estate in Yorkshire, I'm told. Let him return to it. He soon will—if I have my way."

"Let us hope that your word will carry some weight, John," Lady Elizabeth said sternly. "We have enough pretenders in society as it is. Do you not agree, my dear Vanessa?"

"Yes, I certainly do. People ought to know what manner of man he is. One can so easily be taken in by a pleasant address." She started for the stairs and paused. "Pray excuse me, Aunt Elizabeth, I must rest a bit. You remember that you promised to accompany Phoebe and me to Hyde Park Corner at five this evening?"

"I remember." Lady Elizabeth nodded. "Will you be coming with us, John?"

"No, I do not think I should," he said gloomily. "If you will excuse me, Aunt Elizabeth?" Abruptly he hurried up the stairs, and a moment later his door slammed loudly.

"Oh, dear." Lady Elizabeth exchanged a speaking glance with Vanessa. "Dear Charles ought to be told."

"Yes," Vanessa agreed. She did not linger to discuss the situation as she knew her aunt would have preferred, this in

spite of the futility of such a conversation. As she mounted
the stairs, her head was beginning to throb. She hoped that
the threatened ache would not materialize. She also wished
that she had not promised to go driving with her aunt and
Phoebe. They would surely talk about John and Charles, and
Phoebe would weep and need comforting.

If the truth were to be told, she was weary of comforting
Phoebe. She had her own frustrations and there was no one to
commiserate with her. She paused in her thinking and was
amazed. She was not in the least frustrated. Furthermore, she
did not need anyone to commiserate with her. She was not in
love and nor was she likely to be, ever again. She frowned,
realizing that there was something radically wrong with this
particular notion. In order to be in love *again*, one would
have needed to have experienced that tender emotion before,
and that had never happened either. Truly, her brains were
wanting this afternoon. Reaching the head of the stairs, Vanessa
hurried down the hall to her chamber, and the slam of her
door was even louder than that which had been accomplished
by her brother.

"Another green gown! And this one is even more beautiful
than the one you wore last night—if one can compare an
afternoon dress to evening attire. And how well it goes with
your cloak. I do love that deep green velvet and the red fox
collar," Phoebe commented brightly as Bernard, Lady Elizabeth's preferred coachman, expertly maneuvered her barouche
into the line of vehicles making a stately but necessarily slow
progression in the region of Hyde Park Corner. The long
stretch of ground was crowded with barouches, curricles, post
chaises, and even a coach or two. Riding amidst these equi-
pages were numerous gentlemen on spirited thoroughbreds,
pulling up to converse with this or that lady as well as some
who could lay no claim to that particular designation, but
who were even more popular with the riders than the Duchess
of Bray or the Countess of Lancaster.

Vanessa had already exchanged greetings with several
friends, and so had Phoebe, who, having commented on her

friend's gown, had lapsed into silence again. Vanessa did not attempt to break that silence. If her friend were determined to ignore the purple bruise on her cheek, she must not continue to remark on its origin. She was glad that John was not present to see this shocking emblem of Charles's anger. The fact that he had been, according to Phoebe, contrite to the point of tears would have held little weight with her brother, even given his fury over Philip Langhorne's botched operation. It had been the unexpected appearance of the surgeon at the ball that had occasioned Charles's fury, the fury he had turned on poor Phoebe. John must not hear of it. She agreed with Phoebe on that count. Yet, what could he do if he did learn about Charles's latest outburst? He could not call Charles out, and if he were to stop seeing him, poor Charles would be friendless.

"Poor Charles." Vanessa winced. She had known Charles all of her life and it was terrible to think of him as "poor" and to regard him as an object of pity. He would have hated it, if he could have read her mind. Until he had been sent back from Spain, he had seemingly never known a single day's illness! He had been bold and daring, taking impossible risks, riding untrained horses, subduing them with ease, scaling terrifying heights for no other reason than to get to the top first. He had always been first, but not in any arrogant way. He had been proud, true, but it had been of his superb physical strength and fitness. Now, to see him painfully making his way down the street, leaning on his cane, his eyes so darkly circled they seemed bruised, and deep lines of pain etched on his forehead and around his mouth, was an agony to herself, to Phoebe, to Johnny, and to all his friends. And could those terrible sufferings have been prevented? Had he lost his leg merely because a surgeon was "too busy" to give his injury the consideration it required? Her brother's words came back to her. "He asked for a knife and a saw immediately."

It seemed very difficult to connect Philip Langhorne with such heartless negligence. Of course, he must have been extremely overworked, but that was no excuse. There could be no excuse for him, none! Unless the situation had been other than Johnny believed. That was unlikely. Johnny would never have made so serious an accusation unless he had good strong reasons to back it up, and nor, she knew, would Charles. Consequently, she must needs believe them.

"Lady Vanessa . . ."

She glanced up quickly, to find Sir Peregrine Moffett mounted on his white stallion Agamemnon beside her. "Sir Peregrine, good afternoon." She smiled at him pleasantly. He was one of the young men who persistently pursued her. He was an excellent marital prospect, rich and from an old aristocratic family. As they exchanged pleasantries, she found herself comparing his blue eyes with those of another hue, deep and dark, surprisingly so. One would have thought that a man with corn-gold hair must have eyes of Sir Peregrine's color or . . . She caught herself. She had no incentive to dwell on Sir Philip's eyes. He had no place in her life and ought not to occupy so much as a second of her thoughts!

She exchanged a few more words with Sir Peregrine, agreeing that the Farr ball had been a great success, that the weather was mild for late October, and yes, it was a mercy that most of the festivities attendant upon the allied victory were at an end and the trampled grass in the parks given a chance to grow again. Finally he rode away and someone else took his place. Meanwhile, Lady Elizabeth was conversing with an elderly gray-haired gentleman, one of several ancient gallants with whom she might have danced the minuet forty years ago. Surveying them out of the corner of her eye, Vanessa was conscious of a strange yearning to be magically transported some forty or even fifty years into the future— when her life would be behind her. Fifty years would bring her to 1864.

In 1864, she would be seventy-one, two years older than her aunt, and no doubt she, too, would be involved in some organization like the Philharmonic Society or she would be playing cards with several other widowed or unmarried cronies like herself. Unmarried? She considered the notion. She had never contemplated life as a spinster, but there was no reason for her to wed unless she were in love. She could not imagine being in love with any of the young men she knew. Perhaps she *would* remain single and act as hostess for her brother, who had given his heart into Phoebe's keeping forever, she knew.

"Lady Ventriss . . ." The voice was pleasant and deep. She had heard it before and knew where when she looked up into the face of the man who had freed her from the basket—the despised Sir Philip Langhorne! He was wearing well-fitting riding clothes and he was mounted on a spirited chestnut with the small head that signified an Arabian breed. He controlled his steed well, she thought, and was about to smile when she fortunately remembered that a smile was not in order. She regarded him with chill disdain. "I do not believe I know you, sir," she said in freezing accents.

He flushed but instead of responding to her set-down, he actually persisted in continuing the conversation. "We have not been introduced, Lady Ventriss. However, your name has become known to me through a mutual friend, Sir Alastair McLean. I am Philip Langhorne."

"Indeed?" she said coldly. She added, "I fear you have me confused with another, Mr. Langhorne."

His dark gaze mirrored hurt and confusion. "I . . . did not think so, but yes, I expect I have. Pray accept my sincere apologies, Lady Ventriss."

She gave him a frosty nod. "A pardonable error, sir." She turned away and was grievously annoyed at a sudden blurring of her eyes—a condition she immediately blamed on the October breeze.

"Vanessa . . ." Phoebe put a hand on her arm. "Who was that?"

Vanessa glanced around and saw that he had ridden away. She thought she caught sight of him threading his way through the massed vehicles, but she could not be sure. "His name is Philip Langhorne," she said between stiff lips, and saw Phoebe blanch and turn pale, emphasizing the purple bruise on her cheek, which, Vanessa thought bitterly, could be laid directly at Philip Langhorne's door!

"Oh!" Phoebe exclaimed. "The butcher."

"The same."

Lady Elizabeth, who had been conversing with another old friend, leaned forward. "Who was that young man? Did I understand you to say . . ."

"Sir Philip Langhorne, Aunt Elizabeth," Vanessa repeated doggedly.

"He seemed to know you," Lady Elizabeth had a sharp, probing look for her.

"We met briefly at the ball last night," Vanessa explained.

"You did not mention that to John."

"I saw no need to inflame him further."

"Very wise," Lady Elizabeth commented. "You did give him a strong set-down, I see."

"He deserved nothing less," Vanessa responded coldly.

"He seemed most crestfallen," Phoebe murmured.

"It serves the rascal right." Lady Elizabeth glared at her. "Do I detect a note of sympathy in your tone?"

Phoebe flushed. "He does not look like a butcher."

"How can you judge anyone by looks?" Vanessa inquired hotly. "Napoleon Bonaparte does not *look* like a man who is responsible for the deaths of millions." She added. "It's passing cool. Do you suppose we might leave?"

"I'd be quite willing, myself," Lady Elizabeth agreed. "The wind is growing colder."

"I've noticed that too," Phoebe said softly.

"I'll issue the order to Bernard, then." Lady Elizabeth leaned forward.

Lady Maria Glazebrook was seated next to one of her dearest friends, Miss Belinda Compton, blond like herself, but sharp-featured and turned thirty, consequently an agreeable companion and foil. Miss Compton was speaking with Sir Peregrine Moffett, who had just ridden away from Lady Vanessa's equipage. He was being moderately amusing about the Farr ball, but Maria heard only a word in three. Her attention was riveted upon Sir Philip Langhorne, as, riding away from Lady Vanessa's carriage, he seemed to want to go back the way he had come. Unfortunately for him, his progress was halted by the crush of vehicles and he had necessarily to come forward, which would bring him within hailing distance. She was debating as to whether or not she ought to hail him. She had had a good view of what had taken place once he had attempted to speak to Lady Vanessa. However, she was quite sure he did not understand that pointed rejection. Undoubtedly he had not yet heard the gossip. Judging from what she knew of him, he was quite at sea in this confusing world, and considering the tale that was currently making the rounds, he would continue in that watery environment.

She wondered if it were true and was inclined to believe that an error had been made or even a libel perpetrated. Philip would never have wantonly hurt anyone. She remembered only too well the reason for the accident that had lamed him. He had climbed the tree to rescue a stranded cat! However, Lady Vanessa evidently credited the *on-dit* and, of course, she would—being a close friend of Lord Carlton as well as of his fiancée, Lady Phoebe Galliard. A small smile played about Lady Maria's mouth. She could not sympathize with Philip over that chill rebuff. She had glimpsed them the previous night and seen the immediate interest in his eyes as he had gazed upon Lady Vanessa. She, Lady Maria remembered, had been laughing. Her own smile vanished. She did not want to dwell on her conjectures at this moment in time. She was only pleased that an insurmountable barrier had been erected between them. A sigh escaped her.

It had been a rude shock meeting Philip last night. It had brought back a whole flock of bitter memories. She had adored him once, and her adoration had been returned. He had loved her and he had proposed to her, impulsively, without even consulting her parents.

They had been rightfully angry about that. They were even angrier about his lack of prospects. Oh, if only she had not listened to them! If only she had been brave and had agreed to run away with Philip, as he had daringly suggested. Unfortunately, there was no use wallowing in that particular pool of spilt milk. It had long ago soaked into the ground and she had yielded to the argument that, as a lowly doctor's bride, she could not hope to take her proper place in society. And, of course, Tom had been mad to have her and the engagement ring had been so satisfyingly large. She glanced down at her little hands. Were she prone to vulgar display, she could have worn diamonds on eight fingers and her two thumbs as well. They did not make up for the loss of Philip—*Sir* Philip!

His baronetcy was far older than that of Tom, whose grandfather had owned coal mines and whose great-grandfather had been a lowly but ambitious miner. Philip came from a long line of landed aristocrats, but he had been a younger son, and his father before him. She had told her parents that there was a remote chance that he might inherit and they had laughed in her face. And indeed, who could have foreseen the demise of his cousin even before his great-uncle—and poor Desmond, also. It was too, too depressing!

She looked in Philip's direction and experienced a surge of panic. He was no longer where she had seen him before. Had he managed to brook the tide? No! She had caught sight of him again and he was much closer to her carriage than he had been earlier. Was he coming to see her? No, he was merely trying to ride on ahead and escape the crowds. He looked very grim. Undoubtedly he was brooding over that late encounter with Lady Vanessa. And now he was within hailing distance! She must, must, must summon him to her side. She glanced at Miss Compton. She had better ask her not to tell Tom . . . but if she made such a request, dearest Belinda might suspect . . . and Philip was much closer now. Tom would not approve of her summoning him, but she did have to tell Philip what she had heard. It would be a kindness, and furthermore, it would serve to turn him from Lady Vanessa forever.

At the same time, she must impress upon him that she, Lady Maria, did not credit the slander. She would add that she was prepared to defend him to anyone who would listen. He would be grateful to her, and then, who could tell what might happen? After all, she was still young, and if she were a mother, at least she was not breeding at present. She was really at her best. Everyone said that she was much more beautiful than she had been, say, five years earlier, when a distraught Philip, in utter, utter dispair over her refusal and subsequent engagement, had dashed off to the wars. She had preserved his letter, half-protest at her heartlessness and half-apology for that protest and telling her that he understood her dilemma. Lady Maria wasted no more time in cogitation. Leaning forward, she called, "Philip! Philip! Sir Philip!"

"Maria!" Belinda protested. In shocked accents she added, "What are you about?"

"I know him," Lady Maria said over her shoulder. "Since we were the merest infants. Oh, dear, I do hope he's seen me. I must speak to him. I simply must!"

"He seems to be riding on ahead," Belinda commented.

"Yes, no . . . no, he's not." Lady Maria smiled triumphantly. "He's coming in my direction. I thought he must." Summoning up her most sympathetic expression, she happily prepared herself to tell him the worst.

3

"The butcher!" Sir Alastair, sitting in Philip Langhorne's suite at Grillons Hotel, repeated in disgust. His eyes roved over his friend's downcast face. "And Lady Vanessa believes that to be true?"

Philip nodded gloomily. "She's Greysham's sister and Lord Carlton's lifelong friend, but I expect you know that."

"I do." Sir Alastair rose and took a turn around the small parlor, stopping to glare at an unoffending and innocuous vase on the mantelshelf. "But damned if I put two and two together. It has been a long time since Albuera." He was silent a moment, staring moodily into space. "Damn the pair of them 'Tis a great pity you cannot call them out!"

"Would that muffle the gossip?" Philip demanded wryly. "No, 'twould only add more fuel to that particular blaze." He was silent a moment before adding, "It would not convince Lady Vanessa that Lord Carlton would have perished, and painfully, of gangrene had I not removed his shattered limb. The irony of it all is that I could not even remember the episode at first. Maria was shocked at my callousness, I fear, though she did not say so. She was most sympathetic and, bless her, she told me that she knew I could never have wantonly injured any living creature."

"Ummm." Sir Alastair found himself unmoved by Lady Maria's touted sympathy. However, it was no time to discuss her possible motives, not with Philip so deeply hurt and so incredibly misjudged by a goodly number of the *ton*. He did say, "I imagine you spared Lady Maria a description of your life in the surgeon's corps at the front and the long parade of 'episodes' with which you were confronted nearly every minute of every hour?" He scanned Philip's face. "I expect you offered no defense whatsoever."

"I told her only what I could recall, which was precious little, unfortunately." Philip fixed rueful eyes on Sir Alastair's face. "As you have just said, Lord Carlton was not the only wounded man I attended nor the only amputation I performed while we were at Albuera. But I do remember that his friend pleaded that I let him die, which, of course, I could not do. Maria agreed that I acted for the best, but though her acquaintance with Carlton is slight, she has said that some of his friends have told her that he cannot adjust to his infirmity. Lord, I understand that and I do sympathize with him, despite the havoc it has wrought in my life." He paused and shrugged. "Oh, well, do they not say that fortune's capricious, giving with the one hand, taking with the other?"

"It's the injustice that angers me!" Sir Alastair exclaimed. Before Philip could respond, he added, "And so your mind's made up? You'll be shaking the dust of London from your shoes and returning to Yorkshire?"

"I have not changed my plans in the ten minutes since you've been here, Alastair. There's nothing to hold me in London."

"Nothing? What will you do about your house?"

"I will make arrangements with my man of business to have it let for the rest of the Season. I would prefer to sell it, but—"

"You cannot sell it!" Sir Alastair protested. "It has been in your family for a hundred years and 'twas built on the site of a mansion that burned down—"

"Spare me a history I know full well," Philip interrupted impatiently.

Sir Alastair grimaced and then said, "It's unlike you to flee the field."

"Flee the field?" Philip repeated sharply. "What do you mean by that?"

"What other construction will be placed on this hasty departure, other than that the gossip is true and you wantonly maimed Carlton because you were in a hurry?"

Philip's brows drew together. "They will think what they choose to think, whether I go or stay. 'Tis a shame, for it makes the whole profession suspect. That is what angers me."

"And what of Lady Vanessa?"

Philip colored and looked away. "What of her? I have described her reception of me."

"She does not know the truth," Sir Alastair reminded him. "As you know, I am acquainted with the family. Lady Elizabeth, her aunt, is a most reasonable woman when presented with all the facts in a given situation."

"She is still the close relative of Lord Greysham, who . . ." Philip paused and stared at Sir Alastair. "Lord Greysham, if you'll remember, pleaded with me to let Carlton die."

Sir Alastair was silent a moment. "Yes," he said finally. " 'Tis true. I, too, remember that. And your refusal was taken in very bad part."

"Yes, but do you not see? His arguments suggest that he knew amputation was necessary. Can he have forgotten that?"

"He and Carlton are fast friends."

"Yes, but what has that to do with the situation?"

" 'Tis likely that Carlton's reasoning powers are in abeyance. He has needed to blame someone for his plight, and naturally the choice has fallen upon you. 'Tis easier than to face the situation squarely and admit that his reckless behavior on the field of battle was one of the underlying reasons for his injury. If I were so close a friend and felt as sorry for him as Lord Greysham must, I could probably convince myself that he was right."

Philip was silent for a moment. Then he said slowly, "Yes, that does make sense. And consequently, all London will believe them and continue to dub me a butcher. 'Tis better that I leave for Yorkshire while the roads are still passable."

"When will you go?"

"As soon as I have seen to matters here."

"Very well," Sir Alastair sighed. "I will bow to the inevitable. But will you ride with me in the park tomorrow morning? That stallion of yours could use the exercise."

"And shall have it," Philip said readily. He visited a long look on Sir Alastair's face. "I beg you'll not call me coward. I never have enjoyed large cities, as you know, and while I cannot but regret the stigma attached to my name, I shall welcome a sight of the country again. And . . ." He paused and sighed.

"And what?" Sir Alastair prompted.

"I do not enjoy a life of idleness. I was trained to be a physician. 'Tis not easy to relinquish my work in favor of a life of idle pleasure."

" 'Tis not all pleasure," Sir Alastair protested. "You have vast properties to manage."

"And agents to manage these vast properties. From my conferences with them, I have found that they resent my suggestions. Why would they not? They believe, and rightly, that I am a novice in such matters."

"That would set me thinking," Sir Alastair mused. "Agents, you know, are not always trustworthy. Your uncle was ill for a long time. They might have seized the occasion to feather their own nests. That's a matter you might pursue."

"I fear I am not equipped to find those plumes." Philip smiled wryly. "If 'twere not for these rumors, I would be inclined to set up a practice." He shook his head sadly. "But I fear I would have very few patients, and without my work, Alastair, I am a man at sea in an open boat with no rudder and no sails to catch the breeze."

"Ah, Philip, do not despair." Sir Alastair clapped him on the back. "There might come a large and unexpected wave to bear you safe to shore."

On leaving the hotel, Sir Alastair, turned thoughtful, walked slowly down the street. He wished that he knew Lord Greysham as well as he knew Lady Elizabeth. If that were the case, he might have been able to talk some sense into him. He toyed with the notion of bringing the matter to Lady Elizabeth's attention, but discarded it. She knew nothing of Philip and she would certainly side with her nephew. It was a damnable situation because, as he well knew, it was not only the gossip that was occasioning Philip's departure for the country, it was Lady Vanessa. Though Philip had said very little about her beyond describing his earlier encounter and his meeting this evening, Alastair had little doubt that his friend had been badly hurt. Philip had been ripe to fall in love, and fall he had, with a woman who would have made him an ideal wife.

Unlike many of her contemporaries, Lady Vanessa knew her own mind. He knew that from his conversations with Lady Elizabeth, as well as from his own observation. It was a good mind, too. She was intelligent and she was beautiful. Furthermore, she was a country girl at heart, and if she would suit Philip, he had a strong feeling that Philip would suit her—far more than the idle sprigs of fashion with which she was surrounded. And now what could have been an ideal couple had been driven apart by Carlton's unconscionable accusations, seconded by Greysham! Impossible to understand Carlton's thinking—but it was *not* thinking! It was, it had to be, a matter of insane pride, as if even the loss of a limb must be attributed to human error rather than to his own heedless actions on the field of battle. He snorted. Had Carlton an inkling of his folly? Was that the fuel that stoked his wrath? Possibly, it might be, on one level, but he doubted that the man was consciously aware of it. And Carlton did not matter. What mattered was Philip's happiness, he who had had such a damnably scant share of it in his short lifetime. Inadvertently Alastair thought of Lady Maria, and a sarcastic smile pulled at his lips. That was one little nose that was certainly out of joint, married to her clumsy Johnny-come-lately baronet for whom she had renounced Philip's love. How she must have enjoyed explaining those rumors!

"Bad cess to her!" he muttered aloud, and turned his mind back to Lady Vanessa. She and Philip deserved each other, and they must be brought together. That was why he had insisted that Philip ride with him in the park. To his certain knowledge, Lady Vanessa rode there every morning until the snows came. If she and Philip happened to meet tomorrow, nothing might come of it, but again, something might. He could only hope that Sir Peregrine Moffett might be her escort and not her brother. Moffett was an agreeable lightweight and could not possibly vie with Philip upon the field of love.

It was one of those mornings when the sky was almost an iridescent blue. It was patterned with pink-tinged clouds in shapes that approached definition. Vanessa, glancing upward, saw some sort of bulky animal with paws outstretched in close proximity to its heavy chin. It had floppy ears and then the wind chivvied it into scattered fragments. It was followed by a crab with well-defined claws. She laughed at her fancies, remembering that her governess had once chided her for them, saying that she was far too dreamy. That comment had always puzzled her. She expected that Miss Wellstood distrusted dreamers, not understanding the wild flights imagination could take. In those years, she had dreamed of romance, of bold knights and captive maidens out of *Le Morte d'Arthur*. Miss Wellstood had disapproved of that, too. She had appropriated the volume, saying, "You must think of your place in your world, Lady Vanessa. You have a great name and 'tis your duty to do justice to it."

And how did one do justice to a great name? By marrying well, had been her governess's quick response. Poor Miss Wellstood, she had left years ago, and consequently she would never know that her pupil would never be wed. Beneath her, Vanessa felt movement. Vulcan, her horse, was also impatient of dreamers and wanted to be on his way down the bridle paths of the park. There was a wind blowing and she would ride in it. She glanced over her shoulder at Johnny, just behind her.

"Race you!" she called.

He had been looking gloomy, his habitual expression these days and one which made her very glad he had not found out about Phoebe's bruised cheek. It would have shocked and distressed him, and nothing would have been gained by that knowledge. She suddenly loathed pity. Pity chained Phoebe to Charles and pity kept Johnny from telling his best friend about his feelings for . . . But she could not dwell on that now. Johnny was urging his horse forward.

"Very well, let's do race," he called. "Where's the finish line?"

"To the Serpentine and . . ." She paused, seeing two other early-rising horsemen coming up behind him. She did not usually meet many people at this hour. She wondered who they were and caught a glimpse of flaming hair under a high-crowned beaver. Sir Alastair McLean, she identified. His companion had dark brown eyes and corn-gold hair. Sir Philip Langhorne!

"Well, come, then, slowpoke. Are you racing or are you not?" Johnny demanded.

"I am racing, of course," she responded. With a flick of her crop on Vulcan's rump, which brought a startled snort from his mouth, she was off.

She was not concentrating on the race, however, but on the man she had just seen. The butcher. She had an interior wince for that nickname. It seemed very hard to believe that he could be guilty of the sort of negligence described by her brother and by Charles. Even in that brief glance, she could not help noticing his fine features set in a frank, open countenance. Furthermore, there was a gentleness about him which, if one were ill, would prove very soothing. Judging by his looks and his manner, she would have believed him a very good physician. She swallowed a sudden obstruction in her throat. In her mind's eye, she was regrettably, regretfully, witnessing their second encounter. He had been hurt by her coldness. She had been hurt too. She had been thinking about that brief moment off and on since it had taken place, and each time she had conjured up a vision of his expression as he had turned away, she had wanted to weep. She wished that he would pass her now—and disappear into the distance. She did not want to see him again, but she was racing Johnny. Very well, she would outdistance him, outdistance them all! Unthinkingly, she brought her crop down on Vulcan's rump a second time and was appalled. He did not appreciate such treatment! He did not have the stubbornness of Hercules, her other saddle horse. He needed only a word, and now he demonstrated his deep displeasure with a whinny that was close to a scream as he reared up, his eyes rolling and his front hooves flailing.

Vanessa made a futile effort to pull him in, but to no avail. He was determined to lose her, and lose her he did, dashing away as she hit the ground, hard. She was briefly conscious of a crack as if a branch had snapped beneath her, and then everything went black.

"Good God, Vanessa!" Sir Alastair, a few paces ahead of Philip, who was purposely staying back, brought his horse to a halt and swung down from his saddle. In that same moment, Philip, applying spurs to his horse, caught up with Sir Alastair and dismounted. Clutching his reins in one hand, he hurried to the fallen girl, noticing with some concern that her left arm was lying at an unnatural angle. Even without further examination, he was sure she had broken it. He looked ahead in search of Lord Greysham, but obviously he, riding pell-mell onward, was unaware of his sister's mishap.

He glanced up at Sir Alastair. "Fetch Greysham," he commanded. "I'll see to her."

"Her arm—" Sir Alastair began.

"I think it must be broken," Philip said.

"Oh, God, poor girl!"

"Ohhh, dear, what happened?" Vanessa spoke groggily. Opening her eyes, she stared up at Philip in surprise. "You!" she exclaimed. She made an effort to sit up, but he gently pushed her back. Calmly, matter-of-factly, as if, in fact, nothing had ever happened between them, he said gently, "You'd best lie still. You'll jar your arm."

Her thoughts had been in a turmoil, but at this suggestion, she forgot what she had been thinking. "My arm? Is . . . is there anything the matter with it?"

"I fear you may have hurt it. Not badly, but you'd best not

try to move it about at this moment—your left arm." He spoke soothingly.

"I'll go for your brother," Sir Alastair told her, and vaulted into his saddle.

"He's headed for the Serpentine," Vanessa explained. "He must be practically there by now."

"I'll find him. Meanwhile, you're in good hands." Sir Alastair rode off.

Staring ruefully up at Philip, Vanessa said, "We were racing, you see. And I applied the crop to Vulcan. He's not Hercules."

His lips twitched. "No, I'd say that they had very little in common."

She gave him a puzzled glance. "How would you know?" Before he could respond, she added with a little laugh, "Oh, I see what you mean. Actually, you are right. They do not. Hercules is my other horse. He is very stubborn. Vulcan is mercurial . . ." Again she laughed. "I do seem to be centered on the gods. I expect he ran away."

"He did," Philip corroborated. "However, we'll retrieve him for you. Now, let's see to this arm. I will have to ease back your sleeve, if you do not mind."

"I do not mind," she assured him. "You'll find the buttons very pesky, I fear. They're so small."

"No matter."

His fingers were deft, she noticed. He slid the sleeve up and then his light touch was on her arm. He nodded. " 'Tis as I thought."

"What . . . did you think?" she asked, trying not to sound as alarmed as she was beginning to feel. "It does not hurt," she added defensively.

"It will not, for the nonce. Fortunately, 'tis not your right arm. You'll need to keep it in a sling for some six weeks."

"I've broken it, then?"

"You have, but I beg you not to worry. 'Tis not serious. It wants only setting." At the sound of hooves, he glanced up quickly, saying on a note of relief, "Here's your brother."

Lord Greysham was down from his horse in a trice. Winding the reins around his hand, he came to his sister's side, looking at her with concern and saying abruptly, "What's this, Vanessa?"

Sir Alastair, also dismounting, exchanged a look with Philip in which concern was mingled with anger. He seemed on the verge of a comment, but did not voice it as Vanessa said, "As you see, Johnny, I was thrown. And Sir Philip seems to believe that I've broken my arm."

"Are you sure?" Lord Greysham had a cold look for Philip.

"I am sure, my lord," Philip said equably. "However, from what I can discern, 'tis a clean break. It must be set immediately."

"I'll take her to Harlock. He's our man," Lord Greysham stated.

"I'd not advise moving her until after I have set it," Philip protested. "She—"

"Why not? He's an accredited physician with an unblemished reputation."

The implication was clear, and Vanessa winced. She opened her mouth to protest, but in that same moment Philip said, "Moving her would jar and possibly bring further injury to the limb. If you will allow it, I will set the arm."

"No," Lord Greysham protested. "I'll not have it!"

"I want him to set it, Johnny." Vanessa made an effort to sit up.

"Please." Philip pushed her gently back. "You must lie still."

With some asperity Sir Alastair said, "I think you must admit, Greysham, that Sir Philip, who has served as surgeon with the armed forces on the Peninsula and in France, is quite qualified to set a broken arm. He has done as much for me." He held out his right arm and flexed it. "I've never had a day's trouble from it since."

"And," Vanessa added, "I do not need my brother's permission. I am twenty-one and my own mistress."

Lord Greysham reddened and frowned. "You cannot do it here. This path is much frequented by other riders."

"We will move her beyond the verge, of course," Philip said. "But carefully." He looked at Sir Alastair. "You'd best help me."

"I have said you cannot do it here!" Lord Greysham repeated angrily.

"On the contrary, my lord," Philip said calmly, "I can, and since I have received Lady Vanessa's permission, I will. I need only bandages and splints, which you, again, Alastair, can fetch for me if you will. My instruments are in my luggage at the hotel. You will find the splints in the same bag."

Lord Greysham stared at him wide-eyed, and Vanessa, in spite of a growing discomfort, was both surprised and impressed. Sir Philip's shyness had vanished. His tone had become crisp and authoritative. He reminded her of someone she knew but whom she could not quite place. In a moment, the name came to her. Mr. Harlock had much the same manner. A sense of security she had not even recognized made itself known at the same time that it grew stronger. "That does seem an admirable plan," she approved. "Do go, Sir Alastair, if you do not mind."

"Of course I do not mind. As soon as we've moved you, I'll be off."

With infinite care Sir Alastair and Philip brought Vanessa to a small glade. Seeing that she was comfortably situated, Sir Alastair moved back. "I'm off." He smiled, and mounting hastily, urged his horse back along the bridle path.

Lord Greysham still eyed Philip mistrustfully. "I expect," he began in no conciliatory tone, "that you *have* treated a good many similar conditions."

"I have," Philip acknowledged. He turned away from his lordship and looked down at Vanessa. Shrugging himself out of his coat, he folded it, and kneeling beside her, slipped it under her head. "I hope this will make you feel more the thing," he said concernedly.

"It definitely does," she acknowledged. Meeting his dark gaze, she had an uncomfortable recollection of the previous day. She longed to say something by way of apology, but she was having trouble in sorting out her thoughts. One conclusion had emerged, and that concerned his competence as a physician. Despite all that her brother and Lord Carlton had said, she found herself doubting them. She was sure that Sir Philip would never make a wrong decision. He commanded trust. Immediately, upon that conclusion, her arm began to ache. She swallowed a moan, and not wanting to acknowledge the hurt, she managed a smile. "You'll think me entirely cow-handed, I fear."

"No," he said gently. "You have an admirable seat on a horse." He added. "I expect your arm is beginning to be rather painful now."

She regarded him amazedly, wondering how he had guessed. "Not really," she demurred, half-raising it in an effort to prove that she felt nothing. Unfortunately, that movement sent little barbs of pain coursing through it.

Philip put his hand down on her wrist. "You must remain still," he ordered.

"You are sure it's a clean break?" Lord Greysham asked anxiously.

Vanessa started. She had forgotten that her brother was nearby, and no wonder! He had been extremely quiet. She guessed that he, too, had been impressed by Sir Philip's manner, and with a little thrill of anger, she guessed it was not the first time he had observed it.

"It is, my lord." Philip spoke soothingly. "She is fortunate that she fell as she did. Though"—he had a warm, reassuring smile for Vanessa—"she may not believe it at this moment."

Lord Greysham regarded his sister with a concern blended with censure. "I have told you that Vulcan has an uncertain disposition."

"It was not his fault," she said quickly. " 'Twas entirely mine. He's not used to being struck."

"You did that?" Lord Greysham raised his eyebrows. "Sure you know better, Vanessa."

She stifled a sigh. All too clearly, she remembered the reason for that untoward action. However, since it was one she could not explain, she contented herself with saying merely, "I was too desirous of maintaining my lead."

"Silly gudgeon," he scolded gently. "No race is worth this!" With a frown he added, "You might have broken your neck."

"But I did not," she pointed out. "Gracious, Johnny, such a pother over practically nothing!"

" 'Tis not nothing," he protested. "I should never have tried to race you."

" 'Twas not your idea. 'Twas mine, if you'll recall," she said comfortingly.

"You should not have suggested it. And I should never have acted upon that suggestion. And—"

"I think you must not argue now," Philip interposed.

Vanessa tensed as she saw her brother's face darken at the reprimand, but then he surprised her by saying gruffly, "You are right, Langhorne. She ought not to be excited at present."

"I am not excited," Vanessa assured him.

"You are," Lord Greysham insisted. "Your face is flushed and . . . But your physician has said I must not argue with you." He turned to Philip. "I hope that Sir Alastair will not be too long in returning. We should get her home as soon as possible."

" 'Twill depend upon the congestion in the streets," Philip said. "Fortunately, 'tis early."

"Yes, that is fortunate," Lord Greysham agreed. He further surprised his sister by adding, " 'Twas well that you and Sir Alastair were abroad at this hour."

"I am glad of it too, my lord," Philip responded.

"And I." Vanessa smiled and was silent, struck by the thought that if Sir Philip had not been present, she never would have suggested the race to her brother. Yet, on the whole and despite her accident, she was not as regretful as she might have been. She had come to know Sir Philip better and she doubted that acquaintance would end once she returned home. He would come to see her, and judging from Johnny's less antagonistic attitude, he would not forbid that visit. And when the opportunity presented itself, she would try to make amends for her cruel slight of yesterday. And . . . Before she could speculate further, Sir Alastair returned.

In spite of her trust in Philip, Vanessa was conscious of qualms as, taking his satchel from Sir Alastair, he opened it and began to remove rolls of bandage and other items. She had never broken a limb, but Johnny had, she remembered, and it seemed to her that she recalled his saying that the process of setting had been "deuced uncomfortable." She moved restlessly as Philip knelt beside her again, and once more he seemed to have divined her thoughts.

"You must relax," he said softly. "You must not be afraid, you know." His dark gaze caught and held her eyes—so that she could not seem to look away. "I promise you it will not hurt. Do you believe me?"

His low, uninflected tone of voice was much at variance with the way he had been speaking earlier. His dark, unwavering stare continued to command and hold her attention. A fugitive memory stirred, something her brother had said about Lord Carlton in connection with . . . in connection with . . . She could not remember, because Philip was still speaking, was saying, "You are tired. Your head is very heavy. You must rest, must rest, must rest . . ."

"Rest? I do not want to rest." Rest, indeed, was the farthest thing from her mind. Yet, even as she endeavored to explain that to him, she found herself unable to speak. She also felt tired and sleepy, which was odd. She had not felt tired before . . . or had she? She was finding it very difficult to concentrate. Her thoughts seemed to be like the clouds overhead, constantly changing shape before she could identify them.

"*What are you doing, Langhorne?*"

There was both alarm and anger in Lord Greysham's question.

Hearing it, Vanessa wondered vaguely why he should be so angry, but she could not bring herself to question him. She was too weary. Her eyelids seemed strangely weighted and heavy, far too heavy for her to keep them open, and yet she did not want to sleep, not at all, but *he* wanted it.

"Sleep, you must sleep," he was saying.

"I do not . . ." she managed to whisper, but doubted if he had even heard her, for he still urged her to sleep, and evidently her brother had ceased to remonstrate with him, for she could no longer hear his voice. Indeed, as her eyes closed, she no longer heard anything at all.

4

"Now, this is the sort of setting I approve for you, Philip."
Sir Alastair stood in an airy drawing room hung with fine
paintings and furnished with pieces from the workshops of
Chippendale and Adam. French doors opened on a small
garden with patterned walks and trees caught in autumn's
palette of colors. There were marble busts set on mahogany
pedestals between windows draped in beige damask. There
was also a pianoforte in the corner near the door, indicative
of the former owner's love of music, also expressed in the
well-equipped music room down the hall. "Are you not
comfortable here?"

"I do find it to my liking," Philip admitted as he drew on
a pair of new chamois gloves.

He was, Sir Alastair noted with an amusement tinged with
admiration, dressed with especial care in a new brown coat of
superfine. His stockinette trousers were tan and his waistcoat
a gold brocade. His hessian boots were polished to a high
shine and the greatcoat he had flung over a chair bore several
capes. His starched cravat was so intricately tied that it
suggested a valet of exceptional talent and imagination. However, to his certain knowledge, Philip had yet to hire a
valet, which made his sartorial efforts the more laudable.
Still, despite his new and felicitous background, he did not
seem entirely at ease in his surroundings. Consequently Sir
Alastair felt impelled to say, "But for me, you'd have been
tooling down some chill stretch on the Great North Road.

Admit that 'twas well I persuaded you to go riding three days ago.''

Philip's dark eyes gleamed. "I cannot deny it. And was it you forced her horse to bolt?''

"I cannot claim responsibility for that, but if you'd not been there when it did bolt, you'd have soon been shivering in the winds from off the moors. I rest my case, your lordship.''

"A point well taken, O learned judge.''

"Not judge but advocate," Sir Alastair contradicted. "All joking aside, I am delighted that your differences are at an end.''

"With Lady Vanessa, at least." Philip nodded. "I, too, am heartily glad of that, but I do not believe that Lord Greysham is entirely in favor of my visits.''

"Greysham's slow to change his mind on any count, and having cast you as the villain in this work, he is loath to hand you another side.''

"Side?" Philip questioned.

"Another word for 'part,' as in a play. I expect Carlton, being apprised of this situation, is also disturbed. He'll need to con another playscript.''

Philip regarded him in some surprise. "I had no idea you were so addicted to the theater, Alastair.''

"I am not, my friend, but it provides a proper analogy. To my mind, actors do not imitate life, they parody it with their wordy declamations. Even Kean's posturings fail to impress me. But I do digress. I should not discuss or deplore acting techniques. I should applaud a leading lady—and of such stuff is Lady Vanessa.''

"Yes," Philip agreed. He added softly, "She has been very brave.''

" 'Tis her nature . . . and she was fortunate, also.''

"Fortunate?''

"In finding so excellent a surgeon. But do not let me detain you any longer. I know you are bound for Greysham House.''

"And you also, I thought.''

"Do you still want my company?"

"Of course."

Sir Alastair's eyes filled with laughter. "I suspect you of hoping that I will keep Lady Elizabeth amused and, if he is present, Greysham as well, while you examine or, perhaps, entertain the beautiful Vanessa."

"You've ferreted out my devious designs." Philip grinned.

"I could wish you were more devious, Philip, especially when you enter a den of wolves."

"I have counted only one wolf," Philip responded. "And I hope to draw its teeth."

"You were not trained as a veterinarian," Sir Alastair said meaningfully. "I hope you do not get bitten in the process."

" 'Twill not send me mad if I do." Philip shrugged. "The rewards surpass the risks."

Several streets away, Lady Vanessa, ensconced on a sofa in the sunny second drawing room of Greysham House, glared up at its present lord. "I have promised to receive him. You knew that, were here the day before yesterday when I saw him last. And still you are full of these ridiculous objections! I do not understand you. Or rather, I do. You've been with Charles and he's been upbraiding you, obviously."

Lord Greysham said stubbornly, "Harlock is due any minute. He is your physician."

"Sir Philip is my physician on this occasion," Vanessa retorted. "I cannot understand why you took it upon yourself to summon Mr. Harlock. I have suffered very little pain in my arm."

"All the same, I require a second opinion."

"I do not! Furthermore, you had no right to bring him here without consulting me."

"Aunt Elizabeth agrees with me."

"Aunt Elizabeth's not my guardian, and neither are you. I am my own woman. And Sir Philip is my physician."

"I must say that your opinion of him has undergone a rapid reversal!"

Vanessa glared at him. "You are being totally unreasonable, Johnny. I do not see how you can speak in such a manner after you *witnessed* his treatment of my arm!''

He frowned and said angrily, ''I do not trust the man. Charles's experience—''

''I am inclined to believe that Charles's condition warranted the treatment he received,'' Vanessa cut in.

''I am inclined to believe that that witch doctor has mesmerized you into liking him. I do not approve of that treatment in particular!''

''Even though I experienced no pain from the setting, a process which Phoebe, who has suffered a similar injury, describes as hurtful? I think it was next to a miracle, myself. And as for his powers of mesmerism, they do not extend so far. I liked him the first time I met him, which, as I explained to you, was at the Farr ball. Furthermore—''

A tap on the door silenced Vanessa and caused her to cast an eager look in that direction. ''Yes?'' she called.

The door was opened by Soames, the butler, a tall graying and pompous man in his early fifties. ''Mr. Harlock,'' he announced in tones that relegated the physician to a position considerably lower than those who were awaiting him.

Hearing that lofty but denigrating announcement, Vanessa thought of Philip with regret. He, too, must have received many such slights from so-called ''superior'' servants, and she had added to them herself that afternoon in the park. She wondered if he had forgiven her for that. She had offered no apologies but she had tried to make amends in manner and address. Still, it seemed to her that he seemed a trifle withdrawn, and she sensed that he was also on guard. Her thoughts reverted to Mr. Harlock. Much as she resented the reasons behind his arrival, she must greet him pleasantly if only to make up for Soames's arrogance.

Harlock, a pleasant-faced and unassuming man in his mid-forties, came in quickly. He had a smile for Vanessa and a respectful bow for Lord Greysham. After a polite exchange of greetings, he came to the sofa. ''Well,'' he said affably, ''what is this, Lady Vanessa? I am told that you suffered a fall from your horse.''

She extended her hand to the physician, saying as he took it, "I did, and 'twas through pure carelessness."

"Surely not," he said politely, releasing her hand and looking at the sling. "When did this accident take place?"

"Three days ago, Mr. Harlock," Vanessa said.

"Three days?" He regarded her quizzically. "And why was I not summoned sooner?"

"There was a physician present, as it happened." Vanessa glanced at her brother. "He was able to attend to my arm."

"But I wanted a second opinion, Mr. Harlock," Lord Greysham explained.

"I see." A crease appeared between Harlock's brows. "You do not trust this other person?"

"I do," Vanessa said cooly. "And—" She paused at another tap on the door.

"Yes?" Lord Greysham called.

The butler appeared on the threshold a second time. "Sir Alastair McLean. Sir Philip Langhorne," he announced with that subtle shading of respect that had been absent from his prior introduction.

"Please admit them, Soames," Vanessa said.

"*Sir* Philip Langhorne?" the physician inquired, raising his eyebrows in evident surprise.

"Are you acquainted with him, then?" Lord Greysham demanded. Before he received a response, the two men entered. Another exchange of greetings was interrupted as Harlock, staring at Philip with surprise and pleasure, strode forward, extending his hand.

"My dear fellow!" he exclaimed.

"Alden . . . Alden Harlock!" Philip said with similar pleasure. "Well met, man. I had planned to look you up."

"Well, you are spared the search." Oblivious of his employers, he added, "And you are *Sir* Philip now?" As Philip nodded, he continued. "So they knighted you for your services abroad. Well, there's none deserved it more!"

Philip reddened. "Nothing of the kind, Alden. 'Twas not an honor, 'twas an inheritance."

"You know each other, I see," Lord Greysham commented.

"Indeed we do, my lord," Harlock said enthusiastically. 'This young man was at the top of his class in Edinburgh. We met when I came to pay a call on my old friend Sir Hartley Manners, who, you may know, is one of the heads of the school. Sir Hartley had nothing but the highest praise for him, which he went on to fully justify by his services on the Peninsula." He had a quizzical look for Philip. "And now you have retired?"

Philip sighed. "As to that, I've not come to any decision, but of late my practice has been limited to only one, I fear."

"And I am that one," Vanessa said with a triumphant glance at her brother.

Harlock glanced at Lord Greysham and then back to Philip. With some amazement he said, "Am I to understand that you attended Lady Vanessa?"

Philip nodded. "Fortunately, I too was riding in the park that morning, and even more fortunately, I was not far away from her when she sustained the fall. The break—in the humerus about two inches above the elbow—was fortunately clean."

"I see." Harlock nodded. "A minor injury, but painful in the setting, I expect."

"No," Vanessa contradicted. "I felt no pain. Sir Philip put me to sleep."

"To sleep?" Harlock gave him a knowing look. "Mesmerism. I understand that you practiced that in Spain and Portugal."

"Yes," Philip said. "It proved most effective in many cases."

" 'Tis not easy to master. I have made the attempt myself, but with little success."

"You approve the work of Mesmer?" Lord Greysham inquired.

"Indeed I do, my lord. Though, of course, it does not always work."

"When does it not?" Lord Greysham demanded.

"The patient must be receptive and suggestible. There must be a definite rapport between the two."

"The patient and the mesmerist?"

"That is my belief, my lord."

"And if there is no such relationship?"

"In some cases, the treatment may still prove effective, depending upon the condition of the patient."

"If this patient is weakened by a wound and has suffered a considerable loss of blood, might that not cause him to be more receptive than ordinarily?" Vanessa asked.

Harlock had an approving look for her. "Exactly. In those circumstances, his defenses are down and he might, though not always, yield to the persuasions of the mesmerist."

"I can understand that completely." Vanessa did not look at her brother, or, indeed, at anyone in the room. The audacious course upon which she had decided to embark rather took her breath away, but she was determined to see it through. Fixing her eyes on the physician's face, she continued. "Would you, Mr. Harlock, imagine that Sir Philip, through the exigencies attendant upon operating during the heat of battle—and with many other casualties requiring his immediate attention—ever amputate a man's leg without giving the alternatives due consideration?"

"Vanessa!" Lord Greysham exploded.

She took no notice of his interruption. Calmly she continued, "This, because he was in a hurry to attend to those others who needed him?"

Harlock stared at her incredulously, his face paling, his gaze angry. "Good God!" he burst out, then paused, making a determined effort to control himself. "I assure you, Lady Vanessa, that the very thought of such a lapse is unthinkable in any surgeon, much less a man of Philip's caliber and integrity! He has always been dedicated to the saving of life and, if possible, limb."

"That is entirely my feeling," she said softly. She turned to her brother. "I am sure that anyone who has been fortunate enough to be a patient of Sir Philip's must agree with me."

A small silence was broken by Lord Greysham. He moved toward Philip, saying gratingly, "It seems that I owe you an apology, sir." He paused and cleared his throat. "I will also speak to Charles. You see, we . . . we have been friends since childhood, and to see him in such straits, limping along so painfully, where he used to leap . . .'' He swallowed and paused briefly. ''I fear that I agreed with him that you were too hasty in your decision that day in Albuera. It did not mend matters for him to believe that, nothing could, but it did provide a . . . a diversion of sorts. Consequently I must beg your pardon and, at the same time, ask your understanding.''

''I do understand,'' Philip said gently. ''He was a very active man.''

''Active and rash,'' Vanessa amplified. She fixed her eyes on Lord Greysham's flushed face. ''Charles has always been in love with danger, which can be a most exacting mistress.''

''Vanessa!'' Lord Greysham protested.

''Quite right, and very well put, my child.''

Everyone in the room turned to find Lady Elizabeth standing in the doorway. She came in, smiling at them. ''And so the air is clear, is it? And this young man exonerated.''

''Exonerated?'' Harlock cried, and flushed, looking at Lady Elizabeth. ''I beg your pardon, milady.''

''Exonerated from the charges of being a butcher, yes,'' Vanessa said clearly.

''Good God!'' Harlock exclaimed. ''I had heard something of that rumor, but knew not to whom it had been affixed. 'Tis unthinkable in connection with Philip.''

''So we are all agreed, I hope,'' Vanessa said. She turned to Philip and found him flushed. ''And,'' she added, ''I beg that he will forgive me for my unkindness of a few days ago.''

'' 'Tis forgotten quite,'' Philip said softly.

''Good, very good indeed,'' Lady Elizabeth said approvingly. ''I was about to suggest tea—but I think we might all be the better for a glass of wine.''

''An admirable suggestion, Aunt Elizabeth,'' Lord Greysham approved. ''I think we must toast Sir Philip.''

''And so his sins are forgiven and Sir Philip Langhorne is received into the heavenly spheres of Greysham House and all the privileges accruing?'' Lord Carlton said challengingly.

They were in the spacious but gloomy library of his town house. The room was made even more gloomy by reason of the draperies being drawn against the bright autumnal light of a day in mid-November.

"I would have told you the whole of it sooner, Charles," Lord Greysham said defensively. "But you were ill and feverish."

"And you feared to raise my temperature even higher with the news of your capitulation?" Carlton questioned sarcastically. Wrapped in a dressing gown of heavy scarlet satin stitched with gold, he lay supine on a long leather couch. His eyes, Greysham noted, were unnaturally bright, almost feverish. He had seen him in similar states and guessed that he had been smoking opium, an addiction that was growing on him.

Greysham stifled a sigh. At times like these, he was uncomfortably reminded of the years before they had been sent to the Peninsula. Then Charles would have been horrified at the thought of sequestering himself in this dark overheated chamber. He would have been equally horrified at the idea of inhaling the smoke of the poppy. However, that Charles was not the man he had once been was only too obvious. He had not made the effort to rise above his infirmity. Instead, he had surrendered to it, and though Greysham could not find it in his heart to blame him, he could not help but think of poor Phoebe, sharing Charles's gloom and being all but stifled by it.

She had been looking very wan and unhappy of late, and he had longed to hold her in his arms and comfort her, but he dared not dwell on that. Phoebe was forever beyond his reach and he must remember why he was here. It was for a reason he would have preferred not to discuss, but there was no help for it. Phoebe, again, had made reticence impossible. Charles knew that Sir Philip was being welcomed at Greysham House.

Greysham said coolly, "I did not fear to disturb you, Charles. As I have explained, I was primed to give you the whole of it when it took place . . . but you had gone to the country. And, as I have also explained, I am of the opinion that you . . . that we both reached an erroneous conclusion regarding Sir Philip."

'Hear, hear . . .'' Carlton drawled.

'From what I have been able to observe,'' Greysham continued stubbornly, ''Sir Philip is a man of considerable integrity. I am also assured, by those whose opinion I value, that he could not have operated on you without due consideration and the conviction that he had no alternative.''

'I see!'' Carlton bit the words off. He continued coldly, 'And are you prepared to receive this . . . paragon of integrity into the bosom of your family—or rather, the bosom of one specific member of your family?''

'That is not at issue.''

'Is it not? I was given to understand that your sister seems infatuated with the man. At least that is the impression I received from Phoebe. And your aunt admires him, as does Phoebe also. She prates of his gentle manners, finding them, no doubt, infinitely preferable to mine. In other words, my dear Johnny, Sir Philip, like Caesar before him, has come, has seen, and has conquered. The butcher is no more. In his place stands a . . . possible benedict. When will this felicitous coupling take place?''

'There are no such plans in the offing,'' Greysham responded.

''But if there were, what would you say?'' Without giving him a chance to reply, Carlton continued. ''Judging from your present beneficent attitude, I would say that you are more than prepared to give them your blessing.''

Greysham frowned. ''I have no jurisdiction over my sister, as you well know. She is her own mistress. However, I think I can safely say that she and Sir Philip, who have known each other a little more than a month, are good friends and nothing more.''

A mocking smile curled Carlton's lips. ''I fear that observation is not your strong suit, Johnny. Dearest Phoebe is all atwitter over Sir Philip's sterling qualities, the which she would have been delighted to enumerate when I returned from the country last week. Unfortunately, I did not give her the opportunity. Still, I had the distinct impression that she and her mantua maker are poring over the designs for the gown she will have made for the wedding.''

"Nonsense," Greysham responded uncomfortably. "I tell you, they are only friends.''

"And I tell you, my dear Johnny, that men and women cannot be friends. They can be only enemies or lovers, and the charming Vanessa could do worse. The man is wealthy, wellborn, and a skilled physician. Imagine the benefits that must arise from such a connection. You and whatever bride you ultimately choose must profit too.''

"I am not contemplating marriage, and neither, I believe, is my sister.''

"Is that a belief or a hope? Can it be possible that now you've allied yourself with the angels, you are finding heaven a trifle uncomfortable?''

"Damn you!" Greysham burst out. "I tell you I could do nothing else than accept the man, what with Harlock singing his praises, and my sister as well. I do believe him a skilled physician. He spoke of gangrene, Charles, and said that if he'd not operated, and soon, you'd have died in days. I see no reason to disbelieve that diagnosis.''

"And nor do I!" Lord Carlton exclaimed. With a bitter look he added, "I anticipated gangrene. I wanted it, damn him.''

There was a long pause while Greysham stared at him incredulously. Finally he said slowly, "Then . . . your accusation that he was getting even with you for some quarrel, that was not true. And also the fact that he acted too hastily . . .''

"That was your contention, Johnny," Carlton reminded him. "Also you reprimanded him for it.''

"And you agreed that I was right, and said as much to all our friends—and dubbed him butcher. Yet you knew there was no hope of saving your leg.''

"Of course I knew," Lord Carlton said impatiently. "And you'd have known it too, had you given it more than a cursory glance. I know the sight of it distressed you, Johnny.''

"You had me believing in his perfidy," Lord Greysham said angrily.

"He should have done as I requested!" Carlton cried.

"He did not want to accept the role of murderer," Greysham retorted harshly.

"Murderer? He'd not have been my murderer, but my savior! Do you think I relish this life he has so munificently returned to me? Can you believe that I was born to hop about like some . . . some filthy toad? Do you imagine that any gently bred female would want to share my bed when she learns she must cuddle up to . . . to this?" Carlton flung his robe aside, baring the scarred stump of his leg. "Am I supposed to thank Philip Langhorne for inflicting life upon me when I wanted . . . when I craved death?"

Lord Greysham winced. He gave Carlton a long look. "I blame myself as well," he sighed. "I let my feelings for you rule my head. No matter how you felt, Charles, your blame was misplaced, and moreover, it was unjust!"

"Misplaced and unjust, blast your eyes!" Unthinking, Carlton sprang from the sofa and, as if he still had two legs to support him, moved forward, only to fall prone at his friend's feet.

"Charles!" Lord Greysham cried, and knelt beside him. "Oh, Charlie," he said brokenly, flinging his arms around him. "Are you hurt, man?"

"No, no, I am not hurt." Carlton half-lifted himself. "Damn you, Johnny, help me back to the couch," he begged.

"Yes, of . . . of course," Lord Greysham said. Tears ran down his cheeks as he lifted Lord Carlton and gently settled him on the couch.

"Oh, Johnny . . ." Carlton pulled his robe around him. "My apologies. I keep forgetting, you see, that I am no longer a whole man, sound of wind and limb."

Greysham swallowed and nodded. "I . . . understand, of course," he said throatily.

Carlton sighed and passed his hands over his face. "Sometimes I think 'twould have been better for me to have put a period to my existence so as not to distress my friends with my ravings, or poor Phoebe, who is so patient, so valiant, so kind, and such a damned little liar.''

"Phoebe a liar?" Lord Greysham regarded him half in anger, half in confusion. "You . . . you do not know what you are saying, Charlie. You are mad.''

"No, my dear, dear fire-eater, and I beg you'll not spit your flames at me. I am not mad. She does not love me, you see. And furthermore, I think you know what I am talking about. Also, Johnny—and may God help me—I do not love her, either.''

Greysham said incredulously, "You *are* mad!''

"I swear to you that at this present moment I am as sane as I ever shall be. I cannot bear the pity she so desperately tries to conceal from me. I grow angry and lash out at her. Once I was so furious I actually struck her!''

"You struck her!" Lord Greysham paled and moved back, glaring at him, his fists clenched.

"Do not pummel me to a pulp, Johnny. 'Tis after the fact and 'twill not happen again.''

"You'd best make damned sure it doesn't," Lord Greysham growled.

"Calm down, my dear friend. I tell you this only to show you my damnable state of mind where poor Phoebe is concerned. I do not want her here. However, until now I have lacked the resolution to tell her the truth. No . . .'' He actually looked sheepish. "As long as I am in the mood to be absolutely honest, let me say that I, out of my own frustration and misery, have wanted her to suffer too, and Langhorne as well. They say that an infirmity can either improve your character and make a saint out of you or undermine it and turn you into a devil. I fear I have chosen the latter course, and in the doing of it, I have served the one I love above all other a very bad turn.''

"Phoebe . . .'' Lord Greysham began confusedly.

"Not Phoebe. I mean you, Johnny. Your good opinion, your kindness, your friendship . . .'' Carlton's voice faltered and he stared down at his hands. "I know I have tried them sorely recently. It seems that the devil I have mentioned has been sitting on my shoulder, prompting me to wound all those whom I love or have loved the most. And I think I have hurt you, who have always been my champion, worst of all."

"No, Charlie, no, no, 'tis not true," Lord Greysham assured him.

"Hear me out before you contradict me. Know also that I have known for a long time that you love Phoebe, and furthermore, I also know that she loves you. I imagine 'tis an open secret between you."

"I have never spoken . . ."

"I know that too, Johnny, just as I am sure that she has kept her own counsel. You are both saints and should have nothing to do with devils."

Greysham came nearer the couch. In a voice turned husky once more, he said, "I am far from saintly, Charlie."

"My friend . . ." Carlton smiled up at him. "My dear, dear friend, for God's sake, marry Phoebe and make her and all of us happy! And do not imagine that I will become a hermit, a prey to opium and other squalid vices. I intend to go away."

"Go away?" Lord Greysham repeated fearfully. "Where?"

"To the country, to my estate, and . . . my mistress."

"Your mistress!" Lord Greysham regarded him in amazement. "You have . . . ? There . . . there is someone in residence at—?"

"Yes," Carlton interrupted. "And has always been there. You know her, as do Vanessa and Phoebe as well. Possibly you'll not recall that scrawny little waif who used to fetch birds for us when we went shooting?"

"I do not think I remember . . ." Greysham began.

"Think hard, Johnny. Think how often you used to order her away, and if you did not, I did, when she would tag after us like some shadow."

"I . . ." Lord Greysham paused and then said incredulously, "You'll not be meaning that freckle-faced, carrot-topped little—"

"The same." Carlton smiled. "Anne Tompkins, the housekeeper's daughter." His voice softened. "Only she's neither scrawny nor carrot-topped now, Johnny. Her hair is tawny and she's slim as a fairy. Her freckles have almost faded, and though you may not call her beautiful, she is most beguiling. When I was brought home, 'twas she who sat by my bed for hours, soothing and cosseting me. Later, when I was on the mend, she came to that same bed and begged me to love her. I did, Johnny. She . . . We have a son. He is a most bonny infant, a felicitous blend of us both. And very bright. Though I've not seen him as often as I should, he knows me. A fortnight ago . . .'' He shook his head. "I will not bore you by a recital of his charms. His name is Michael Charles John, and before long he'll be Carlton as well.

"I do not know why I have not gone to them before, save that perhaps my resident devil wanted to make Annie suffer too, because I love her. I do love her, Johnny. All this has somehow cleared the air and my head as well. Your tears have made me see what I am doing to you, to myself, and to Phoebe. Go to her, my dear friend, and I will go home to my Annie.''

5

"Ten weeks . . . two and a half months—is that long enough? It ought to be," Vanessa whispered to herself. Garbed in a new walking dress of dark green kerseymere, trimmed with silken floss of a lighter green, she rotated in front of her bedroom looking glass, critically surveying her person. Letty, her maid, stood behind her holding up another glass so that she might get the full effect of her new coiffure. Her curls were drawn back in a style which her maid called "ala Greck," causing Vanessa to wince and smother a giggle. Greck or Grecque, whatever, it was becoming. And perhaps Sir Philip would let his eyes stray to her hair, her face, and her shape. She did not think he was entirely oblivious of these assets—but even though her arm had been in the very pink of condition for a full month, he had confined his comments to it alone. "If only . . ."

"Yes, milady?" Letty asked.

"Nothing," Vanessa replied self-consciously. Recently she had fallen into the regrettable habit of talking to herself. It was two and a half months since she had fallen from her horse and in love with Philip Langhorne, two events which had happened almost simultaneously. She was not entirely sure that immediately upon gazing up into his concerned brown eyes, she had been afflicted by that most tender of all emotions. However, it had happened within that period, give or take a day, and it had grown by leaps and bounds! She could compare it to the wild spread of crabgrass that, according to Mr. Heathersage, the head gardener at Greysham's Hold, their country estate, "spreads without no encouragement nohow. An' when you uproot it, 'twill come back as quick as anythin'."

She had tried to uproot it, at least in the beginning, before the feeling had gotten completely out of hand. She had told herself that she could not have possibly fallen in love so quickly and with no spoken encouragement from the object of her desire. True, he looked at her in a way she fondly hoped denoted a special interest. However, he confined his remarks to the weather and the state of her arm, varying these with references to the political upheaval taking place during the Congress of Vienna or the possible conclusion of the British-American hostilities. It was very frustrating. Vanessa turned away from her mirror with a fleeting smile at her abigail. "You may go, Letty."

"Yes, milady." Letty bobbed a brief curtsy and left.

As the door closed behind the girl, Vanessa breathed easier. In the moments before Sir Philip arrived to take her driving, she wanted to be alone with thoughts that, in her present state of mind, might inadvertently be expressed out loud. These would not require comments, particularly those which Letty could offer. Furthermore, anything she confided to Letty would be mulled over by her fellow servants, who would whisper it to friends in other houses, with the result that a goodly part of London would be aware that Lady Vanessa Ventriss cherished an unrequited passion for Sir Philip Langhorne.

"And why is it unrequited?" She turned her back to her mirrored image.

Her image looked blank. Sir Philip *was* more at ease with her, Vanessa thought, more at ease in general now that the harmful gossip had been largely scotched by her brother in his desire to make amends. Charles had also helped before leaving for the country.

So much had happened, so very much, she thought amazedly, and a great deal of it had been engendered by Philip's arrival, if only inadvertently.

Phoebe, for instance, had ceased to remind her of an early Christian martyr within three steps of a lion-filled arena. Johnny, too, was relaxed and happy now that the announcement of their engagement had been inserted in the *Morning Post* and, even more amazing, Charles was reported to be equally happy. Johnny, who had posted to the country to be present at his friend's wedding to one Anne Tompkins, daughter of his late housekeeper, had brought Vanessa this news. Needless to say, the Marquess of Carlton's nuptials had *not* been announced in the *Morning Post*. Instead, the town gossips, primed by Lord Greysham, had whispered of a secret marriage, which had taken place months earlier, resulting in the birth of a son and heir. Johnny, who was not particularly fond of children, especially those no more than a year old, had pronounced the youthful heir to be adorable and the image of his father. Lord Carlton was described as infatuated with both son and wife.

"In less than three months, everything has changed!" Vanessa murmured, gazing around her chamber. It was a sufficiently pretty and comfortable room. Flowered chintz curtains hung at the windows, and their colors, green and gold, were duplicated on the carpet and bed hangings. An ormolu clock ticked on her mantelshelf and over it hung a portrait of her long-dead mother. The likeness had been made at the time of her marriage in 1778, when she was a mere seventeen. She had been a fragile beauty, and who, Vanessa had often thought, would not be fragile, encumbered and well-nigh engulfed by the garments of the period? Her wide skirts were tricked out by hoop petticoats and her hair piled high over horsehair forms and surmounted by a tulle cap. No wonder her mother's slender body had collapsed under all those weighty garments. She had spent the last years of her short life clad in diaphanous negligees and lying on a sofa similar to the one that stood in front of her own fireplace and which she herself rarely used.

Vanessa did not have very happy memories of her late mother. Lady Greysham had never welcomed the sight of herself or her brother, fretfully moaning that they gave her the headache. Their father, beyond sternly counseling them not to disturb their mother, had also ignored them. He had been seldom at home. He, Vanessa knew, preferred a score of less fragile females. He had been notorious for his liaisons. Consequently, it was strange that her brother, beyond a few wild oats, cared only for Phoebe, while she herself, with no oats to her credit, had loved only one among the many young men who had pursued her in the four years since she had left the schoolroom. And until she had met Philip, she had fully intended to devote her life to Johnny.

It would not have been a bad life. Their winters would have been spent visiting various friends in the country and here in London. Their summers would have been similarly divided. She would also have helped Lady Elizabeth plan musicales and launch some of her more promising protégés. This last year, she and Johnny had spoken of going to France in the spring. By the spring, he would be married. He had spoken of spending his honeymoon in Paris, but part of it would be at Greysham's Hold. And where would she be? She could also go to the Hold, but it would no longer feel like her home, even though she knew Phoebe would be welcoming. Yet, what bride, however friendly, wanted to be a perennial hostess to her bridegroom's unmarried sister?

"Clearly, I must be married too," Vanessa muttered, and thought once more of Philip or, rather, she did not actually think of him, he had been there in the place he had occupied, off and on, for quite a while. She called that area "the back of her mind." However, it was a most misleading description. Philip was situated far closer to the front and edging ever forward, to the point that he was near to bestriding her life like a Colussus or, to use a less Shakespearean analogy, he was like a disease, a disease that carried with it a cure that only he could administer.

And why did he not effect the cure and offer for her? He gave every sign of being interested—more than merely interested. In her years of dealing with the protestations of infatuated young men, she had come to recognize certain signs. Philip Langhorne displayed them all: the brightness of eye,

the fixed stare, the flushed face, the softened glance, the
unfinished sentence, the importance he attached to her every
stated opinion and, of course, his frequent visits!

In his capacity of physician, he had come to see her at least
three times a week. This, even though his diagnosis of her
condition did not vary from day to day. Indeed, there were
times when they did not even discuss her arm. They talked of
the court, with Vanessa giving him lively word pictures of
her presentation and how the Prince Regent's stays creaked as
he bowed to her and how weary and cross his mother, Queen
Caroline, had seemed as she greeted the procession of
debutantes.

They touched on the scandalous elopement of Bysshe Shel-
ley with the daughter of Mary Wollstonecraft, whose ponder-
ous volume, *Vindication of the Rights of Women*, Philip had
read and with which he agreed in principle, stating that in his
opinion, women were quite as intelligent and capable as men.
He had not turned that observation into a compliment. Instead, he had cited the camp followers who had worked as
nurses in the surgeons' tents and who, he seemed to believe,
could be organized into a corps, with the ranks and some of
the pay allotted to soldiers. The suggestion had half-shocked,
half-intrigued her. She had wondered aloud if women could
bear the sights they must necessarily view, being so close to
the battlefield. He had responded that from his own observation of those same camp followers, women could be as strong
and as reliable as the bravest of soldiers.

Strong, reliable, intelligent, and capable. Remembering
these opinions, Vanessa wondered what he must think of her
life, her round of social activities, routs, balls, banquets,
literary teas, lectures at the museum, her aunt's musical
evenings, the theater, the opera, the Philharmonic Society.

She sighed, remembering a conversation with Phoebe, who
had been very comforting when she had decried the effects
her idle existence must have upon Philip. Her friend's words
came back to her:

"I cannot think that he takes such matters into account, my
love. When a gentleman seems oblivious of everyone in a

radius of ten feet, as he was last Sunday, when he happened to arrive at St. Martin-in-the-Fields for Sunday service because you mentioned you went there, it seems to me that he approves everything about you, not excluding your so-called 'idle existence.' You are not a frippery miss. You are intelligent and beautiful too. How could he help but be interested in you?''

"I think he is interested mainly in my arm."

"Pooh to that!" Phoebe had said very rudely, for her. "I would not need a telescope or even a quizzing glass to discern his sentiments whenever you are present. The man is clearly smitten!''

"Then . . . Why?" Vanessa had begun reluctantly. She had not wanted to confide her innermost feelings to anyone, not even Phoebe, but having no other confidante she could trust, her soon-to-be sister-in-law was the logical choice. Felicia, though one of her dearest friends, would have lent an interested ear and possibly advice more worldly than that which Phoebe dispensed, but Felicia had also sent many a rumor speeding on its merry way. Phoebe, on the other hand, was closemouthed and, on this occasion, very comforting.

"He looks at you, my dear, with his heart in his eyes, but he is shy. Do not forget that he has only recently been introduced to society. He has spent a great deal of his life as a hardworking physician. It must be very difficult for him to make the transition to a gentleman-of-leisure.''

That was true. Vanessa knew, also, that she would have arrived at this conclusion herself had her understanding not been clouded by emotions most of her friends had experienced at least three years earlier. Forced by her father into the engagement with Lord Rothmore, something even Johnny had condoned because of his friendship with her fiancé, she had experienced nothing but frustration and resentment as she had vainly endeavored to free herself from the entanglement. In the years since his death, she had been well on the way to believing that she would never be attracted to anyone. She had never anticipated falling in love at first sight! However, if she were to be absolutely honest with herself, she must needs admit that her attraction to Philip had begun in the moment when he had freed her from the basket. She did not believe herself overly conceited in guessing that something of that same nature had also happened to him.

"I wish he would speak his mind and have done!" That had been Lady Elizabeth's comment. "This fiction of your arm wearies me. Your arm has been in fine working order for at least a fortnight." The implications of that observation were twofold. Her aunt agreed with her concerning Philip's intentions and, also, she had tacitly given them her blessing. Nor would Johnny erect any barriers between them, were Sir Philip to offer for her.

Would he?

Glaring at her image in the glass, Vanessa stamped her foot. "Damn all men!" she said explosively. "But at least he has asked me to go driving with him this afternoon—and alone. Does he understand the implications of that?"

She had an instant and unwelcome memory of Lord Rothmore escorting her out to his waiting curricle and tooling up St. James's Street and thence to Hyde Park. Later, Felicia Beaufort, her very best friend in those years, had told her that her unwanted engagement was now official. "Lord Farr drove me through Hyde Park last week," she had giggled. "Mama was discussing bridal clothes with a mantua maker even before he came to ask Papa for my hand."

It occurred to Vanessa that Sir Philip might not be aware of the aforementioned implications. Yet Sir Alastair must certainly have explained them. She grimaced. Sir Alastair was not in the city. He had been summoned back to Inverness a week earlier. Sir Philip must miss him. As far as she could judge, he had not made any friends among the *ton*. Of course, he had been much occupied with getting his house in order. And— The chime of the clock interrupted her cogitations. Glancing at its golden face, she found that its hands indicated thirty minutes past the hour of three! He ought to have been here by now, and why was he not? Generally, he was more than punctual. A little pulse began to beat in the bottom of her throat. She had grown to depend upon his punctuality, she realized. Had something happened to him?

"Do not look so frantic, my love," Lady Elizabeth said comfortably as Vanessa moved to the window for a third time in as many minutes.

"He is forty-two minutes late," Vanessa said between stiff lips. All manner of uneasy speculations were chasing through her mind. They ranged from the possibility that some interfering friend of whom she knew nothing had explained the aforementioned implications of taking her on a drive through London's streets and discouraged him from making so positive a "statement." Or had he been called out of town? Or had he met with an accident, or had he been seized with a sudden illness? She turned to her aunt, saying in a voice which was not quite steady, " 'Tis unlike him not to be on time."

"And 'tis unlike you to be so concerned, my dear. Anything could have held him up. The streets are mightily congested at this hour, and 'tis a pleasant day, especially for this time of the year. A great many people will be enjoying the sunshine. I wonder what his opinions on Jenner are. I have been intending to ask him whether he has ever met the man, but I always forget."

"On *Jenner*?" Vanessa repeated, startled by Lady Elizabeth's abrupt change of subject.

"The cowpox man," her aunt clarified. "My mother, you know, was a dear friend of Lady Mary Wortley Montague. Poor Lady Mary, she would have been fascinated by his discovery of that vaccine. She had smallpox, you know. It quite ruined her beauty. That's how she happened to become so interested in inoculation. They had some sort of system in Turkey, whence she went with her husband, who, as you must know, was our ambassador to that heathen spot. They used human pus from smallpox victims in inoculation. She had both her children treated in a like manner—but Mr. Jenner's method is much more effective. In my day, smallpox was a scourge. Nearly everybody contracted it. I escaped with a light case, thank the good Lord. That's why I insisted that you and Johnny be vaccinated immediately, even though the treatment was in its infancy then. You cried and screamed, do you remember? Vanessa, are you listening to me?''

Vanessa said blankly, ''Of course. What is it?''

''My dear, I beg you'll not be so impatient.''

''Impatient? He is very late. I do not understand it. He is usually on time to the minute ''

''And you are generally considerably more self-contained,'' Lady Elizabeth observed tartly. ''I beg you'll not let your anxieties overmaster you. I admit—''

Whatever she might have admitted was to remain undisclosed, for at that moment the butler announced Sir Philip Langhorne. Vanessa, who had been standing near the window, immediately sat down, leaning back in her chair and turning to her aunt, hoping to give the impression that they had been engaged in a casual conversation.

Sir Philip came in hastily, an apologetic look in his eyes and his garments somewhat disordered. There was a brownish stain on his knee, which to Vanessa's eye appeared to be blood. ''Good God!'' she exclaimed, rising. ''What has happened? An accident?''

''No, not to me,'' he assured her quickly. ''But directly in front of me as I turned off Charles Street. A post chaise collided with a dray and I stopped to see if I might be of assistance.''

''Very proper,'' Lady Elizabeth said approvingly. ''And were you able to help?''

''Yes, there was a young woman—''

''Young woman?'' Vanessa questioned, and could have bitten her tongue for that inadvertent response.

He nodded, evidently oblivious of her reaction. ''She was in the dray with her father, who was delivering . . . I am not sure what. He was unconscious and her speech was very difficult to comprehend, being a dialect of some sort. 'Twas necessary to bring the man to a hospital, and she, of course, was far too upset to manage alone. The occupant of the post chaise, an elderly and crotchety gentleman, was being most abusive, too, though judging from the position of the two vehicles and the attitude of the young girl, I would say 'twas the fault of his coachman, who, I might add, was contributing a very loud voice to the altercation. Consequently''—Sir Philip gave Vanessa a rueful look—''I was constrained to act as peacemaker and ambulance driver as well. I could do nothing else.''

"Of course you could not," Vanessa agreed.

"I trust that the drayman was not badly injured?" Lady Elizabeth inquired.

"As to that"—he frowned—"I am not quite sure. He was still unconscious when I left him. I expect I will have to look in on him tomorrow."

"Can the people at the hospital not attend to him themselves?" Lady Elizabeth asked.

"No, I feel that I must see him," Sir Philip responded. "I fear that the pair of them might be given short shrift by the attendants, and I doubt that they can afford the services of a physician."

Despite the apologetic air he had worn upon arriving, Vanessa discerned an unfamiliar eagerness about him, but, she realized a half-second later, it was *not* unfamiliar. He had displayed that same eagerness upon a former occasion, and that was when he had met Mr. Harlock all those weeks ago. At the same time, she recalled the encomiums visited upon Sir Philip by that physician.

Until his change in fortunes, he had been dedicated to his profession, and it must have been very hard for him to give it up. With a little twinge of fear, she wondered if that same reluctance might not have engendered the many visits he had paid to herself? She also recalled something he had said upon Harlock's asking if he had retired. He had denied that, saying that his practice was limited to one. And now that his one patient was fully recovered, he had found another who had prevented his coming to see her at a time when she had hoped . . . no, when she had *expected* that he might or, rather, that he would make known his feelings toward herself. Well, he had made his feelings known, had he not? And they did not

concern her. Instead, they were concentrated upon an unconscious drayman and his inarticulate daughter!

She said coolly, "I am glad you took no hurt from this
experience, Sir Philip."

He regarded her regretfully. "I did not escape entirely
unscathed."

"You were hurt?" she asked quickly. "Your leg . . ."
She pointed to the stain on his knee.

"No, no," he assured her. "That is only dirt from the
street. I meant that, as you can see, I am rather disheveled. I
should not have appeared before you in such a condition, but
I did not wish to take the time to go home and return.
However, I fear it is too late for our drive."

"Yes." Vanessa nodded. She was annoyed with herself for
that quick expression of what had turned out to be wasted
sympathy. She continued, "It is close on five and I am
expected at Lady Farr's for supper." She avoided looking at
her aunt, hoping only that she would not evince any untoward
reaction regarding this falsehood.

"Perhaps," Sir Philip said eagerly, "we can go tomorrow
afternoon?"

Vanessa shook her head. "Tomorrow is out of the question, I fear. I am due at a rout at Lady Townsend's."

His face fell. "Oh, I am sorry. Perhaps we might meet
after church on Sunday next?"

She had, she decided, denied him enough. "Sunday after
church," she mused. "Yes, that would be satisfactory, I
think."

"Sunday after church." Lady Elizabeth's eyes sparkled.
"If it is a fair day, I will accompany you."

There was a second's pause before Sir Philip smilingly
said, "That would be delightful, Lady Combe. I shall count
myself twice fortunate." He bowed over her hand and a
second later bore Vanessa's hand to his lips.

The door had scarcely shut upon him when Vanessa rounded
on her aunt. "You will most assuredly not come with us on
Sunday!" she hissed.

"Of course I will not," Lady Elizabeth said calmly. "But at least I have laid your ridiculous fears to rest."

"My . . . ridiculous fears? And what would you be meaning by that?"

"My sweetest Vanessa, you are so deeply in the throes of passions which you should have experienced three years earlier at least, that you are quite deprived of your lively intelligence!"

"My intelligence?" Vanessa said indignantly. "I do not understand you."

"I see you do not," Lady Elizabeth sighed. "But since I am well-acquainted with your engagement calendar and know for a fact that you are promised neither to Lady Felicia for tonight nor to Lady Townsend on the morrow, I have deduced that you are trying to punish poor Philip for what you consider to be an unforgivable slight on his part. It was not. He acted very properly. Furthermore, that young man adores you. It is evident in his every word and look. And I, for one, am delighted. Each time I see him, I am the more favorably impressed. I was not impressed by your reactions, which seemed selfish in the extreme. He is not putting his patients first and you second. That is utter nonsense!"

"How did you—?"

"Give me credit for learning something in my three-score and nine years of life, my love. You had your answer to that ridiculous assumption when I told him I would come driving with you, thus preventing him from saying what is obviously on the tip of his tongue. Of course, I'll not come driving with you, my dearest numbskull. I wonder, Vanessa, if you understand how fortunate you are?"

Tears stood in Vanessa's eyes. Impulsively she ran to her aunt and embraced her. "Oh, I do, Aunt Elizabeth, believe me that I do. And thank you."

She had never known a sermon to last so long! Vanessa, sitting between her brother and her aunt, hardly listened to the minister. She had glimpsed Sir Philip as they entered the church, and it appeared to her that he had regarded her in a particularly meaningful manner. She could still see him, if she shifted her gaze to the right. At least she could see the back of his head in the third pew from the front of the church on the side. However, she resolutely kept her gaze on the benign face of the minister and denied herself the privilege and pleasure of watching the sunbeams shifting through the stained-glass windows to throw their particolored glow on his fair hair. However, it was also impossible for her not to be aware that a great many people were looking at her. That they were mainly gentlemen had once been a source of envy to her friends. That concentrated masculine admiration had long ceased to excite her.

Indeed, it had early become a nuisance, keeping her at her desk writing polite notes thanking this or that young man for the roses or the violets or the tulips and other floral offerings that had utilized most of the vases in the house. That admiration had also been expressed in passionate notes, in sweetmeats and even jewelry, this last rigorously returned to the senders by her brother or her aunt and accompanied by curt notes.

At assemblies, her ball card was filled from the moment she stepped on the floor. She was similarly besieged at routs, garden parties, fetes in the park, and balloon ascensions. It was only the vigorous protest of her aunt that had saved her from the dubious distinction of being voted an Incomparable by the dandies who sat in the bow window at White's. Furthermore, she was popular with royalty as well. She had been bidden to the palace for tea with Queen Caroline and one or another of the unmarried princesses. Fortunately, she had escaped the honor of being chosen as a lady-in-waiting, though she had come perilously near it. She had also danced with the Prince Regent during the course of several balls at Carlton House and at Brighton, an honor she decried, since his highness was not above patting and pinching various areas of her person. Beau Brummell, who also counted himself her friend, had teased her about that, as had Lord Alvanley.

Yet, at present, all her popularity and acclaim were as dust and ashes, because despite the propitious signs outlined by her aunt, she still wondered if Sir Philip Langhorne were really going to offer for her. She herself did not see why he should. In her estimation, her social success did not work in her favor. She had done nothing to merit his admiration—other than be beautiful. For the past three years she had followed the crowds, she had danced, ridden, hunted, taken the waters at Bath and the sea baths at Brighton. She had visited this and that country house during such holidays as Christmas and Easter, while he had been in the thick of the fighting to bind wounds and to save lives!

Yet, if she were fortunate enough to become his bride, she would be a good wife and a good mother. She wanted to bear his children and she wanted to make him happy. She had come to love him so completely and to respect him so entirely that sometimes of a morning, she wept at her own unworthiness. She had wept this morning, and thinking about that, she was suddenly angry with herself and with Philip too. He had turned her into another person in the short space of two months!

" 'Tis my opinion that he used his vaunted animal magnetism on you," Felicia had recently told her when, against her better judgment, she had confided her qualms to her friend. Felicia had been speaking in jest, but Vanessa wondered if perhaps she were not partially right. She had never expected to love someone quite so completely.

"And when he offers for you, I will give a ball in your honor and I beg the privilege of announcing your betrothal!" Felicia had said.

"If he offers for me, you may of course give one of your famous balls. However, if he does not, you'll need another excuse, for I can see you are in a festive mood."

"I'll not need another excuse." Felicia had winked. "La, but you are a dolt, my dearest. You are beautiful, amazingly good-tempered, kind, and rich. I do not know why I include this last, for he, I understand from little Lady Maria, is as wealthy as the fabled Croesus! There will be many who envy you this match."

"I wish I were as optimistic regarding this match as you are."

Felicia had smiled and kissed her. "One is never optimistic when one is deeply in love, my dearest. 'Tis most dampening to the spirits. Indeed, 'tis a sickness that can be cured only with a proposal."

And will I be cured? Vanessa wondered, daring to glance to the right. Meeting dark sober eyes, she blushed and hastily fixed her attention once more on the minister.

Other eyes, less reluctant than those of Vanessa, were avidly observing the fair sun-crowned locks of Sir Philip Langhorne. Lady Maria, sitting beside her husband, stared at him, willing him to look in her direction. That he did not was regrettable, but she was not surprised. Philip had always enjoyed a good pithy sermon.

"I am fond of words well-used," he had told her once, long ago. So much that he had been wont to tell her was coming back to her. Rather, it had never been forgotten. She put her hand to her bosom. Her heart was beating faster at those sweet and tender memories. She was also swallowing little air bubbles, or "butterflies," as they were dubbed. Images, also unforgotten, flickered in her mind's eye. Herself waiting nervously at the old ruined abbey just beyond the park of her father's estate and Philip galloping toward her. Swinging down from his horse and tethering it to a nearby tree, coming to her eagerly and taking her in his arms, kissing her passionately, rapturously, leaving her breathless. His ardor had surprised and frightened her, but it had also been exciting and exhilarating! She had shyly returned his embraces. To think of those moments was to relive them, but she wanted more than mere memories! She wanted Philip and she had given him up, yielding to her parents' wishes. He had not taken her weeping refusal lightly.

"You have broken my heart, Maria," he had told her.

He had not spoken loudly, but the intensity was present. She had vainly tried to comfort him. Fool, fool, fool! She had not known that in renouncing Philip, she had broken her own heart too. She *had* tried to be a good wife to Tom and she had succeeded. If only Philip had been killed in Spain, but he had not, he had come back, bringing with him memories that kept her wakeful and restless. And now, to see him so polite and distant, as if, indeed, he remembered nothing of the great love that had once existed between them! As if, in fact, they were naught but disinterested strangers!

They were not strangers!

He could not have completely forgotten what they had once meant to each other! She could not believe that Philip's heart could be so easily mended. Hers was not. She tensed. He had turned his head, directing a glance to the right. She looked in that direction as well and saw Lord Greysham, and beside him his sister, Lady Vanessa, who had been looking at Philip. Yes, and now she was hastily staring at the minister. Maria swallowed a lump in her throat. Philip could not be interested in that great, tall, gawky creature! Unlike herself, Lady Vanessa was a good half-foot higher than his heart!

"You are no higher than my heart, Maria," he had told her, adding that that organ was in her possession. "You hold my heart in your two tiny hands, my own dearest." He had kissed one hand and then the other—his lips lingering on her palm, sending wicked thrills through her. And now, was he kissing Lady Vanessa's huge *paws*? She could not imagine it. The very thought of it made her ill!

Felicia! Maria suddenly thought. Felicia was a dear friend of Lady Vanessa's, and she could tell Maria how matters stood between the two of them. Philip could not be in love with her, and if he were, Maria could not imagine that her brother, Lord Greysham, would sanction that match. Lady Vanessa's late fiancé had been a marquess. The Duke of Cales had also been in love with her, God knows why! She had heard that Lord Greysham had been furious when his sister had refused Cales, fool that she was. Imagine turning down a duke!

It would be lovely to be a duchess and have that beautiful crest on the panel of your coach, your linens, your silverware! And you would ride in state at, say, a coronation. There would be one soon, because George III was known to be mad as a hatter and ill besides, and dear Prinny, who had once danced with her and been very naughty with his hands, would be George IV and she would wear ermine and a coronet. It would really be a splendid occasion, or would have been had she been fortunate enough to marry a duke rather than a baronet, who was so far back in precedence that he would be fortunate if he were able to stand at the rear of Westminster Abbey!

She could not imagine that Lady Vanessa would settle for a mere baronet. Probably she was just leading poor Philip on. Though of course she was rather old. She had been out for four years; it would be five, pretty soon, and she would be twenty-two, might already have arrived at that age, which was not really advanced if one were married. She herself was twenty-four, though no one dreamed she had reached that age. Again, it was all right to be twenty-four if one were married.

"Maria," Tom muttered.

She directed a startled look at him and then saw that the congregation was leaving. "Oh, dear"—she raised soulful blue eyes—"I was so deep in my prayers that I did not notice that the service was at an end." Rising, she took her husband's proffered arm and as they came out into the aisle, she glanced about for Philip but, much to her disappointment, did not see him. She did see Lady Felicia and made a mental note to visit her on the earliest possible occasion.

They met on the steps of St. Martin's, and Vanessa, feeling a cool wind, drew her brown velvet mantle about her, rather regretfully. She had donned a gold silk chemise robe with tiny gold buttons running from throat to hemline, and even Johnny, who took little notice of fashions, had pronounced it most becoming. However, upon greeting Sir Philip, such minor disappointments faded from her mind.

He, too, had elected to wear brown. He had dressed with care in garments which, she guessed, were new. He had doffed a beaver hat as he came toward her, and his golden hair, ruffled by the wind, curled about his face. However, if he made an uncommonly handsome figure, he was supremely unaware of it, unaware also of the many admiring and flirtatious glances he was receiving from ladies going down the stairs or congregated on the pavement below. His attention was all for herself.

"Good morning, Lady Vanessa," he said shyly.

"Good morning, Sir Philip. I—" Vanessa broke off as Lady Ingram, an old friend of her aunt's, pounced on her, clutching her arm determinedly. Stifling a sigh, Vanessa looked into a thin countenance dominated by small, piercing brown eyes. "Good morning, Lady Martha. Have you met Sir Philip Langhorne?"

"Good morning, my dear Vanessa." Lady Ingram darted a glance at Sir Philip, and without acknowledging the introduction, said in loud penetrating tones, "I was ever so surprised to learn that your brother had offered for that poor little dab of a Galliard chit."

Vanessa tensed. "My brother is very happy in his engagement," she said coldly.

"I should not think he would want Carlton's leavings . . . and he's wed some manner of . . . nursemaid, I believe? I vow—"

"Martha!" Lady Elizabeth, emerging from the church with the minister, moved forward and tapped Lady Ingram on the shoulder. "If you need any particulars on a matter which is clearly no concern of yours, you'll not have them from my niece. Now, come away, please."

"But . . ." Lady Ingram protested, and was still protesting as inexorably she was urged down the steps by a purposeful Lady Elizabeth.

"Oh, dear, people are so unkind." Vanessa looked up at Philip. "I do hope that my aunt will give her a strong set-down."

"I would think it more than likely." Sir Philip nodded. He added hastily, as if fearing another interruption, "May I hope that you will come driving with me?"

She regarded him gravely. "I would be delighted," she said softly, thinking anew how very handsome he looked and how beautiful his eyes under his well-shaped brows. It was no wonder he could use them so effectively.

"Will your aunt be joining us?" he asked.

"No, she must return home."

"I am sorry." His smile suggested that his comment was mendacious. "Come, then." He took her arm, and with an expertise she appreciated, went down the steps, skirting the small groups of friends and acquaintances who might have drawn her into conversation.

His curricle, drawn by a pair of matched grays, had been left in the capable hands of a thin, small boy whose narrow face was dominated by huge black eyes and surmounted by an unruly crop of blue-black hair. These and the brownish tint of his skin suggested a Gypsy heritage to Vanessa. He was clad in red livery, lavishly sewn with gold braid. A row of big brass buttons ran from collar to waist. He wore his attire, Vanessa noticed, with an almost palpable pride. Seeing Sir Philip, he stared at him with an almost doglike affection, and still clutching the reins, leaped down from his high perch. He offered them to Philip.

"Thank you, Gabriel," his master said. He added punctiliously, "May I introduce Gabriel, Lady Vanessa? He is a lad of few words, but these, addressed mainly to Zephyr and Storm here, have made me believe that in addition to being a 'tiger,' he is also a wizard."

"I am delighted to know a wizard." Vanessa smiled at the boy, who looked gravely back at her before nodding and grinning widely.

"Ah, he approves of you," Sir Philip said. "In fact, he approves of you most heartily . . . for he has both nodded and smiled."

"I am complimented." Vanessa had another smile for the boy, who bobbed his head, and waiting until Philip had assisted Vanessa into the curricle and taken his place beside her, handed him the reins and went running back to his seat in the rumble.

"Gabriel looks to be of Gypsy origin," Vanessa commented as Philip urged his horses forward.

"As to that, I'd not be knowing. Nor, I would guess, does he. I found him working at the stables where I kept my post

chaise while my house was being readied. He was knocked
about by the other boys, who were all bigger and heavier than
himself. I saved him from a drubbing one day and he began
to follow me about like a dog.''

"You were kind to take him on," she approved.

"On the contrary, I did myself a great service. Quite by
accident I found that he has a remarkable way with horses.
They respond to him as to no one else and there's nothing he
does not seem to know about them." He gave her a whimsi-
cal smile. "I'd say that if he did have a family, they'd be a
mare and a stallion.''

Vanessa laughed. "And did you provide him with that
remarkable livery?''

Philip flushed. '' 'Twas of his choosing. I would have had
him fitted out in the colors of my house—blue and gold—but
he saw a bolt of red cloth at the tailor's shop and appeared so
smitten with it, I could not refuse to buy it. The superfluity of
gold, I fear, is my own idea. I thought if he were so attracted
to red, he would be made equally happy by the gold.''

"And of course, you were proved right.''

"Yes, he was quite pleased." Philip glanced at her. "The
wind is cool." He drew a wool robe over her. "I hope you
will be warm enough.''

"I am very cozy," she assured him. Meeting his eyes, she
looked down hastily, feeling the power of his gaze anew. A
little thrill of fear ran through her as she wondered if it were
possible that the feeling she had for him might have come
from his willing of it. However, that was utterly ridiculous!
Mesmerist or not, he was no sorcerer. If there was power
here, it was the power of attraction—mutual attraction. Felicia
had once told her that upon meeting Lord Farr, she had been
drawn to him like a rabbit to a stoat. The analogy had sent
Vanessa into a fit of the giggles, but for once Felicia had not
been amused.

"I was only attempting to explain that when I met him, I
knew that he was for me," she had retorted huffily. "But
until you have had a similar experience, you'll probably
continue to laugh at me.''

She did understand now. She understood and could absolve Philip from exerting any arcane influences over her. She could not have been so comfortable with a sorcerer if, indeed, such persons did exist. She could not remember ever being quite so happy. It was a totally different kind of happiness, she knew. With Philip beside her, she felt completed.

'Should you like to drive into Chelsea and along the river?" he inquired.

"That would be very pleasant," she replied. She looked down, thinking how strong his hands were and how well he controlled his horses. Those hands, with their slender, supple fingers, were also able to set broken bones and administer to the wounded. Inadvertently she thought of Charles, whose life he had saved. He had received small thanks for that. Yet she was sure that Charles was happy now. She did not want to think of him. She looked at her companion and flushed as their glances locked again. Then it was he who looked away, expertly maneuvering his curricle through the heavy traffic.

Finally they reached the Thames. The river was turbulent and the small boats were being tossed upon the choppy waters. The shouts of the rivermen, rude and profane, reached them as they halted near London Bridge. Across the waters, she could see the tree-ringed bulk of Vauxhall Gardens.

"I've never been to the gardens," Vanessa remarked, breaking a silence that was beginning to be slightly oppressive.

"Nor I," he answered. "I've not spent much time in London, you know. My leaves were mainly taken in Yorkshire."

"I remember your mentioning that. I have lived here a long time and my . . ."—she gave him a deprecating little smile—" 'leaves' have been mainly taken at the Hold in Sussex. I have always wanted to see Yorkshire."

" 'Tis a chill place, but very beautiful."

"I am sure it must be. And Scotland, also."

'Scotland, also," he agreed absently, his eyes straying toward the river.

Vanessa wished heartily that she had never mentioned Vauxhall. Perhaps he had been planning to break his silence with a remark of an entirely different nature, and now they seemed launched upon a discussion of places. However, she effortfully held to the course she had inadvertently charted. "I am told that the lakes in Scotland are beautiful, but Loch Ness, I have heard, is inhabited by some manner of monster."

"One cannot dispute that," he said with a twitch of his lips.

"You've seen it?" she demanded in some surprise.

"Never, but I have never tarried by Loch Ness's fabled waters."

"Then you are suggesting that you might believe in the monster?"

"I am saying that since I have never been there, I cannot attest to the fact that it inhabits the lake, yet, at the same time, I cannot dispute with those who insist that it does. I, however, am inclined to be a doubter."

"I. too." She smiled. "I cannot believe in monsters."

"Can you not?" His dark gaze grew somber. "I can believe in some monsters."

"And which would they be?"

"Napoleon, for one. He is a greater monster than any that might inhabit the peat-filled waters of some Scottish lake. They are reputed to be singularly shy. He is not."

" 'Tis well his claws are clipped," she agreed.

He gave her a long, grave look. "Claws," he said finally, "in common with fingernails, require constant cutting, else they grow again."

She tensed. "And you believe that Napoleon's claws might grow again?"

"It does seem possible, logical as well. The eagle's a bird of prey and must needs attack in order to survive."

"Ah, but this eagle's caged and well-fed by its keepers."

"They'd best watch their hands," he said grimly, and fell silent, staring across the water. After a moment he turned back to her. "The winds are blowing cold. I hope that you are not chilly?"

"No, not in the least." She shook her head. "I rarely feel the cold."

His smile was approving. "You do seem to enjoy good health."

"I always have."

"I wish some of my patients . . ." He broke off with a rather rueful smile. "I am referring to some of the patients I used to tend. Many of them would have been the better had they shared your attitude."

With a sudden flash of insight she said, "I think you must miss your work."

"I have," he admitted. "In the beginning, I did not think I could accustom myself to this radical change in my existence. I had intended to buy into a practice, you see. However, of late I have found this way of life considerably more to my taste."

His eyes were on her face. She felt excited and breathless, but she managed to say with a calmness that surprised her, 'Really? I am glad of that."

Under his hands, the horses snorted and moved restlessly at a sudden tug of the reins as, impulsively, he leaned toward her. He murmured to them soothingly and then said, "There's a reason for it, you know. May I tell you about it, Lady Vanessa?"

"Yes, I would like to know your reasons," she said softly.

He paused and cleared his throat. "I . . . we . . . have not been acquainted very long. Yet, it . . . does seem to me that I have, indeed, known you far longer than you might imagine if we go by dreams. You have invaded my dreams at night and . . . and in all the hours we've not spent together, you, and you alone, have ruled my thoughts. Indeed, I have been able to think of little else. I do hope you will not think me importunate if I tell you that I have come to love you with all my heart and soul and that my dearest wish is that you might agree to become my wife." He loosed a long quavering breath.

Vanessa, too, breathed deeply. She wondered if he, as did she herself, felt as if a heavy weight had been lifted from his heart. "Oh, my dear, my dearest Philip, 'tis my wish too, and soon—as soon as possible!'' She paused, suddenly appalled at her uncharacteristic boldness. "I mean . . ."

He seized her hand and bore it to his lips. "I hope, my love, my dear, dear love, I hope that you meant exactly what you said."

"Well . . ." She paused, and meeting his dark, compelling gaze, she could only respond, "I did."

with
the

6

---•◆•---

"Another ball, dear Felicia? And what, pray, is the occasion?" Lady Maria, sitting in Lady Felicia's small parlor, blinked against the winter sunshine flooding through the tall windows. Her eyes were bright with surprise, and if Felicia had looked closer, she might also have discerned a lively suspicion in those pale depths. She was, however, not gazing directly at her visitor. Her own eyes were fixed on a point above Maria's head. She looked, the latter thought, not unlike a cat who had climbed on the banquet table and drunk all the cream as well as partaking of some choice bits of pasty. Clearly Felicia had been party to an *on-dit* that had yet to make the rounds. Furthermore, Maria was also convinced that whatever it was had a direct bearing on her projected ball. She was finding her hostess's reticence most peculiar. And, she realized, Felicia had not answered her question. "Might one know the occasion for the ball?" she repeated.

"Must there be an occasion?" Felicia's eyes sparkled, and the cat look was even more apparent to her guest.

Maria mentally added a hapless canary to that feast. "There usually is," she pursued.

"Is there?" Felicia said maddeningly. "Well, my love, say that I am doing it in honor of Christmas."

"But you are giving it on the fifteenth of January!"

"Oh, dear, so I am. Christmas is such a cluttered time of the year! Then 'tis in honor of the season or of Twelfth Night. *Twelfth Night; or: What You Will.* That is an odd title for a play, is it not? I expect that Shakespeare wrote so many that he ran out of proper titles. *As You Like It* is another, but I do *not* like it. Rosalind is a dead bore and her Orlando was plain stupid not to recognize her, even if she were clad in male attire. Do you not agree, Maria?''

Maria was concealing her impatience with some difficulty. "So many people will be in the country at that time. I am referring to your ball."

"Then it will be a small ball and we shall have much more room for waltzing. However, I am of the opinion that we'll have a sufficient number of guests."

"I hope so," Maria murmured. She added, " 'Tis wonderful that Phoebe will be wed to Lord Greysham. I never thought 'twould happen."

"Yes, it is indeed wonderful!" Felicia said enthusiastically.

"However, it must be very difficult for poor Vanessa."

"Difficult?" Felicia fixed wide eyes on Maria's face. "I should not think so. Vanessa is delighted that her brother is so happy, and as you must know, she adores Phoebe."

"But where will she live?" Lady Maria pursued. "Surely she cannot continue to reside at her present address—once the nuptial knot is tied."

"No, I shouldn't think she would want to do that." Felicia's eyes were bright with secrets.

"She will either have to set up a separate residence or . . . marry herself. But 'tis a long time since one has heard her name linked with that of any gentleman."

"Yes, it has been a long time."

Felicia's cheeks were pink and Maria's suspicions, already piqued, increased. "She is very beautiful and I cannot think she will be single much longer. In fact, I would not be surprised if she were to follow in her brother's footsteps very soon, would you?"

Felicia looked at her narrowly. Then she said, "Really? You must have heard something that has not yet come my way."

Maria stifled a sigh of pure annoyance. Generally her hostess was not so closemouthed. She decided to try another tack. Daringly she said, "Of late I have had the feeling that Lady Vanessa has a decided penchant for Sir Philip Langhorne."

"Oh?"

"But I do not believe that anything could come out of that, certainly."

"Why not?"

"Well, I cannot imagine that Lord Greysham would let his sister wed a baronet—especially one who has been a practicing physician!"

"As to that," Felicia said tartly, "being a physician is an honorable calling. Lord Pickering was a solicitor's clerk before a succession of happy deaths raised him to the marquessate. Lord Allenby was in debtor's prison."

"Oh, well," Lady Maria said tolerantly. "Many gentlemen get into debt."

"And that is considered more honorable than being a hardworking and respected physician? I have heard Greysham say that Sir Philip ought to have been decorated for bravery."

"Indeed?" Maria raised her eyebrows. "His opinion of Sir Philip has certainly undergone a swift reversal."

"He has had an opportunity to know him better."

"And now he approves of him? How pleasant for Philip . . . with all the barriers down."

"Barriers?" Felicia inquired. "What barriers would you mean?"

"I am speaking about a possible understanding between dear Vanessa and Sir Philip," Maria pursued, the while she was all too aware of a sinking feeling. Felicia was looking more self-conscious than ever. Evidently she had been sworn to secrecy, but it was a secret that she was having great difficulty suppressing—as for herself, she had dug for gold and struck a rich vein of that precious metal! "Perhaps there already is an understanding?"

Felicia's wide eyes were filled with spurious innocence. "Not that I know."

Her attempt at dissimulation was really laughable! However, her guest was not amused. Maria glanced at the little gold-and-enamel watch pinned to her bosom and rose swiftly.

"Oh, dear, I must go!" she exclaimed, the while a swift glance at her hostess's face told her that Felicia was extremely relieved by this statement. She added, "I fear I have stayed too long already. Dear Lady Connington is expecting me."

"I will see you out." Felicia smiled radiantly.

A half-hour later, Maria stood before Sir Philip's imposing mansion on Charles Street, her hot eyes on an edifice which was at least twice the size of her own residence and in a much more felicitous location.

The term "landed aristocrat" came to mind. One had to have been of an old family—far older than Tom's—to have secured a grant of land in this prestigious spot. And she had renounced all of this—been forced to renounce it, rather, she recalled, thinking of her parents' relentless persuasions. They had not actually put her on bread and water, but endlessly, endlessly, *endlessly* they had told her that Philip's chances of inheriting his family's wealth and title were moot and her mother had said, "One baronet in hand is worth two in the bush," and laughed at her own feeble wit. But it did no good to think about the regretted and regrettable past. Philip could not have totally forgotten their love with its stolen meetings and passionate letters, the latter discreetly burned immediately upon perusing! Oh, why had she not kept them to remind dearest Philip of all, all, *all* they had once been to each other? But perhaps he would not need reminding, were she to come to him now. Of course, there would have to be a divorce, and that meant total disgrace. She shuddered a little at that.

Still, now that hostilities were at an end, they could live on the Continent—in Rome, no, not Rome, *Paris*, where everyone was going now—though Tom would not, because he distrusted the Frogs, as he called them—and the Paris modistes were so much more accomplished than London's mantua makers! Just to read about the divine styles that originated in the French capital was exciting! How much more exciting to be there and have an armoire full of them—two or even three armoires! She could envision blue satin or silk edged with the very finest Chantilly lace or, as a fallen woman, she could wear low-cut gowns to display her beautifully shaped *poitrine*, so clever of her to have insisted upon a wetnurse, nearly everyone she knew did. Tom had not approved, but that only showed his low origins.

She would have to leave her infant behind, of course, but she did not see him very often and he would be just as happy with Mrs. Hollis, his nurse, who did not like her anyway, nasty creature. There was no need for her to spend time in the nursery—why else had she hired a nanny to perform those duties? She saw him mornings and evenings and that was enough! In Paris, she would not have to see him at all—and she could have her own coach and four. She would purchase matched grays. She would insist on that, and Philip was a good judge of horseflesh. And she would have drawers and drawers of kid gloves and shoes of morocco leather and jewels, diamonds of course, and sapphires and emeralds and rubies too. She would have a tiara, a glittering tiara such as she had recently seen at a Carlton House ball. The female who had worn it had a face like a monkey—but on her own fair curls . . . With a little sob of pure anguish, Maria hurtled across the street, and reaching the front door of Philip's house, she breathed, "He cannot have forgotten!" In that same moment, she clutched the knocker and with all her strength threw it against the plate.

Philip, informed by an astounded and patently disapproving butler that a lady had come to call, had been similarly astounded. Because of his preoccupation with Vanessa, his acquaintance with ladies was slight and certainly not conducive to unheralded visits. It must be Vanessa, and what had happened? His heart throbbed with alarm. What could have occasioned her arrival? They were to have gone to the opera that night. One of Lady Elizabeth's young protégés was singing in Pergolesi's *La Serva Padrona*, but why was he thinking of such matters when *she* was awaiting him? It must be a matter of very great moment to bring her to his house.

His heart was pounding even more heavily as he came into the drawing room, whence he had instructed the butler to bring her.

She was standing near the fireplace gazing up at a Tintoretto his grandfather had purchased in Rome some fifty years earlier. He stared at her in consternation. "Maria!"

"Oh, Ph-Philip!" Her face a mask of tragedy, her eyes were drowned in tears, her soft mouth was quivering. "Oh, Ph-Ph-Philip!" she wailed, and running to him, she threw herself against his chest, clutching his arms with her tiny hands. "I had to come," she sobbed.

After the first moment of utter and speechless amazement, he gently extricated himself from her frenzied clasp and said, "My dear Maria, what is amiss?"

"Philip, Philip, Philip," she moaned. "I have been in utter, utter, utter *torment* since your return. I know you must have felt the same but dared not confide your misery in me—because of T-Tom. Oh, God, to think of you here in London, so close, so very close and yet separated by . . . boundaries of steel! At home, we were also separated, but we could meet. Do you remember those meetings, Philip, dearest, do you? I know that I cannot forget them. They are enshrined in my memory—those sweet, wild moments at the edge of the moors, those moments which have given me the little happiness I have experienced in life! Do not tell me that you have forgotten them, Philip? It seems to me as if they happened only yesterday. You riding across the moor on your chestnut stallion and I awaiting you, terrified because my parents did not know where I was going—and yet knowing that I had to see you, had to or I would have gone mad with misery! And—"

He finally managed to stem the tide of reminiscences. "That was a long time ago, Maria. And now—"

"I beg you'll not speak of the 'now,' " she wailed. "Oh, Philip, I am so very miserable *now*!"

As she gazed up at him, he looked beyond her, caught in his own memories. Six years ago, he had been as distraught as she appeared to be at present. Maria had filled his dreams and dominated his waking hours. He had lived between the heights and depths of emotion—happy at her smiles, agonized at her rejections.

She had nearly driven him to despair with her tantalizing little touches and frightened tears when, in the heat of passion, he had overcome her not very determined resistance and had come perilously close to ravishing her. That he had not was something for which he could thank God and herself. Seeing her now and mentally contrasting her with Vanessa, he could scarcely credit his good fortune. The one was all pretense and surface emotion, making play with tear-tipped lashes and woeful mouth. He could not imagine Vanessa resorting to such tricks. She would never weep. Her emotions would be concealed, and nor would she have led him on as Maria had all those years ago. Vanessa was neither a torturer nor a teaser; a man would always know where he stood with her. All in all, he owed Maria a debt of gratitude for not succumbing to his passionate entreaties.

"Philip, my dearest Philip," she moaned. "Why are you so silent? Do not tell me that you have forgotten all, *all* that we used to mean to each other?"

He was feeling acutely embarrassed and uncomfortable. He hardly knew how to respond to her unexpected and unwanted onslaught of passion. "My dear Maria, of course I have not forgotten, but—"

"I knew it, knew it, *knew* it!" she cried triumphantly. "And nor have I ever forgotten. Our meetings, our embraces, our love have been all that I have ever known of joy. Oh, Philip, once you begged me to run away with you, and poor me, I was so young and so frightened . . . but believe me when I tell you I am a different person now. I have learned through six long hard years what a stupid little fool I was! Oh, God, God, God, to have renounced the one love of my life—but 'twas not my fault, Philip. I was forced to it by my parents. They never let me alone. Night and day they tormented and threatened me, they said they would send me to my aunt in Newcastle if I did not reject you. And then we never could have met. But that is all ancient history. I am a different person now. I am strong. There's none can intimidate me. I am willing to come to you now. I could go this very night, we could flee to D-Dover and thence to France—to P-Paris.''

"My dear Maria," he said gently. "We are not the same people we were six years ago. You are wed. You cannot honestly mean that you would leave your husband and your child—"

She reached up a little hand and pressed it against his lips. "I would, Philip. I would make any sacrifice if we could be together." She removed her hand from his mouth and clutched his arm again. "Philip, Philip, take me, I beg you!"

"I am sorry, Maria," he said firmly. "I could not approve such a sacrifice and nor could I base my happiness upon another's misery."

She was silent a long moment, the anguish fading from her eyes, to be replaced by anger. Accusingly she cried, "You could not refuse me if you still cared for me the way you once did. You vowed eternal love—but it seems that this eternity's been curtailed. You do not care for me anymore. That's the truth, is it not?"

"My dear Maria, of course I care . . ." he began uncomfortably.

"Then, if you do, Philip"—she grabbed his hand—"come away with me. The world is wide."

"No, my dear. However, I do want to be your friend," he said soothingly. "I hope that we will always be friends, but surely—"

"Damn your friendship!" she said shrilly, whirling away from him now. Then, turning back, she stared angrily up at him. "I expect that you imagine you can, with impunity, woo that great cow of a female Lady Vanessa Ventriss. I am told that you have been pursuing her, and I tell you, you are wasting your time. Her family will never countenance your suit. Furthermore, I seem to remember telling you that she was engaged to Lord Rothmore, who was one of her brother's best friends!"

"I remember that, but Lord Rothmore's dead."

"I'll warrant he's not dead to her, who mourned him even longer than some women grieve for a husband. She was absolutely draped in black—but that is beside the point. He was a marquess and she is daughter to an earl. She could have had a duke—so do you imagine that her brother will allow her to wed a mere baronet, and one who was practically in *trade*?"

Her soft manner had deserted her completely. There was a shrewish note in her voice that Philip had never heard before. He had a moment of feeling very sorry for her husband, who might have encountered this side of her whenever she was thwarted. More than ever he was grateful for the poverty that had stood between himself and his "love" for Maria, but of course it had never been love. It had been only a callow approximation of that emotion. Love, real love, was what he felt for Vanessa. He knew, too, that despite Maria's assertions concerning the late Lord Rothmore, Vanessa loved him, Philip Langhorne, as much as he loved her. He was not a conceited man, but the change in her expression when he came to see her, and the change in her voice as well, conveyed her feelings more than any words could do. This, however, was not the sort of intelligence he wished to share with Maria. Nor was he minded to tell her about his engagement. It was time she left. She never should have committed the extreme indiscretion of coming here. He hoped devoutly that his butler and housekeeper would not discuss her folly with their cronies in other establishments.

He said, "Be that as it may, my dear, I do feel 'twas most unwise of you to have tempted fate and the gossips by coming here unescorted. Is your coach awaiting you? If not, perhaps—"

"I beg you'll not concern yourself with me," she cried. "Oh, Philip . . ." She stared up at him tearfully now. "Does it not matter to you that you have succeeded in breaking my heart?" She sniffed twice and finally managed a sob.

"Maria"—he put his arm around her—"I beg you'll—"

"Philip, ohhhh, Philip, I cannot believe that all is over between us!" Standing on tiptoe, she wound her arms around his neck and kissed him passionately.

He stood rigidly for a second. Then, as she moved back, he said with acute embarrassment, "My dear, you must try to forget the past. 'Tis not something that can ever be revived. And for both our sakes—"

"Say no more!" she cried loudly. "Oh, cruel, cruel, *cruel*!" Whirling, she fled from the room, wailing loudly.

"Maria!" Philip hurried after her, but as he reached the hall, he heard only the loud reverberating slam of the front door.

The butler, coming hastily out of a passageway, looked at that portal in some surprise and then prepared to go back the way he had come.

"Harding," Philip said hastily, "I think 'twould be best if the lady's visit remained a secret."

Harding's expression was an artful combination of surprise and reproach. He bowed slightly. "But of course, sir." He left Philip feeling that it would have been far better had he said nothing at all. He was uncomfortably reminded of what Sir Alastair had described as a "dangerous situation." However, he could, he thought, reassure himself that Maria would not be inclined to repeat the indiscretion that had brought her here this afternoon.

"When I see you in green, I think you must always wear it, and when I see you in gold, I am positive that no other shade becomes you half so well, and now I am all amazed at your russet velvet. I can only say that you wear every color well, Vanessa, dear," Phoebe said admiringly.

Vanessa laughed. "You've mentioned only three colors and I might tell you that I abhor pink, loathe orange, and am not particularly fond of blue and believe that white is only for blonds like you."

Phoebe glanced down at her white gown and said deprecatingly, " 'Tis well enough, I expect, but no one will think me out of the ordinary. They will stare at you so!" With a mischievous smile, she put thumb and first finger together and held them up to her eye, quizzing-glass-style.

"Oh, Phoebe, how you do exaggerate!" Vanessa chided. "You have always put me in the shade."

"I have not, and certainly I shall not tonight. I've never seen you so radiant, my dearest. You are glowing. Look in your mirror. You would outshine even the beautiful Duchess of Devonshire in her heyday or . . . But I cannot think of any more comparisons. Sir James Carmody must paint you!"

"Cease, cease with these encomiums, I pray you," Vanessa begged. "You do not need to heap excessive praise upon your sister-in-law-to-be. I love you as it is."

"I am not doing it for that, and well you know it," Phoebe chided. "And speaking of in-laws, I do think it tremendously exciting that you and Philip have agreed to join us for a double wedding. Only I do wish it were taking place next month rather than April, which is months away!"

"Three months and some twelve days, and we both have thousands of things to do. Bridal clothes and choosing—"

"Bridal clothes be damned!" Phoebe interrupted uncharacteristically. Even more uncharacteristically she continued, "I could wed Johnny in my shift!"

"Phoebe!" Vanessa put both hands to her ears. "I vow I am shocked. You sound like Mary of Scotland, who said something to the effect that she could follow the Earl of Bothwell around the world in her nightie."

"Poor foolish woman," Phoebe said soberly. "She did lose her head over him."

"Actually, she really did." Vanessa also spoke soberly. "Certainly her passion for him was one of the main factors contributing to her downfall."

"Oh, dear, I wish you hadn't mentioned her," Phoebe said with a little shiver.

"It was all a long time ago." Vanessa shrugged. "As a child, I used to play Mary of Scotland going to her execution." She laughed. "I thought it was all very romantic."

"One does, at that age. I used to pretend I was Cleopatra applying the asp to my arm."

They laughed and looked at each other fondly. "Isn't it nice that we've grown up?" Vanessa commented.

"Particularly nice tonight." Phoebe giggled. "Felicia is in ecstasy. Not only is she giving one of her famous balls, but she will amaze the polite world with her news. It was kind of you to let her announce your engagement, and to my certain knowledge, she has sat on that news for the entire month of December and fifteen days into January, which, you must admit, is scarcely to be believed!"

"I know." Vanessa smiled. "Felicia is a true friend."

"She really is. She tells me that she cannot wait until we have joined her in the married state."

"That sounds as if she thinks we are moving to another country."

"Well?" Phoebe flushed a lovely pink. "Are we not?"

"I expect we are, a wonderful country, to live with someone whom you really love. That does not always happen."

Phoebe nodded soberly. "I never thought it would happen to me."

"Nor did I," Vanessa agreed. "I was so miserable at the idea of wedding poor Rothmore. I do not think I knew what love meant until I met Philip. Oh, Phoebe, I am so utterly happy that I am frightened."

"Frightened?" Phoebe looked at her in surprise. "Of what, my dearest?"

"I do not know." Vanessa frowned at the floor. "It all seems too perfect, every barrier down, Johnny pleased, and Aunt Elizabeth also." Vanessa's eyes twinkled. "She is particularly pleased. She sounded Philip out on music and discovered something I did not know. He plays the pianoforte. In fact, he gave her a demonstration with Mozart's Fantasy in C Major. She was amazed, and so was I. He is a fine musician. He tells me that many physicians of his acquaintance are even more accomplished. When he was studying in Edinburgh, he and several friends used to gather together of a night and perform chamber music!"

"Really, that is interesting," Phoebe said. "Your Philip is certainly a many-faceted young man. He's a breath of air in this jaded world."

"Yes, but sometimes . . ." Vanessa's frown deepened.

"Sometimes what?"

"I feel that he is unhappy. I had that impression when he came back from Yorkshire last week. You know, he also went up to Scotland."

Phoebe nodded. "Yes, he mentioned that, and so did you. He wanted to recruit Sir Alastair to be his best man."

"He also visited some of his old teachers and says that while they congratulated him on his inheritance, they were disappointed that he was not going to set up a practice."

"I expect it has been difficult for him to renounce his profession—especially since he is so capable a physician," Phoebe said.

"Yes," Vanessa agreed moodily. "And he still misses his work. He told me what his teachers said for a reason. He wanted to hear what I would say."

"I guessed as much," Phoebe murmured. "And what did you say, dear?"

"I said what I thought he wanted to hear—that he ought to set up a practice, if he so desired, to which he replied that he had no such intention."

"Really?" Phoebe looked surprised.

"He . . . he does not believe me enthusiastic about it, you see." Vanessa moved away from her, adding in a low, worried tone of voice, "And he is right. I am not."

"Why not?" Phoebe asked. "Because you consider it socially demeaning? I know that is the belief, but I cannot imagine you would agree."

"I do not agree, but . . ." Vanessa reddened. "So many of his patients would be females, bedridden females, suffering with minor complaints and wanting attention . . . his attention."

"Vanessa!" Phoebe cried. "I have never heard anything so ridiculous. He loves you. He would not look at another woman. You know that."

"I know it in my heart," Vanessa said miserably. "I know he loves me and I feel terrible about this—it's unlike me."

"It most certainly is!"

"But you see, I love him so *much*. When he went up to

Edinburgh, I was worried, thinking he must have known other women there while he was at school, and I find myself jealous even of little Maria Glazebrook because he used to know her." She stared at Phoebe. "You are looking shocked. I should never have unburdened myself on this subject."

"I am glad you did, my dear." Phoebe shook her head. "But I am surprised. I would never have suspected you of being jealous of anyone. You, of all people, have no reason for it."

"I know, I know, I know . . ." Vanessa paced up and down the room. "This is a side to my nature I never realized I had."

"Darling, you must exorcise these feelings. Being in love can do strange things to one's nature, but jealousy must be avoided at all costs. It is dangerous. It can warp and distort our feelings."

"I know. I know, too, that Philip is unhappy because he is deprived of his life's work. He is a dedicated man, and maybe . . . maybe I am even jealous of that dedication."

"Dearest, you are being possessive. You cannot possess anyone. Charles tried to possess me, you know. I did love him once—in the beginning, before he went to war. When he returned, so hurt, I felt I loved him even more, but he did not believe I did. He felt that I only pitied him. He was always trying to test my love, and he was so jealous. It colored his every action, until I thought I must go mad—and, of course, I began to dislike him. I was near to hating him when everything came to an end. He was so totally unreasonable."

"And I am being unreasonable too, I know. I do not want to drive Philip away."

"I cannot think that you will, my dear. This is only a phase, I am sure. You will get over it."

"I hope so," Vanessa sighed. "I do not like myself. Oh, I pray you'll not think hardly of me, Phoebe. I had to tell someone how I felt."

"I know, and of course I do not think hardly of you, I do understand. In spite of all your beauty and charm, your life has been lonely, I know—and now to fall so deeply in love.

It is a wonderful experience, but it does take getting used to.''

"Oh, it does, it certainly does!" Vanessa exclaimed. "I fear that it has even robbed me of my sense of humor."

"There's no help for it, my dearest. You must get married as soon as possible!"

"I wish I could," Vanessa said moodily. "I wish we did not need to wait so long."

"Now you are beginning to agree with me."

"I think I always have, but I wanted to put a good face on it."

"Perhaps we could tell our respective swains that—" Phoebe paused at a tap on the door.

"Yes," Vanessa called.

Letty appeared on the threshold. "Beggin' yer pardon, my lady, but 'is lordship's wonderin' when yer comin' down. The coach is 'ere."

"Immediately, tell him," Vanessa said. As Letty closed the door, she glanced into her mirror again. "Do I really look well?" she asked.

"My very dearest, all the females will turn pea green the minute you step onto the floor, and all the men will match them in hue—after Lord Farr makes his announcement. Now, do stop being nonsensical—in all ways. And let us go."

Vanessa smiled at her. "You are good for me, Phoebe."

"I hope I have been." Phoebe caught her hand. "You are very foolish to be so uncertain of Philip. I would sooner believe that the earth would stop turning rather than that he would ever be unfaithful to you."

"I expect that I believe that too," Vanessa said.

"You must, my dear." Phoebe threw open the door and they hurried out.

7

The first of the waltzes had begun. Vanessa, dancing with her host, Lord Farr, while Felicia whirled about in Lord Greysham's arms, saw Philip at the edge of the floor. He was wearing new evening clothes and, as usual, he had followed Beau Brummell's dictum. Simplicity became him, she thought lovingly. He was so incredibly handsome that he appeared resplendent even in that understated black and white. Also he seemed more at ease than he had been when they first met. He was becoming used to his position in society, and also, judging from the pedigrees of the men who stopped to exchange a word or two with him, he was well on his way to being accepted into that exclusive stratum known as the *ton*.

She was pleased at that, but less pleased by the languishing looks he was receiving from its female contingent. Still, he did appear oblivious of the inviting and beguiling smiles visited upon him. His dark eyes were directed toward the dancers. She guessed, or rather she knew, that he was actively looking for her. She wished that she were with him, but Lord Farr had claimed the privilege of the first waltz, and of course she could not refuse her host. Lord Farr was a pleasant man and fortunately he was not given to idle chatter as he guided her around the room. Consequently she was spared the ordeal of making conversation when her thoughts were elsewhere. He, in fact, was sparing of words, not surprising with Felicia for a wife, but they were admirably well-suited, just as she knew that she and Philip would be.

At first sight of him, her earlier fears had entirely disappeared. He was so obviously delighted to see her and so entirely in love with her. That was evident in the cadences of his voice when he addressed her, and there was a bemused look in his eyes, as if, in fact, he could not quite believe his good fortune in having won her. In those moments she had been entirely secure, and the feeling lingered. She was glad of that. As she had told Phoebe, she had not liked the jealousy that had sprung up like some bitter weed that must poison an entire garden if not checked. She had never experienced such a sensation and hoped she had managed to vanquish it. It was unworthy of her and it was also baseless. Philip would never give her cause for such anxiety. In her heart she was totally convinced of that.

The dance finally ended and Vanessa came off the floor, to be claimed by Philip. "Finally," he said delightedly.

"You did not dance?" she said.

"How might I dance without a partner? I am not a member of the corps de ballet."

"Silly! There are many ladies present and not partnered."

"Are there? I saw only one, and she was partnered."

"You will turn my head with this flattery."

"I never flatter. I am entirely sincere."

"That is a virtue—or it might be that you, being relatively new to London society, have yet to learn its ways."

"I am a poor student. I may never learn them."

"I pray you are right, sir." She had spoken teasingly, but then she wished she had not turned the conversation in that direction. A somberness flickered in his eyes. She had a feeling that despite the lightness of his tone, he was speaking that true word so often uttered in jest, at least according to the aphorism. Reluctantly she recalled her conversation with Phoebe and wished devoutly that the months might speed by. It did seem a long time to wait—when she wanted to be with him now, with him in every sense of the word, and judging from his attitude, he shared that wish.

The music was in her ears and Philip said, "My dance, milady."

She moved into his arms, glad that it was another waltz and not a country dance. She did not like to be separated from him, even for a few moments. As they moved onto the polished dance floor, Vanessa stifled a sigh. Once more she was uncomfortably reminded of the changes knowing Philip had wrought in her nature—or had it been love? They were one and the same thing. She did not believe—indeed, she knew full well—these changes were not for the better. She must make a strenuous effort to banish them from her mind. For the second time in as many minutes, she wished devoutly that January would magically change into April.

Across the room, Lady Maria was dancing with a faceless partner, faceless because she had hardly glanced at him when he had asked her to waltz with him. Her eyes had been all for Philip, standing with Lady Vanessa Ventriss at the edge of the floor and, a few minutes later, as the pair joined the other dancers. Philip, she noted with surprise, waltzed very well, this despite the limp that had kept him from training with his father's old regiment. Or was it that which had prevented him? Might he not have been afraid to fight? No, she amended. Much as she longed to find fault with him, she had been party to his despair when he had learned he could not be accepted in the regiment. She frowned, noting that he was totally absorbed in his partner and she in him. That was surprising, an earl's daughter, an earl's sister, with a lowly physician, but she must remember that he was no longer forced to work as a physician. And he had never been lowly. His family tree was well-known to her. She had once been able to recite it, branches and all, from its Saxon roots through the reigns of thirty-eight rulers and the Lord Protector Cromwell.

She grimaced, remembering that she had garnered this knowledge in order to present it in an argument she had intended to have with her parents, and which she had ultimately lost, for they, while acknowledging that Philip's tree was hung with aristocratic fruit, had also pointed out that he had no fortune and no prospects of ever amassing one. Consequently, though his rank might be lower than that of Vanessa

Ventriss, his line was rooted in deeper soil than that of the
Ventriss clan, which, to her certain knowledge, dated back no
further than the reign of Edward II, with some suggestion that
the Ventriss of that period had been enobled less for his
prowess on the battlefield than for an exceptionally handsome
face and fine manly figure.

She glanced at the mirrors and saw that Philip and Vanessa
were reflected in those silvered depths. He was gazing at her
so lovingly! It was an expression Maria remembered only too
well, for once she had been the recipient of those soulful
glances. Anger coupled with misery coursed through her as
she recalled their last meeting. She wished she had not accepted Felicia's invitation. Tom had not wanted to go.

"Another ball?" he had growled. "That woman lives upon
the dance floor. I suppose you'll be wanting to attend?" He
had glowered at her. "And no doubt you'll be purchasing a
new gown for the occasion?"

"Of course I will," she had replied lightly. If she had not
given him that anticipated answer, he might have wondered
why she was acting so untypically and probed for reasons.
She had been sure she would see Philip at the ball. She did
not want to see him, but at the same time, she did, and
decided to have a blue satin gown made—a color a younger
Philip had much admired when she had worn it, telling her
that she went garbed in garments clipped from the sky.

She had been dreaming of him incessantly, dreams of the
past, dreams of secret meetings and wild kisses, dreams of
walking across the moors in springtime hand in hand with
Philip, and he looking at her the way he was now staring at
Lady Vanessa, a curiously fixed stare. A Mesmer stare. She
recalled when Philip was studying that method. He had called
it "mesmerizing," a word only recently coined, he had told
her. Perhaps, she thought bitterly, he had mesmerized Lady
Vanessa. Felicia had described her accident and how Philip
had quelled the pain in her arm. That had been the beginning
of their friendship, but surely it was more than a mere
friendship? The waltz was coming to an end. She bestowed a
beaming smile on her partner and allowed him to escort her

off the floor. She was prayerfully glad that she had not
emerged in the vicinity of Philip and his ladylove. *Was* she?
"Of course" was the answer to that. One would have to be a
blind fool not to read what was printed on both their faces.

A country dance was next, and she was engaged for that
too. Her partner was coming toward her, and out of the
corner of her eye Lady Maria caught sight of Philip and
Vanessa returning to the floor—together! Lady Vanessa had
promised him another dance, two in a row!

Lady Maria put her hand to her bosom. Her heart was
pounding violently. Her breathing was uneven—two dances
in a row with the same partner, and Lady Vanessa evidently
not caring what construction her friends might put on that!

Maria took her place beside her partner. As luck would
have it, she was not in the same grouping as Lady Vanessa
and Philip, but, she decided some few minutes later, it would
not have mattered had they been side by side! Neither Philip
nor Vanessa would have noticed her. Even going through the
complicated patterns of the dance, they contrived to lock
glances and seemed unaware of anyone else on the floor.
Philip's attitude toward herself was fully explained. He was
in love with Lady Vanessa and she with him, shamelessly in
love and not caring who knew it! As she came off the floor
after the country dance, Lady Maria's head was whirling. She
felt faint, but she never fainted, not really. She wondered
where Tom was, but of course she knew where he was. He
was in the card room. She was sadly scatterbrained—no, not
scatterbrained. Her mind was centered on Philip and Lady
Vanessa! Philip and Lady Vanessa? It was not possible. Her
family would never countenance it. That was a cheering
thought. Vanessa might make a fool of herself over Philip,
but, old family or not, the Ventrisses would look elsewhere
for her husband! She was convinced of that—and when he
found that his suit was futile, he might well turn to an old
friend for comforting. No, she was deluding herself. He
would never turn to her, never, never, never again!

"Milady . . ."

Lady Maria, dragged from her thoughts by a polite and

obsequious tone, looked blankly into the face of a servant proffering a tray on which stood a glass of champagne. She goggled at it.

"Champagne?" she blurted.

"Yes, milady, for a toast."

She took it mechanically. A glance around the ballroom showed her that champagne-bearing servants in the fanciful Farr livery were circulating through the ballroom. Soon everyone would have a glass in hand. "And whom are we . . . ?" The words died on her lips as she saw that the servant had moved away.

"What folderol is this?"

Lady Maria heard her husband's gruff tones and glanced up at him blankly. "I do not know."

"I did not think you would," he said unnecessarily. "Are you enjoying yourself, Maria?"

She made herself smile. "Of course, I love to dance. And are you?"

"I was until I was summoned from the tables." Tom's small eyes were resentful. "I had just been dealt a damned good hand, looked as if my luck were on the upswing at last."

"Surely this is very unusual?" someone behind them remarked.

"You know Lady Felicia," came an amused response. "The unusual is usual in her lexicon."

"But whom are we toasting?" Lady Maria wondered aloud.

"Whom indeed, and let there be an end to it," Sir Thomas snapped.

"My friends . . ." Lord Farr, tall and bright-faced, stood across the room with his wife beside him. He spoke loudly, his voice cutting through the murmured speculation instigated by the champagne. "My dear friends," he repeated. "My wife and I have selected this moment to extend our felicitations to our dear friend Lady Vanessa Ventriss and her bridegroom-to-be, Sir Philip Langhorne! I trust that many of you will be present at their wedding next April—a twice-blessed occasion, since Lady Vanessa's brother, Lord Grey-

sham, will be wed to Lady Phoebe Galliard at the same time.
A toast, I say, a toast to the bright future of these two happy
couples!''

There was a round of applause and a mounting murmur of
congratulations, but amidst these Lady Maria moaned, "No,
no, no, it cannot be, not with him . . . 'tis impossible. Philip,
oh, God, no!''

Sir Thomas stared down at her in consternation. "What's
that you are saying, Maria?''

"Oh, Tom." She clutched his arm. "It must not happen. It
cannot happen." Her voice rose. "It cannot happen, do you
hear?''

"I damned well do hear," he growled. "But I'm damned
if I understand. What do you mean?''

Meeting her husband's eyes and reading suspicion in them,
Lady Maria quailed inwardly. In that same moment, she
realized that she had been very, very foolish and she would
be really in trouble if she did not think of a logical explanation for that inadvertent outburst. Tom would think the worst!
If only she had not blurted out Philip's name in her deep
shock, but she had—and having done so, she must needs
provide an explanation convincing enough to assuage his
jealousy and allay his suspicions. There might be others who
had also heard her shocked cry.

"Oh, Tom," she moaned. "I . . . I had not m-meant to
tell you.''

"Tell me what?''

"I never dreamed he would do it . . . offer for Lady
Vanessa. Oh, the poor, poor girl. I must save her. I must not
think of the . . . the cost to me, the scandal.''

"The . . . scandal? What are you saying?" Putting his arm
around her waist, he drew her apart from the crowd and
stared down at her. "Tell me, Maria!" he commanded. His
eyes had grown intent, his mouth turned down. He was
beginning to breathe hard. In another moment he would be in
one of his rages.

Lady Maria clutched his arm. "P-promise you'll not think

hardly of me for . . . for what I am about to s-say," she breathed.

"What do you mean?" he demanded harshly. "You and Philip Langhorne . . . you knew each other well, once. What is there between you?"

"Nothing," she whispered. "Nothing at all. But that is only because I . . . I was able to escape from him that day."

"Escape?" he repeated. "You *escaped*—"

"Shhhh." She put her little hand over his mouth. "You must not speak so loud, Tom. You will attract attention."

Oblivious of her remonstrance, he continued loudly, "I want to know what you meant by 'escape'? Tell me."

Lady Maria sagged against him. "I . . . I will tell you, if you will p-promise not to . . . to create a scandal or call him out. I would not have you harmed, Tom, my dearest, because of my own folly. I trusted him, do you see?"

"I see nothing," he rasped between gritted teeth. "What happened?"

"I . . . encountered him a short time ago. 'Twas on the street just after I had come from Lady Felicia's house. He told me he was redecorating his house and . . . and would like my advice on the color scheme, he remembering that I had an eye for color, which you know I do, Tom."

"Never mind that," he growled. "You went to his house?"

She nodded. "I did. Oh, I know 'twas rash, but we were such old friends and . . . and I never dreamed he would . . . would . . . Ohhh, I do not want to . . . to tell you the rest, Tom."

"But you will!" he exclaimed.

Her husband's face was unpleasantly red, his eyes bright with fury. She loosed a quavering breath. "I must impress upon you, Tom, that I *trusted* him." She stifled a sob.

"That was damned foolish . . . going to his house, damned foolish. What happened?"

"Once . . . once we were there and I looking at the d-draperies, he suddenly fell upon me. He . . . he . . ." Lady Maria achieved another sob. "I struggled, but . . ."

"But what?"

"He looked into my eyes and I . . . I went all weak. I . . . Oh, 'tis impossible to . . . to describe the sensation. I could not struggle longer. He lifted me in his arms and b-bore me to . . . to the couch. He . . . f-fell on me and I could not r-resist him, not . . . not at first, I mean. I had to . . . to suffer his horrid kisses . . . but then that f-feeling wore off and I s-saw my peril. I p-pushed him off . . . he lost his b-balance and f-fell to the floor, and I ran from the house . . . he did not pursue me."

"Good God!" Sir Thomas exploded. "Why did you not tell me?"

"Because I . . . I was afraid you would do something . . . d-dreadful, like calling him out. I was afraid for you, Tom. 'Twas why I kept silent. I did not want anything to . . . to happen to you, and knowing your temper, knowing, too, that Philip is an expert shot and almost as accomplished with a sword, I f-feared to speak. I was afraid of what you might do. Oh, T-Tom, dearest, take me away from here."

"You are telling me the *truth?*" he demanded harshly. He was breathing deeply and his face was totally suffused with color.

"I would swear to it on my mother's grave!" Lady Maria said solemnly.

"Damm it, Maria, your mother's not dead yet!"

"Oh, T-Tom, you know what I mean, and I would if she . . . she were."

"You should have told me," he said heavily.

"I have explained why I . . . I did not, and also I . . . I did not want to cause a horrid scandal. But that poor girl he is to wed, she must know the truth."

"And will," he said between his teeth. "I will fetch Lord Greysham, and you may repeat your story to him!"

"N-now?" Lady Maria paled.

"Now."

"Oh, Tom . . ." She caught at his sleeve. "Do let us go. I do not want everyone to know . . . they will suspect that he . . . that I . . . there must not be a scandal, Tom."

"There'll be no scandal. And everyone will not know.

only Lord Greysham, at present." He escorted Lady Maria to the chairs that were pushed against the wall. "Sit here," he ordered. "I will be back shortly!"

With considerable if concealed satisfaction, Lady Maria, lying limply against her chair, her head drooping, her eyes half-shut, watched her husband stride away through the curtain of her lengthy lashes. Mentally she was congratulating herself upon a scene that would have easily equaled if not surpassed Miss O'Neil's much-lauded performance of *Isabella* at Covent Garden last month. She had not only managed to convince her husband, but she had also or would soon have scotched Philip's chances of wedding the fair Vanessa! Furthermore, she was happily positive that Tom would call him out. Philip, as far as she knew, was proficient with neither gun nor sword. His childhood infirmity had precluded that. Of course, he could deny his complicity, but that, she was positive, would not stick. He was still new to London society . . . She paused in her thoughts. Miss Belinda Compton, having quaffed her champagne and toasted the happy pair, was returning to the seat she usually occupied at a ball. She was rarely sought as a partner, and in a few more years she would undoubtedly join the ranks of the chaperons. Lady Maria saw surprise flare in her friend's eyes.

"My dearest Maria," she gushed. "Fancy finding *you* here. Are you not feeling well?"

Lady Maria sighed deeply. "Alas, no, I . . . I have had a rude shock."

"A shock? But what happened?" Miss Compton sat down next to her.

"Oh, I cannot tell you. 'Tis too terrible, and no one must ever, ever know," she said provocatively.

"Surely you can trust me," Miss Compton murmured.

"You are inclined to gossip, Belinda. And no one must know about *this*—no one!"

Miss Compton looked affronted. "I have never gossiped about you, Maria. You know I am your true friend." Her eyes were alight with curiosity.

Lady Maria scanned the dance floor. She did not see Tom.

If she were to speak quickly, dearest Belinda would have the tale and it would spread like the proverbial wildfire. "If I do take you into my confidence, Belinda, you must swear that you will not repeat a word!"

"I will certainly swear that I will not, though I must say you needn't have demanded that of *me*," Miss Compton reproved.

"Very well." Lady Maria leaned forward. Fortunately, she was finished with her tale well before Lord Greysham, with an even more irate Tom, came over to her.

To do Belinda justice, she did not betray by word or look the shocking story she had just been party to. She moved away and sat at the far end of the row of chairs, not even glancing in Lady Maria's direction.

Lady Maria, looking up at Lord Greysham, found him frowning. She drew a deep breath. Everything depended upon his crediting her. However, Tom had believed her, and so had Belinda, who must be bursting to give birth to this juicy scandal. She drew another breath and realized that she might be experiencing what actors were known to feel when they faced a difficult house. However, under the stern gaze of a most attentive audience, she warmed to her subject and was even able to add a few artful embellishments that she had not imparted to Tom. Watching the play of expressions on Lord Greysham's face, she realized that she was making a definite impression. She did experience some qualms when, after a brief silence, he said grimly, "I will fetch Sir Philip." Still, though new to the acting profession, she had the most satisfying feeling that her "public" was with her.

Philip, standing with Lady Vanessa and still receiving the congratulations of her friends, wished heartily that these were at an end. He would like to be alone with her. She, he noted, was looking radiantly happy. Her obvious joy warmed his heart. Yet, even now, it seemed to him that he must be living in a dream. No, that was not an adequate description of his feelings. Never, even in dreams, had he envisioned himself the chosen bridegroom of this beautiful, this perfect woman. She *was* perfect, he thought ecstatically. She had no faults, none at all. She was everything a woman could be, noble, beautiful, honest. She was far more honest than women were purported to be. She had none of, say, Maria's artful little tricks. A man knew exactly where he stood with her!

"Langhorne!" Lord Greysham strode up to him. "Might I have a word with you, please?"

"Certainly." Philip smiled at his future brother-in-law. He did not receive an answering smile. Greysham, he noted, was frowning.

"Johnny," Vanessa said. "You look like a veritable thundercloud. What's amiss?"

His frown grew even blacker. "Everything or nothing," he said in clipped accents.

"Gracious!" Phoebe, who had evidently heard him, came to stand by his side. "What can that mean?"

"No matter," he snapped. "Come with me, Langhorne."

Vanessa said on a breath, "Something *is* the matter. What is it, John? Tell me, please."

"This does not concern you, my dear," he said heavily. "I want but a moment of your time, Langhorne."

"Might I know why?" Philip demanded.

"I think we should speak privately," Lord Greysham rasped.

"John," Vanessa said purposefully, "what has happened?"

"Very well," he capitulated. "Since you are determined to know, and possibly ought to know—if there is anything to know—you can come with us, Vanessa."

"Come where?" She looked from her brother to Philip. "I do not understand."

"No more do I," Lord Greysham burst out. He glared at Philip. "But if 'tis true I . . . I . . ." He paused. "I had best say no more, as yet."

Philip regarded him incredulously. "I would prefer it if you said a great deal more. You appear to be deeply disturbed and angry. Your anger seems directed at me. I would like to know the reason."

"You will know it soon enough."

"Oh, John, for God's sake," Vanessa protested. "Out with it, please. I loathe mysteries!"

"This one may soon be solved, and not to your liking, I fear." Lord Greysham moved forward. "Follow me, please." He added, "I can only hope that you are not culpable, Langhorne. I do not like to be mistaken in my judgments."

"Culpable?" Philip repeated. "Of what?"

Lord Greysham did not answer. He strode forward. Philip, following him, looked at Vanessa. Some of her lovely color had fled. She exchanged glances with him and he found her eyes full of concern and even fear. He wanted to reassure her, but his own fears stood in the way, and yet, he reasoned angrily, he had nothing to fear. He had done nothing to occasion this reaction on the part of Greysham. His attitude reflected his former antipathy, but that was supposedly at an end, with Lord Carlton purported to be a new man, happy with bride and son.

Lord Greysham came to a stop. "You had, I believe, an understanding with Lady Maria Glazebrook some time back?"

Philip stared at him incredulously. "Lady Maria . . . I knew her years ago." He nodded and heard Vanessa sigh. He added quickly, " 'Twas never an understanding. I did believe myself in love with her, but I was very young—"

"Oh, God, do not say any more!" Lord Greysham exclaimed. "You . . . you would have married my sister!"

"What can you mean?" Vanessa cried.

"Come," he ordered, striding ahead of them, stopping near the chairs.

"You, Philip, you and Lady Maria Glazebrook?" Vanessa said in a low voice.

"Vanessa, my love, it was over years ago. And 'twas only a boy's callow passion. I cannot understand why 'tis mentioned now!"

"Your . . . confusion will be at an end—and soon," Lord Greysham said caustically.

Philip looked at Vanessa and received no look in return. Shock went through him. She was frowning, and her mouth was actually grim, as if, while still in ignorance of his possible offense, she had already passed judgment on him, or, if that were too strong a supposition, as if she were already doubting his veracity. A chill went through him. Coupled with it was indignation. How could she make judgments without knowledge? She had heard a name and immediately arrived at an erroneous conclusion.

This was not the Vanessa he knew, but how well did he know her? Was the image he had formed of her accurate, or was it merely an idealization? He must not think about that now—but rather of Maria Glazebrook and what could have lifted that ancient connection, severed by herself, from the dust. He would know soon enough, for there she was, sitting or rather half-lying on the chair, with one young woman, Miss Compton, he remembered, fanning her and several other people gazing down at her. Her husband, his full face appearing thunderous, stood by her, and now, as he approached, that lowering gaze was fastened on himself—and he thought of a maddened bull that had once charged him when he had attempted to take a shortcut through a meadow. Philip's consternation increased. Coming closer, he was aware of a whole battery of looks directed at him, and another analogy, equally uncomfortable, sprang to mind. He was like a criminal in the dock, judged by his peers even before the trial had commenced. He glanced at Vanessa but failed to catch her eye. And then he was facing Maria, who looked up at him and shuddered. She also moaned piteously.

He stared down at her, concern melding with confusion. "You are ill, then, Maria?" He moved toward her.

"On your life, do not come any nearer to my wife," Sir Thomas growled. "Do not touch her again!"

"Philip," Maria whispered. "Oh, Philip, how could you expect to wed poor, poor Lady Vanessa. Did you think yourself safe?"

"Safe?" he repeated numbly. "What can you mean, Maria?"

"Oh, Philip," she moaned. " 'Twill do you no good to lie. I have told them everything."

"Everything?" he demanded confusedly. "I do not understand."

"You understand!" Sir Thomas accused. "Do not dare to say you do not!"

Philip turned toward him. "I do say that I have no idea what she is talking about."

"Oh, cruel, cruel," Maria sighed. "I did not believe that you, of all people, could ever be craven, Philip." Her eyes were wide and filled with tears.

"Craven?" he repeated incredulously, wondering if she had gone mad. "I beg you will tell me what you mean, Maria."

"Montebank!" shrilled Miss Compton.

"Aye, montebank, but this simulated innocence will not protect you," Lord Greysham snapped. " 'Tis time and past that you admitted your complicity."

"My . . . complicity?"

"The other day, Philip . . ." Maria said. "At your house. I have told them the whole of it. I could not keep silent . . . no matter what the . . . the disgrace to myself, not when the future happiness of Lady Vanessa was at stake."

He regarded her blankly. "What are you talking about, Maria?" he demanded angrily. "What nonsense is this?"

"Nonsense, is it? I'll give you nonsense, you foul miscreant, you nobody from nowhere!" Sir Thomas moved toward him, fists clenched.

"Stay, Sir Thomas!" Lord Greysham caught his arm.

"Will you deny everything, Philip?" Maria cried. "Will you ever deny that I was in your house alone?"

"I'll not deny that," he began. "But—"

"Philip, oh, Philip!" Vanessa whispered.

To his ears, that whisper was as loud as a shout or a scream. " 'Twas nothing," he said to her. "She—"

"Oh, Philip," Maria exclaimed. "Do not continue to lie. They know the whole of it. Everything!"

"Everything?" His attention was once more fixed on Maria. "And what does 'everything' comprise?"

"How you . . . mesmerized me and . . . and—"

"A devil's game!" Sir Thomas roared.

"Maria." Philip fixed his eyes on her. "Why are you saying these things? Why are you lying—?"

"My wife's no liar, damn you for a white-livered rogue, a brazen-faced cull!" Sir Thomas launched himself at Philip, striking him hard across the face.

Philip staggered back, his cheek stinging and a tooth loosened by the force of the blow. "You . . . you . . ." His own rage was rising.

"You will accept my challenge, Langhorne," Sir Thomas roared. "Or are you a coward who only attacks weak women!"

They were all staring at him. Vaguely he heard Miss Compton's nervous giggle. Maria was moaning. Philip was beset with a sense of unreality. He looked down at his accuser. She was lying against her chair, her eyes wide and wet with tears—the picture of outraged innocence. He would have liked to shake her until her teeth rattled—but that would have availed him nothing. He started at Vanessa and in that moment received a withering look of contempt. Then, turning on her heel, she walked swiftly across the floor.

He was conscious of a pain in his heart. She had not asked to hear his side of the matter, had not wanted to hear it, had tried and condemned him on the strength of Maria's lies alone. It was amazing how quickly, how easily all of them had believed Maria. He stared at her and could understand why. She lay there, half-fainting, her natural paleness standing her in good stead. It would be very difficult for those unacquainted with the situation to believe her the arrant liar that she was!

"You are afraid, are you not, coward?" Sir Thomas said contemptuously.

Lord Greysham nodded. "It does look that way."

"Looks can be extremely deceiving, my lord," Philip said coldly. "I am not afraid." He turned to Sir Thomas. "I accept your challenge. Name the place and the time."

"Tomorrow morning—" Sir Thomas began.

"Oh, Tom." Maria interjected. "Is it not enough that you know him for what he is . . . that all know him for what he is?"

"No, it is not enough!" Sir Thomas snapped.

"But if I am willing to forgive him—" Maria murmured.

"That is most magnanimous, my dear," he interrupted sharply. "And surely it does you credit, but I am not prepared to forgive him." Sir Thomas turned his hot eyes on Philip. "Tomorrow morning, Wimbledon Common, five o'clock. Name your seconds."

"I have no names . . ." Philip began, and frowned. "No, I have, and will send him to you."

"And you, my lord, will you act for me?" Sir Thomas turned to Lord Greysham.

"I shall," his lordship said grimly. He looked at Philip. "Swords or pistols? Yours is the choice."

"Pistols, swords, no matter." Philip shrugged.

"Pistols, then," Sir Thomas said.

"Oh, Tom," Maria moaned. "Must it come to this?"

He glared at her. "Can you actually believe that I will stand by and see myself cuckolded by this damned miscreant?"

"Cuckolded?" Philip repeated.

"It . . . it did not come to that, I told you it did not," Maria cried. "I was able to . . . to fight him off."

"And that must satisfy me?" Sir Thomas demanded, his fists clenched again. He whirled on Philip.

"Enough, Sir Thomas." Lord Greysham stepped forward. He turned his cold gaze on Philip. "You'll have your satisfaction on the morrow. And you, Langhorne, will have your seconds wait on me tomorrow morning."

"I shall," Philip said. He turned and walked across the ballroom. He kept his eyes fixed on the door leading to the hall. He wondered vaguely what the hour was . . . he would need to rouse Harlock, now his only friend in the city. It was a pity that Alastair was still in Scotland. Into his mind popped his friend's warnings about dangerous situations. It was not the first time Alastair's remarks had come back to him; he had recalled them at the time of Maria's visit. His teeth came together with a click as he remembered his surprise and subsequent embarrassment at her protestations and her wild declarations. He also remembered his final words before she went screaming out of the house. He had tried to be gentle with her—but obviously he had been inept. Yet how else could he have handled the situation? No matter what he had said or done, her reaction would have been the same. She had thrown herself at him and he had failed to catch her. She, remembering the lovelorn youth he had been, was much aggrieved, more than that, furious that her daringly overt attentions had received no response. Consequently she had sought revenge, and she had had it!

As for himself, would it have been better had he denied the fact that she had visited him? No, for the servants had seen her come, and heard the violently slammed door that had signaled her departure. Their testimony, circulating through the various houses and avidly repeated by maidservants and valets, would naturally add more fuel to the blaze.

If only Lady Felicia had not insisted on making that announcement, he thought wryly, nothing would have happened. If she had not, Vanessa would . . . His lip curled. Amazingly enough, Vanessa had been disposed to believe the worst! She had not even waited, and nor had she wanted any explanations from him. Why? Did she not know him any better than that? How could she believe that he would ravish or attempt to ravish a helpless Maria? Unfortunately, he had practiced mesmerism on her and so she had credited Maria's statement, but she should not have credited it. She ought to have given him the benefit of the doubt, but had not because . . . because why?

He had an answer for that. In her world, he was yet an outsider. And Maria had sounded most convincing. Still, that did not excuse Vanessa. She ought to have heard him out. But what could he have told her? Could he have described Maria's visit? Could he have provided further details concerning her untoward actions, her embrace? To reveal these particulars to anyone would have been the act of a scoundrel! No, Vanessa must needs have taken his word that nothing had happened between them—and he had uttered that word, if not directly, at least in his surprise and shock. And Vanessa had preferred to believe Maria!

He had reached the entrance hall. He went into a small anteroom and retrieved his cloak. A few minutes later, a servant opened wide the front door and Philip strode out into the blustery winter night. Behind him, the golden glow from the hall was blotted out by the swift closing of the portal—a tacit acknowledgment of what had taken place in the ballroom? Philip smiled mirthlessly. Whether it was or not made no difference. All society had cast him out of its world and into the darkness. Henceforth he would walk alone, provided he survived the meeting in the morning.

8

Philip had chosen to ride rather than to take his curricle or post chaise. The dueling ground lay some six or seven miles from the city proper, but he had given himself plenty of time on this, which might prove to be the last morning of his life.

The hands of the hall clock had indicated half-past the hour of three when he had quietly closed his door. At this moment, he had reached King Street and was riding at a good clip, one he would increase once he reached the road to Wimbledon. It was important that he arrive there betimes, for he must needs act as his own second. No doubt there would be considerable caviling at that, but he had decided against recruiting the man he considered his only real friend in London: Alden Harlock. One dedicated to saving life ought not to be required to officiate at so sorry a business. He himself had always loathed the idea of duels and would have applauded had they been officially outlawed. Furthermore, he intended to remain true to his principles. He was a fair shot, having been instructed in that dubious skill by Alastair, home on one of his leaves and insisting that as a physician serving on the Peninsula, he might need to defend himself. On two occasions Alastair had been proved right. However, this morning, the idea of sending a ball into some portion of Sir Thomas' anatomy because of Maria's lies was definitely repugnant to him. He could not do it. He, at least, would delope. And if Sir Thomas decided to dispatch him, he did not much care. Life, which had been singularly sweet to him in the past two months, had turned bitter, a poisoned cup indeed!

"Vanessa," Philip muttered, and his horse snorted at a sudden tightening of the reins. He stared up at the sky, still dark with a sickle moon flat against that vast canopy. It was a beautiful sight, especially to one who might well be dead at sunrise. And what would she think when that news was brought by her brother? Probably she would agree with Greysham, that he had received no more than his just deserts—and she would congratulate herself on her narrow escape from a villain who had ravished an innocent female. His mocking laughter rang out, startling even himself and, at the same time, annoying him. He was becoming bathetic.

"Help, help, for the love of God, help us . . ." The voice, weak and racked with pain, reached him. He looked down hastily and saw a vague shape on the street, close to the curb and just beyond the glow cast by the gaslight. He reined in his horse.

"Who are you . . . what's amiss?" he demanded warily, for he had heard that the footpads who ranged the streets were adept at mimicry. A good samaritan might find himself in dire straits, were he to offer assistance to one of these birds of prey.

"Here, sir . . . oh, help me. . . . Myself and the . . . the lad were set upon . . . the boy must be unconscious yet."

Philip had ridden closer, and despite the indifferent light, he could see a man lying on the street. His coat was missing and his neckcloth had been torn away. Probably there had been a gem-topped pin on it. Dismounting quickly and winding his reins around his hand, he knelt beside the fallen man, seeing now that there was a bloody welt on his forehead, not far from the temple. He had bled profusely, for his hair was matted with blood and his face streaked with it.

"S-see to . . . to the lad," the man begged. "They must have dragged him somewhere . . . do you see him? He must be found."

"Do you live nearby?" Philip asked.

"Very near. I . . . I was coming home. I . . . chose to

walk . . . the air being crisp and the wind died down . . . damned fool thing to do, but I was half-bosky, I fear. I'd won a large sum, d'you see. 'Tis gone, the lot of it . . . like as not I was followed from the hell. 'Twas not one I was used to . . . to frequenting. B-but no matter . . . the boy, see to poor little Mark. I pray nothing untoward has happened to him.''

Philip looked around. He did not see the boy in question, but there was a space between two of the houses—a narrow alleyway. It was possible that the thieves had dragged him there. Still leading his horse, he went toward it, and producing his tinderbox, he struck the flint against the steel and hastily ignited a match. In the resulting flare, he saw another dark shape, and going to it, found the boy, his shattered lantern lying nearby. His coat, too, had been removed and his shirt torn. Kneeling beside him, Philip put an ear against his chest and found to his relief that his heart was beating strongly. He hurried back to the first victim. "He is not dead, sir. He is only unconscious."

"Oh, thank God," the man said unsteadily. "Mark is the son of my housekeeper. I . . . I could not have borne it if he were hurt badly."

"I cannot think that he is." Philip spoke soothingly.

"Poor child . . . poor child, so willing. Sir, might I ask you to assist me to my house. 'Tis number eighteen."

"Gladly," Philip assented. "I'll tether my horse." Finding a post near the gaslight, he secured the animal and returned to find the man attempting to rise.

"My ankle . . . 'tis . . . I seem to remember turning it when I fell."

Philip struck another match. " 'Tis swollen," he said after a moment. "I will examine it once we are inside."

"If . . . if you will get me to my house, I will not detain you longer. I'll send someone for my physician."

"That will not be necessary, sir," Philip said briskly. "I am a physician. Now, let me bring you to your door, and then I will fetch the lad." He had a moment's qualms but dismissed them immediately. His mission must be life, not death!

The idea had been growing upon her ever since her brother had taken her home. Lying in her bed, Vanessa tossed and turned. There would be a duel, a duel on Wimbledon Common, and would Tom hurt Philip or even slay him . . . slay him for the despoiling of his wife, the attempted despoiling?

Philip's face was etched in the darkness behind her eyes. He had looked toward her as if seeking her understanding, and she had turned away! Had he actually expected her forgiveness for his deed? Vanessa stared into the darkness. It seemed so strange, so unlike the man she had come to know, to attack Maria—but he had not attacked her, he had tried to make love to her, had mesmerized her. Or had he? Was there a chance Maria was lying? She had seemed so convincing. Vanessa started, as she heard her little clock strike the half-hour—two-thirty in the morning. In less than three hours, Philip would be facing Tom on the common!

"No," she whispered, putting her hands to her ears, but not drowning out the sound of the shot reverberating through her head. "No, no, no!"

She slipped out of bed. She had to see him, had to stop the duel. And she must give him a chance to tell her his side of the story. She had not given him that chance. She had turned away—stricken to the heart. It was as if all her unspoken fears had been corroborated. She hurried to her armoire and took out a dark gown and her cloak.

A half-hour later, Vanessa crept out of her room and down the stairs, wincing as they creaked beneath her feet. However, no one would think anything of that, she assured herself. Old houses creaked at night. She must find a hackney, must get to Philip's house, must see him, must stop the duel. He could not face Tom, Tom who was jealous of him and who believed Maria. Everyone believed Maria, but had she spoken the truth? It seemed so incredible, knowing Philip. Incredible and unbelievable.

She reached the hall and started for the door, but in that

instant there were footsteps behind her, coming swiftly down the stairs. She froze, her hand on the doorknob.

"Vanessa," Johnny whispered. "What are you doing here at this time of night."

"It's not night. It's morning. It's nearly three. I must see him. I must stop this duel. I do not believe—"

"My dear," Johnny interrupted. "You are not thinking straight. No man of honor would ever pay heed to you. Tomorrow—"

"What if there is no tomorrow for Philip? Oh, Johnny, I do not believe what Maria said. I do not believe it. I love him."

"Hush . . . hush, my dear. I am not so sure I believe it myself. But Tom's not such a fool as to shoot to kill. He does not want to remove to France for the next six months, I can assure you. By morning he will have calmed down. I doubt that he will do anything except shoot over his head. I expect Philip will do the same. Now, for God's sake, do not be a fool. It is possible that I was too hasty in my denunciation. I, too, have been thinking about it. Now, my dear, come on."

"I am afraid." Vanessa clutched him. "I must see him. I feel I must."

"In the morning, my dear," her brother said firmly. "And as I stand here, I promise you there will be no bloodshed."

It was midmorning before Philip could leave the side of the patient, who proved to be the Duke of Frome. When, at length, he moved from the bedside and came into the hall, he was further delayed by a band of anxious servants, headed by the grateful and tearful housekeeper, who thanked him over and over again for ministering to her son. It was close on forty minutes before he could escape from them. Coming out, he smiled up at a sky which was bright and clear. It occurred to him that he had not expected to view it again and, but for the duke, he might have been lying on the turf with a coat thrown over his face—his second cousin Victor happy in the possession of an unexpected baronetcy, with the competence to match.

Yet, it was not a time for rejoicing, but rather for the resumption of the duel. Fortunately, Sir Thomas was a member of Watier's, which would allay the necessity of going to his house and risking an encounter with the perfidious Maria. Probably another time would be set for the duel. He regretted that. His meeting with the duke had made him even more aware of how much his work meant to him. Years ago, he recalled Mr. Devlin saying to him, " 'Tis not work for me, dear young Philip, 'tis a vocation."

It was a vocation. He could imagine that priests felt much the same way, as if their calling were God-given. In the past two months, his passion for Vanessa had rendered his idle life much more palatable. Yet, even had she remained true to him, he would eventually have longed for the consulting room and the bedside. And now he was free to pursue his chosen profession. Did that mean that he was also free of her? Not yet. The bright sky suddenly blurred. Angrily he blinked those unmanly tears away. It was still so difficult, too difficult, to deal with her lack of faith in himself, her swift acceptance of Maria's facile lies. He swallowed a lump in his throat, remembering that the last time tears had been in his eyes was when Maria had spurned him for Sir Thomas Glazebrook. Twice in his life he had been betrayed by that false emotion called love, he reasoned bitterly. Henceforth, he was through with it. A sense of freedom arose in his mind, but that was instantly blotted out as he recalled that he was still committed to the duel! Springing on his horse, he rode toward that famed corner of Piccadilly and Bolton Street—where Watier's was located.

Surprise was written in large letters on the face of the porter at Watier's as Philip entered. In answer to his inquiry concerning Sir Thomas, he was told that the baronet was not present, but on asking after Lord Greysham, he learned that he was in the card room. The porter looked as if he wanted to say something else, but then he evidently changed his mind. Philip, moving toward the card room, met Lord Alvanley, looking worn and weary. Probably his lordship had been there all the night, and judging from his lowering expression, his stay had not proved profitable. He was about to greet him, but Alvanley did not appear to see him. His gaze turned chill, and he moved swiftly away. Philip looked after him. Evidently his lordship had gone down more heavily than usual. He continued on his way, and a second later he entered the card room. As usual, it was crowded, and from the weary looks of some of the men present, they, too, had been there through the night. At first he did not see Lord Greysham, but a moment later he glimpsed him sitting at a table near the fireplace. As he started toward him, Philip was aware of a sudden diminishing of conversation. It was followed by laughter. He did not look about to discover the cause of what had sounded very like mockery. Had someone cheated? he wondered. That was not his concern. Reaching Lord Greysham, who was sitting playing piquet with one Sir Alan Spoffard, he was relieved to find that neither man was scanning the cards. He said, "My lord, I pray you will excuse the interruption, but I—"

"But," Greysham said coldly, "I do not excuse it. We have nothing to say to each other, sir."

Philip tensed but persisted. "No doubt you are surprised that I did not appear on Wimbledon Common—"

"On the contrary," Greysham cut in, "I am not surprised, since your second did not trouble to come either."

"I must tell you—" Philip began.

"Sir Philip," Greysham said in freezing accents, "I have no interest in anything you might tell me. I do my best to avoid conversations with cowards."

Philip flushed. "I must explain—"

"I have told you"—Lord Greysham rose—"that I will not speak with you, and if you persist in remaining here, I must leave. There is a bad odor about a knave such as yourself, which I cannot stomach!" Turning his back on Philip, Lord Greysham strode from the room.

"If you will excuse me . . ." Sir Alan Spoffard also rose and followed Greysham.

Looking about him, Philip read contempt and derision on the faces of the men at the tables, belatedly realizing that he had been condemned by his peers on supposition alone. Yet, that was not surprising, given the nature of his so-called offense. And now a ripple of laughter was circulating through the room; they were looking at him and laughing loudly and derisively.

"Gentlemen!" Philip said in tones that topped their merriment. "I thank you." Bowing, he strode from the room to the sound of more mocking laughter. On the street, he saw yet another acquaintance, and again he read contempt in eyes that did not seem to see him.

Mounting his horse, he rode away. He found that he was conscious of nothing more than a profound relief. Branded a coward, he need no longer sacrifice his life to Maria's prevarications. He would leave London that night and head for Scotland. The roads were all but impassable at this season of the year, but that was actually a blessing. Given his fleet horses, he would yet arrive in Edinburgh before the mails reached Sir Alastair with the news of his downfall and disgrace. He wanted to see Alastair. He needed the solace of one sympathetic ear and, then, hopefully he could get on with the important business of working and forgetting.

"She is coming here, Felicia?" Vanessa said angrily, "Is *that* why you summoned me?"

"Exactly," Felicia corroborated, not without a touch of defiance.

"Then I will go!" Vanessa exclaimed.

"No, you will not." Felicia caught Vanessa's hand. "I have told you that I do not entirely credit her story. And furthermore—"

"Why do you not credit it? Have the recent events convinced you that Sir Philip possesses so noble a character and is so brave a . . . I have told you I would have forgiven him. I was ready to go to him and hear his side of it . . . but he . . . You know what happened."

"As to his nobility of character or lack of it, I have nothing to say," Felicia responded. "If we are to believe your brother, he is an ignoble coward who turned tail and ran away from a duel. That is not how he struck me, and if you will remember, my love, he served on the Peninsula and in France, too."

"Behind the lines," Vanessa reminded her icily. "He was not a soldier."

"And can you imagine that he was safe behind the lines? Can you not envision what it must be like to be so near the very thick of battle? Physicians are not straw men. They have blood, and 'tis as easily spilled as our own."

"Do not . . ." Vanessa shuddered. She looked down at her hands. "His blood has not been spilled. He avoided the duel. So much for his bravery."

"I cannot believe him a coward," Felicia said insistently.

"Then why—"

"Judging from what your brother has said, no one gave him a chance to explain why he failed to arrive at the dueling ground."

"And his second, also?"

"Oh, Vanessa, 'tis outside of enough that you, who loved him, are his accuser and I his defender, who scarcely knew him. Yet I liked what I saw. And Maria—"

Vanessa rose, her hands clenched tightly. "I do not want to see her!" she cried.

"But, my dear love, she did you a kindness, do you not remember?"

"A . . . a kindness!"

"Did she not expose Sir Philip's perfidy and save you from a most unfortunate alliance? Think what must have happened had Lady Maria not gone to his house. You would have been beleaguered with wedding arrangements—the mantau makers, the furniture houses, for I am sure that not all the furnishings of Langhorne House would have met with your approval, and also—"

"Stop it, stop it." Vanessa put her hands to her ears. "Do you enjoy torturing me?"

"No, I do not." Felicia moved to her and put her arms around her. "And I hate seeing you so utterly miserable."

"I am not miserable!" Vanessa retorted. "I do not see

why you should think I am! And in the last month, I have been exceptionally busy. I have scarce had a single moment to myself!"

"Or one to spare for me. I have been thinking that you've been purposely avoiding me and might even hold it against me that Sir Philip's machinations were exposed under this roof."

"Do not be a goose!" Vanessa snapped. "I have not been purposely avoiding you. I *have* been very busy. And I've not avoided the mantua makers, either, or the furniture houses. Phoebe, if you will remember, *is* getting married in April. And she seems to desire my advice. She is having the most beautiful gown made, all white with little forget-me-nots in pink and blue, fashioned from ribbons and set with tiny seed pearls, stitched to the skirt. There will be blue and pink—"

"My love, you may find these details utterly fascinating, but I do not. And do not look affronted, my dearest. Bear with me and greet our sweet Maria when she appears. Let her chatter on. Above all, do not glower at her as you are currently glowering at me. The poor child is walking on very thin ice, you know. The *on-dit* is that she was almost ravished by that black villain you would have called husband. There is a very fine line between almost and was—and there are some amongst the *ton* who are much less cordial than before. And—"

"Has she been cut? Good!" Vanessa exclaimed.

"That is hardly the attitude you ought to assume. Think how much you owe her. 'Twas for your sake that she voiced her accusations against your intended. She has saved you from a . . . a . . . What is that word? Ah, mesmerist, I think. Imagine being wed to so reprehensible a character. You might want to attend a ball and he with a look would induce you to witness a dog fight or a bear baiting or—"

"Felicia!" Vanessa cried. "That is enough. I am going. I will not—" She paused at a tap on the door.

"Come in, Martin," Lady Felicia called.

The door was opened by the Farrs' polite butler. "If you please, milady. Lady Maria Glazebrook has arrived."

"Good. Show her in here, Martin."

"Yes, milady." The butler withdrew.

Vanessa glared at the door. "I will not remain. I do not want to—"

"Shhhh, 'tis too late, my love. 'Tis time and past that you two met and at least exchanged experiences. Or better yet, listen while she tells you what a narrow escape you had."

"I . . ." Vanessa closed her mouth on another protest as Lady Maria Glazebrook appeared on the threshold. Her pale eyes narrowed as she saw Vanessa, and there was a moment's hesitation before she came forward saying, "My dearest Lady Vanessa, what a delightful surprise! I have been longing to see you."

"Have you?" Vanessa forced a smile. "Well, I am here, as you see."

"Do sit down, Maria." Felicia indicated a chair. "You are looking well."

Maria, slipping into the proffered chair, smiled up at her hostess. "I am very well, thank you. And you, Felicia, are blooming, as usual."

"Thank you, my dear. You are kind to say so. Is that not a new gown you are wearing?"

Maria smiled pridefully, acknowledging a possible compliment. " 'Twas just finished. I do like kerseymere, it is comfortable to wear. Can you imagine that Madame Suzanne told me that no one is purchasing French washing silk this Season—for which I am *très désolée*, it does give such a soft effect, do you not agree?"

"I am forced to agree"—Felicia smiled wryly—"since I have three gowns made from the material."

"Ah, but you can give them to your abigail. That is what I intend to do with mine, provided she does not wear them immediately. I always insist that she wait a decent interval—though, of course, I do not imagine anyone would recognize them on *her*. She has a very dumpy figure. Servants have such big *poitrines*, do you not agree? But no matter." She turned to Vanessa and shook her head. "My dear, I passed one of those horrid print shops on Piccadilly, and the cartoons—

they are still fixed on the scandal. We are both depicted as swooning while *he* stares us down. They have put him in a cap and gown with stars on it, like a sorcerer. He is quite recognizable, but fortunately our features have been cunningly distorted, which is a mercy, is it not?''

"Quite," Vanessa commented coldly. "The tale certainly seems to have taken root."

"I know that only too well," Maria sighed. "Everything seems to be grist for London's gossip mill. I wonder if *he* has seen them? There was a really horrid one of him in the window, fleeing the dueling ground—with a caption to the effect that he is a physician who punctures but is afraid of being punctured. Of course, that is not exactly what it says, it is a pun and quite fiendishly clever. He will really cringe when he sees it, if he does see it, and 'twill serve him right. However, he seems to have dropped from sight. I cannot wonder at that. No one would receive him now! It is too, too terrible, is it not? I never dreamed that Philip would rat on a duel. I expect you were equally shocked, my dear Lady Vanessa."

Vanessa regarded her coldly. "Would you have preferred it if he had died for you . . . or perhaps Sir Thomas?"

Maria's eyes widened in surprise. "But, my dear Lady Vanessa, no one would have *died*," she said positively.

"Oh?" Vanessa questioned. "How can you be so sure of that?"

"How indeed." Felicia raised her eyes. "Such . . . er, mishaps have been known to take place during duels."

"I know my husband," Maria insisted. "He only wanted to teach Philip a lesson he'd not forget. At the most, he might have winged him."

"I see." Vanessa's tone was glacial. "And suppose by some accident Sir Thomas would have been hit in a vital spot?"

"That never would have happened. Philip would have aimed over his head or to one side."

"You mean he'd have deloped?" Felicia inquired.

"Most certainly. He does not approve of duels. He holds

very strong opinions on the subject. I pride myself on knowing Philip far far better than"—Maria darted a glance at
Vanessa—"than anyone currently in London. We were children together, after all, though of course I am much younger
than Philip. Still, I do recall his absolute fury when his elder
brother was forced to fight a duel. Philip tried to talk him out
of it, fancy! He said duels were senseless. He held similar
views on hunting."

"Hunting also?" Vanessa questioned.

Maria nodded. "He would never go hunting. Once he
actually rescued a fox from the hounds. It bit him badly, but
still he took it home and bandaged its wounds. It died,
though, and he was distraught, and of course the hunters
were absolutely furious with him, and his father gave him a
caning. He was very gentle, you see." She laughed lightly.
"People believed him to be a coward even then."

Vanessa was aware of a sinking feeling. She exchanged a
long look at Felicia, who nodded her head slightly. She then
stared at Maria, saying slowly, "You think Sir Philip gentle?"

"Oh, very," Maria acknowledged. "He always insisted
that everything had a right to live, even flies and bats, if you
can credit that!"

"Bats, ugh!" Felicia shivered. "I would dispute with him
on them. I have always loathed the ugly creatures, have you
not, Vanessa?"

Vanessa did not appear to have heard her. She was staring
at Maria. She said slowly, "Sir Philip must have changed a
very great deal since you were children together."

"Not really," Maria said. "I have told you—"

"You have told us that he was very gentle," Vanessa
interrupted. "And yet this very gentle man lured you to his
abode, overpowered you, mesmerized you, and ravished
you—"

"He did not ravish me!" Maria cried.

"I was about to add the word 'attempted.' He attempted to
ravish you," Vanessa amplified. "I would certainly not describe these actions as 'gentle.' "

Maria's eyes were wide with indignation. "That was different!'' she retorted. "He was moved by passion—overmastered by it. 'Twas very wrong of him, of course, considering my married status, but he was . . . he is madly in love with me and has been since we were children. We were meant to be together, you know."

"Were you?" Lady Vanessa inquired coldly.

Maria bridled. "You may not wish to believe me, Lady Vanessa, but 'tis true. 'Twas my parents objected because he was poor and only a physician. They forced me to wed Tom. 'Twas none of my willing. I loved Philip. I always loved him and he felt the same about me."

Vanessa exchanged another glance with Felicia before fixing her eyes on Maria again. "If you feel that way, why do you say he brought you to his house . . . lured you there, in fact, against your will, and attempted to ravish you? Evidently that was what you craved, to be ravished by him!"

"Lady Vanessa!" Maria jumped to her feet. "That's a damnable lie. How dare you . . . how dare you suggest such a thing?"

"Would you care to know what I think?" Felicia addressed Vanessa calmly. "I think she must have invented this sorry tale out of whole cloth."

"That's not true!" Maria shrilled.

"I think it more than likely," Vanessa agreed.

"I tell you it's not true!" Maria stamped her foot. "He did want me, he t-tried to ravish me." She whirled on Vanessa, her eyes big with fury. "You're jealous. You are green with jealousy because we love each other. We've loved each other since we were children. You may think he cared for you, but he did not. He was only dallying with you because he could not have me. He loves me, me, me—and I love him with all my heart and soul. You shan't ever have him, never in this world. He is mine, mine, mine!"

"Oh, God," Vanessa moaned.

"Ohhhh." Maria stared from one woman to the other, her hand flying to her mouth. Appalled by her most indiscreet outburst, she tottered backward and fell fainting to the floor.

There was a shocked moment when Vanessa and Felicia

looked at the fallen Maria. Then Felicia moved to a table and indicated a large bowl of her favorite hothouse roses. "She has swooned," she said loudly. "I will have to fetch my vinaigrette." She started lifting the roses out of the bowl and placing them on the table.

"Or burnt feathers," Vanessa suggested.

"I think a vinaigrette is always more effective," Felicia observed. "And of course there is this remedy, which might be the most effective of all!" She poured the contents of the bowl on Maria's recumbent form.

There was a piercing scream as Maria, her hair and the top of her gown, soaked with water, sat up. "Ooooh, you . . . you . . ." She leaped to her feet. "You . . ." She lunged at Vanessa, her little hands turned talon-shaped.

Moving quickly aside, Vanessa administered a stinging slap to Maria's face.

"You . . . you . . . T-Tom shall hear of this and he . . . he . . . he . . ." Maria babbled.

"What? Will he call me out?" Vanessa demanded mockingly. "Or will you?"

" 'Twill have to be me—since 'twas I who administered the baptism," Felicia said blithely. "What will it be, Maria, swords or pistols?"

"I will . . . I will . . ." Maria turned toward the door.

"You cannot brave the February winds like that, Maria," Felicia said briskly. "I will ring for Minnie. She can dry you off, and since you are much of a size, I will have her lend you one of her garments. Her *poitrine*, I might add, is quite small."

"I will see her and you in hell!" Maria screamed, and dashed out of the room.

"Gracious," Felicia drawled. "I fear she will contract a cold."

"Not if her pelisse is warm enough," Vanessa said. "And I hope she wore a close-fitting bonnet, else she might have some difficulty explaining how her hair became so very wet—on a fair day. I am sure she will not wish to tell Sir Thomas the truth."

"I would say that Lady Maria and the truth are strangers," Felicia observed.

"Yes, strangers." Vanessa sank down on a nearby settee. "Oh, God, Felicia, I have been such a fool!"

"I am afraid you've not been very wise, my dear." Felicia sighed.

An image of Philip's stricken face arose in Vanessa's mind once more. She could see Maria lying on her chair, blurting out her improbable accusations while Philip stared incredulously at her and then at herself. And she, in turn, had stared back at him with all the contempt she could muster before walking away without so much as a backward look, because she had believed all her worst fears realized—but she had had second thoughts that same night. If only she had acted on them, if only she had not let Johnny talk her out of going to him . . . if she had, everything would have been different. "Oh, God, I should have given him a chance to explain!"

"My darling, I wish you had." After a second, Felicia added, "Of course, the evidence did seem damning."

"Still, I knew him," Vanessa burst out. "But I was so jealous."

"I know, my love. I was quite aware of it. And 'twas unlike you."

"Yes, yes, yes, it was." Vanessa sprang up and began to pace the floor. "You see . . . you see, I had been so happy. I had been attracted to him from the first moment I saw him. That had never happened to me before. Then I learned that he was Johnny's 'butcher' and I was so disappointed. And then, there was the accident and he mesmerized me. It was such a strange feeling. It seemed almost as if he were drawing the very soul from my body. I have never told this to anyone before, Felicia, not even Phoebe. I have never put it into words, even to myself. I felt as if I had become his possession, somehow. I had never known what it was to love so deeply. I was frightened of the feeling, frightened of my own happiness. To be so . . . so thoroughly in love and to have your love returned. It was such a new feeling! There were moments when I believed that I was still mesmerized, that he had cast some manner of spell on me. Oh, I know it sounds utterly foolish, but that is what I thought. And then when Lady Maria accused him of mesmerizing her, I thought my worst fears had been realized and that I was one of many.''

"Oh, my poor love," Felicia murmured. "I wish you'd confided in me a long time ago. I would have set you straight.''

"How might you have done that?''

"It was so obvious that he adored you. Why could you not have seen it?''

"I do not know. Well, I did know . . . and Aunt Elizabeth told me the same thing, but I was confused, very confused. It was hard to believe in my good fortune. Oh, Felicia, I have been so miserable. Can you believe that I was actually glad that he did not fight? You see, I had been well on the way to believing I ought to have given him the benefit of the doubt. Then, when Johnny told me what had happened, I was actually relieved. I had been right in my feelings concerning him. I would not need to go to him and devour huge slices of humble pie. I actually preferred to believe him a coward! A coward! No wonder he'd not fight! Why should he sacrifice his life for Maria's lies? And now he's gone. Oh, Felicia, I do deserve it. I deserve everything that has happened." Vanessa buried her face in her hands and burst into agonized tears.

"Dearest love, do not weep." Felicia sat down close beside her, and gathering Vanessa into her arms, she continued, "I cannot believe that you and Philip, so very well-suited to each other, I cannot believe that 'tis an end to everything.''

"I do," Vanessa groaned. "I do, oh, I do, I do.''

"I tell you . . . let us go to his house. We'll leave immediately.''

"He is not there." Vanessa looked up. "Johnny says that no one has seen him. He's left town. Of course he has left town. You could not expect him to remain!''

"Yes, but certainly his servants will know where he is to be found.''

"Do you think they will?" Vanessa asked dubiously. "They are new. He might not have left his direction.''

"I cannot imagine that he would not, my dear. There will be letters arriving. They will need to be forwarded." Rising, Felicia added briskly, "I will order the post chaise. Come my dear, we'll not cry quits—yet."

Vanessa eyed her dubiously, still. "I cannot believe there is any hope," she said.

"There is always hope," Felicia said bracingly.

9

in her present unhappy state of mind, Vanessa had half-expected to find the house shuttered and closed, its gates padlocked and the winter's snow hardened on the walks. However, as the post chaise drew to a halt in front of Philip's house, she was happy to see that the windows were covered only by draperies and that the path leading to the portico was bare of snow.

There was a contraction in her chest. She was breathing shallowly as she and Felicia walked toward the massive front door with its brightly polished knocker. Might it be possible that he had *not* left town, that he had remained shut up in the library that, she recalled, he had praised for its immense number of fine books? No, she thought dolefully as they reached the door. He must have gone. His pride would have kept him from remaining in a city wherein everybody labored under the false impression that he was a vile seducer and a coward to boot. Her hands clenched. If Maria had been beside her at this moment, she would have struck her full in her perfidious countenance! She regretted not having hit her harder for her pernicious lies, for her jealousy, and above all, for her criminal cruelty!

She might have been directly responsible for Philip's murder had he been less intelligent, less brave. It had been much braver not to fight, she realized. Despite Maria's protests, he could easily have been killed. An image of Sir Thomas' mean little eyes came back to her. He had been primed to slay

Philip. He would have shot to kill, and not just Maria, but she herself, Vanessa, would have borne the guilt for his death, because not only had she not listened to his side of the story but also her attitude had borne out the contentions of his accusers. Could Philip ever forgive her for that terrible lack of faith? She doubted it, but if he would listen to her, she could at least try to explain her feelings and, at the least, she could apologize. She lifted the knocker, shivering a little at its coldness, and let it fall.

It was a moment before the door was opened by a tall, pompous butler in blue livery with gold facings. He regarded Vanessa and Felicia with some surprise and a touch of hauteur. "Might I be of service?" he inquired.

Vanessa opened her mouth, but to her confusion and embarrassment, no sound emerged. A second later, Felicia, evidently aware of this impediment, said coolly, "We would like to speak to Sir Philip Langhorne or, if he is not at home, we will leave a message for him."

He regarded them blankly. "Sir Philip is no longer in residence," he said coldly. "He has left the city."

Vanessa's heart plummeted at the chill finality of his tone, but in that same moment she found her voice. She said steadily, "We had believed he must have left town. However, it is imperative that we reach him." Her voice trembled slightly as she continued, "I am sure he would want you to give us his direction."

"He has left no direction," the butler said. He stepped back as if, indeed, he were minded to shut the door in their faces.

"My good man . . ." Felicia raised her hand. "I am Lady Farr and this is Lady Ventriss. We are good friends of your master and you may be sure that he would not reprimand you for having divulged this information."

The butler's mien and tone underwent a definite change, becoming considerably more obsequious. "Your ladyship," he said. "I would be most pleased to be able to oblige you in this manner. Unfortunately, I must assure you that we have no way of reaching him. When he left town, the staff and I were given no information regarding his whereabouts. He instructed us only to shut down the house—we will be gone at the end of this month. I am sorry that I can be of no more assistance than that."

Felicia gave Vanessa a regretful look. "Well, my dear, I see no reason to doubt this man."

"No more do I." Vanessa quelled a rising sigh. "I thank you, sir. Good afternoon."

He bowed. "Good afternoon, your ladyship."

Once back in the post chaise, Felicia put a consoling hand on Vanessa's arm. "I am sorry, my dearest. I thought surely he must have left a forwarding address."

"I am not surprised that he did not," Vanessa said bitterly. " 'Tis only natural that he should want to shake the dust of London from his shoes. You must agree."

" 'Tis a great pity," Felicia remarked. "Shall I take you home, my dear?"

"If you please." Vanessa nodded. "Oh, Felicia, why, why was I so heartless? I could have let him speak. Oh, God, I can still see the hurt in his eyes. Why didn't I listen?"

"Can you imagine that you'd have believed anything he might have told you at that moment, my dear?"

"No," Vanessa groaned. "Consequently, I deserve all that has happened. I, in common with all the others, let him down cruelly, so very cruelly. I drove him from London, too, and from my . . . my life. You cannot argue me out of that!"

"No, I expect I cannot, and nor will I. However, I shall not change my opinion, my love. You and Philip were meant for each other. I am quite convinced of that, and somehow, something will bring you together. I am also convinced of that."

"Meant for each other . . . meant for each other." Felicia's words had come back to Vanessa at intervals through the last six weeks, through all the days, all the hours, all the seconds that had passed before this moment when she stood watching Phoebe, clad in bridal white, exchanging vows with Johnny.

It should have been April, she recalled, but because of events abroad, the date had been changed and outside a March wind howled around the corners of the church, a mournful accompaniment indeed for an occasion which should have been happy but was, instead, fraught with an anguish that turned the bride's lovely countenance pale and brought a falsely reassuring smile to the bridegroom's lips.

Vanessa's own anguish over the situation was increased by the recollection that when originally planned, this wedding would have included herself and Philip. Rather than being a maid of honor, she would have walked up the aisle on her godfather's arm, and Philip, his eyes alight with love for her, would have been waiting to slip a gold ring on her finger.

Instead, he had dropped from sight and no one in London seemed to know what had happened to him. The cartoons and the lampoons that had signaled his disgrace were gone, and, ironically enough, if Sir Philip had elected to stride into Watier's this day, he would have been greeted by staff and members alike. Undoubtedly there would have been apologies as well. If Johnny had been present, it is possible that he would have been among the first to shake his hand, primed as he was by Vanessa's recital of her confrontation with Maria, but more important than that, his own embarrassing encounter with the Duke of Frome.

Frome was an almost legendary nobleman. An antiquarian and a scientist, he was also justly famous for his seascapes, which were considered to rival those of the great masters. He was also a talented amateur musician. Reclusive by temperament, he was rarely seen in polite society. His one indulgence was card games, but generally he did not patronize such clubs as Brooks's, White's or Watier's. Consequently, his arrival at the latter establishment had occasioned no little surprise.

Vanessa envisioned the moment when the duke had entered the club. He had been greeted by the manager with the deference generally accorded the Prince Regent. Actually, the Fromes boasted a pedigree far more ancient and respected than that of the current ruling house. She could imagine the manager's consternation when the illustrious visitor had inquired for Sir Philip Langhorne. She could also envision his stuttering response as he echoed Philip's butler and explained that he was gone, no one knew where. When that piece of intelligence had failed to discourage his grace, he had directed his inquiries to the members, and Johnny had come forward with the information that Philip had been cast out of those hallowed precincts because they did not count cowards among their membership. Frome had been astonished and angry at this indictment; he had demanded further enlightenment and had been given it—how Philip had failed to arrive for a duel on the morning of January 16.

"On the morning of January 16," the duke had repeated. Much to Johnny's surprise, his grace had evinced considerable anger, but it had been directed at him rather than Philip. "Did he give you no explanation as to why he did not arrive?"

The question had amazed Johnny, who had answered with something of the duke's own hauteur, "I am sure there was none that would suffice."

"I disagree with you, Lord Greysham," the duke had answered. "You should have listened to his explanations. Any man deserves an ear, no matter what the circumstances." He had gone on to explain just what had happened on the morning of January 16 and he had concluded, "My physician tells me that without Sir Philip's prompt and, I might add, expert attention, I might have been crippled for life."

Vanessa drew and expelled a long breath. Philip's membership had been reinstated. Even Sir Thomas had concurred. He had been impressed by the illustrious name of Frome and Johnny had told her that Sir Thomas had seemed extremely embarrassed by his references to the reasons for the duel. It was more than possible that he had begun to entertain suspicions of his wife. Maria, according to Felicia, was in the country, whence her husband went to join her shortly after the Frome episode.

There had also been an article in the *Morning Post* lauding what it termed "Sir Philip Langhorne's brave decision," going on to decry the infamous practice of dueling.

Had he been in London, Philip would have been welcomed with open arms, but his whereabouts were still unknown. There was the possibility that he had returned to Yorkshire, but Vanessa did not believe him to be there. Johnny had obtained his direction from Alden Harlock. His home was on the outskirts of Scarborough and the family castle lay near Whitby.

However, letters sent to both places by herself and her brother remained unacknowledged. Of course, his anger and hurt might have precluded a response; that would not have surprised her. Still, she had a feeling that he had gone farther than Yorkshire.

Lady Elizabeth suggested that Philip might have gone to visit Sir Alastair in Inverness or at his other home in Edinburgh. At Vanessa's urging, her aunt had written to him, using the pretext of Johnny's wedding and inviting him to the festivities, moved back from April to late March. She had mentioned Philip only in a postscript, but it had been a long postscript, giving him a summary of what had taken place at Watier's once the duke had put in an appearance. He had not replied, suggesting that he, too, might be traveling. Were he and Philip together? They might be on the Continent—in France. She winced, remembering that Philip had spoken about taking her to Paris on their honeymoon. That wince was succeeded by a shudder. All the English were leaving Paris, traveling overland to Brussels rather than attempting to swell the frantic crowds assembled at the port of Calais.

Brussels was reported to be very gay, despite the new menace of war. Vanessa stifled a groan. Napoleon had escaped from Elba. The alarming news had not reached the British until a week after the fact—on March 8. It had hit London like a blast from a cannon. The terror inspired by the man whom some called the ''tiger,'' others the ''monster,'' now gripped the country. England remembered once again that she was a small and vulnerable island, perilously close to a France which had reportedly welcomed Bonaparte's return almost at the same time that it had sent Louis XVIII fleeing to Ghent.

Thinking of this terribly swift progression of events, Vanessa swallowed painfully. All too easily they could be related to her own family, what with Phoebe's distress and Johnny's immediate decision to return to active service. Concurrent with that resolve had been a missive from the Duke of Wellington summoning him to Brussels, where the duke was at work reassembling his army.

According to Johnny, Wellington would not have the flower of his fighting forces. Many of the most able of his men, veterans of the Peninsular Wars, were still in America. It was reported to Johnny that he must needs recruit the greater part of his army from the ranks of the allies—from Hanover, Holland, Belgium, Brunswick, and Nassau. Wellington, Johnny said, was not pleased with the caliber of these recruits. He would depend, rather, on those Britons who had fought with him before and whom he could trust without question. Men like Johnny and . . . Sir Alastair? Undoubtedly he too would be summoned. And Philip—would he be with the army again? she suddenly wondered. Surgeons would be needed. If he were not traveling far afield, he would, she was sure, come to Brussels.

Johnny and Phoebe would be in that city by the first week in April. Phoebe had asked her to come with them, and she had refused, not wishing to intrude upon her brother's days with his bride, days which might be very few indeed, depending upon the moves of the "monster." She was sure that her brother shared her opinion. He would not want her with them. She must needs remain with Lady Elizabeth, attending concerts and the opera. When the Season ended, she could go to Brighton and in the fall to Farr's Castle, which was in the heart of the hunting country.

She suddenly remembered Maria's description of Philip and the fox hunt; he had rescued a fox which had bitten him. Philip hated fox hunts. He wanted to save lives. Philip, Philip, Philip! Her eyes smarted—well, it was *de rigueur* to weep at weddings. She gazed around a church turned hazy by those same tears and caught a glimpse of red hair on the head of a man standing at the back of the last pew, a late arrival no doubt. She tensed, scarcely daring to hope that the face beneath that fiery thatch might be that of Sir Alastair—but it was!

Lady Elizabeth's message *had* reached him and he had come at her bidding. It was with considerable difficulty that Vanessa kept herself from running up the aisle to join him— and thereby creating not only a disturbance but totally disgracing herself, for she, after all, was a member of the wedding party. She must needs wait until the reception. Would he be there? He would have to be there. Yet, as Philip's friend, he might not come. No, he would have received Lady Elizabeth's explanation, and that might be another reason why he had put in an appearance.

The ceremony was at an end and the newlywed couple had walked up the aisle. Vanessa, looking about her, was dismayed not to see Sir Alastair. And what would she do if he were not at the reception? She came out of the church into a day that was dazzlingly clear but cold. The winds that had howled about the corners of the church were icy, catching at her hair now and creeping under her cloak. She hardly heeded them. She had to find Sir Alastair. He must have hidden his red hair under a curly-brimmed beaver. There were many of these among those men who had attended the wedding and were now offering her their felicitations to present to her brother and his bride. She nodded, giving each of them smiling promises as she continued down the church steps, her unquiet eyes scanning every masculine face that passed her. At her side, her aunt kept pace with her, talking about the organ, which, in her opinion, was sounding very badly and ought to be replaced.

"Oh!" Vanessa startled Lady Elizabeth by suddenly rushing down the rest of the steps and joining Sir Alastair, who was at the bottom and moving away rapidly. "Sir!" she cried, coming up to him. "I must speak to you."

"Lady Vanessa." He halted immediately. There was, she noted with regret, a frown in his eyes and a coolness in his manner, an attitude that was, she guessed, based on his conversations with Philip. "Your servant," he added, bowing over her hand.

"I have wanted to speak to you about Philip," she blurted. "I expect you must know what happened here?"

"I do." His tone remained cool and his expression matched it. Evidently he had been given a description of her actions and as Sir Philip's close friend he could not find it in his heart to pardon them. Still, encouraging or not, she must needs persevere, if only to learn where Philip might be and what he had been doing in these last long, long months, which, in time, numbered only two. She said, "I cannot tell you how much I have wanted to see him again, if only to beg his pardon. Where is he? Please tell me so that I may write to him again. I have written but I have received no response." She paused a moment, scanning his face, but it revealed nothing. She was reluctant to continue, but she had to know. She cast a glance over her shoulder and, to her dismay, saw Lady Elizabeth bearing down on them. In another moment she would be unable to ask her question. "Has he been in Yorkshire?" She all but gabbled the words.

Sir Alastair shook his head. "He . . ." He paused and smiled more cordially at Lady Elizabeth, who in that moment joined them.

"Well, my lad, so you did receive my invitation?" she greeted him.

"I did that and I thank you for it." He kissed her hand.

"Did you arrive in time to hear Mr. Carlson sing?"

"Yes, indeed, a fine voice. I have always admired a good strong baritone."

"As have I. I found him myself. In an obscure . . . But we cannot remain here talking in this cold. My bones are older than yours. You will be present at the reception?"

"I shall be there, of course, Lady Elizabeth."

"Good, good, then we shall talk later." Lady Elizabeth turned to Vanessa. "Come, my dear."

Meeting her aunt's eyes, Vanessa found them censorious. Resentment swept over her. Evidently Lady Elizabeth was primed to take her to task for her wild dash down the church steps. She was in no mood to be chastised. She had reached her twenty-second birthday a week earlier and she did not deserve to be treated as if she were yet in the schoolroom, especially not now when her heart was near to breaking.

Undoubtedly Sir Alastair, who had to be in Philip's corner, reflected his friend's attitude. He was unforgiving, and Philip, too, would be similarly unforgiving—and she still did not know where he was. At least, she reasoned bitterly, her aunt could not send her to her chambers like the naughty child with whom she might be equating her! She fell into step beside Lady Elizabeth and was surprised that rather than censorious, her aunt's only observation contained the fact that she was pleased Sir Alastair had finally arrived.

It was not to be expected that Vanessa would be able to corner her quarry immediately she arrived home. She was needed to help receive the guests. Many of these were Johnny's brothers-in-arms. Phoebe, she knew, had been more than half-fearful that Charles and his bride might make the trip from the country, an encounter which must needs be filled with embarrassment on both sides, if not on Charles's part, on that of his lady, who deserved a kinder introduction to her new world. However, the roads were still very pitted in spots and he did not appear. As she greeted friends of her family and of herself or her brother, she tried to look for Sir Alastair but did not see him. Had he, having made his presence known to her aunt, already gone? Judging from his attitude, there was more than a chance he would not want another confrontation with herself. It was difficult to remain gracious and smiling when all she could think about was Philip, yet she managed it, and finally she did glimpse him and was able to make her way in his direction, with only two or three interruptions as she stopped to agree that her brother was happy and, yes, Phoebe was beautiful and, yes, it was a pity that the wedding journey must bring them to Brussels.

Sir Alastair was standing alone, almost as if he were waiting for her. Yet, as she reached him, she still had the impression that he resented her and would as lief not have spoken with her. She could not dwell on that. His reaction did not matter. Coming up to him, she said in a rush, "I must know where Philip has gone." As he hesitated, she continued, "I know that I have hurt him badly. I cannot go into all the ramifications of why I was so horridly cruel. Let me but say that it had less to do with what had supposedly taken place than with my own stupid fears. And I have suffered for it, I assure you. If I could see him, I would go down on my knees to beg his pardon, if that would only help."

He looked acutely embarrassed. "It is not needful to tell me this, Lady Vanessa. As for Philip . . ." He paused.

"You have seen him!" she cried. "You have spoken with him. You know . . . you know everything. I can tell it from your manner."

"I have seen him. And we have spoken, yes. My dear, 'tis best you put him out of your mind. He is no longer a part of your world."

"But does he know that his name has been cleared and—"

"He knows, but that has made no difference to him. He has made a decision which I know is irrevocable. He has returned to the work he loves. Medicine is more than a mere profession to him, Lady Vanessa. 'Tis, as he puts it, a 'vocation.' And I must agree with him there. He is a fine physician. I would go as far as to say one of the finest."

"I agree with you!" she cried. "And you are telling me that he has had his fill of us, the *ton,* I mean. I can understand that, too. But *where* is he?"

"I cannot think that the information would be of any use to you, Lady Vanessa. Suffice to say that he is well and happy."

She clutched his arm. "Has he told you that he never wants to see or hear from me again? Is that it?"

"No, he did not say that."

Vanessa dropped her hand. "Then why do you not tell me where I can find him?"

"If I tell you, 'twill serve no purpose."

Tears started to her eyes. "It will serve one purpose, Sir Alastair. It will keep me from going mad." In a low voice, she continued, "I must know where he is. I must be allowed to . . . to write to him, at least, to know that he knows I am bitterly ashamed of myself. I have been in agony these last weeks, and today I . . . I wanted to die, because this should have been our wedding day also. You will say that all this suffering is no more than I deserve, and 'tis true, but I pray you, please take pity on me. Tell me, where is he?''

He cleared his throat. He still appeared uncomfortable, and she knew he must be extremely embarrassed by her outpouring of emotion. That would only add to the poor opinion he had evidently formed of her, but she did not care. She was sure he would tell her something, and that was all that mattered!

He said, "Philip has been traveling, but of late he has offered his services to the army. He was in France, but he left when the news came that Bonaparte had escaped from Elba. He is in Brussels. I need not tell you that he will be very busy. Even in peacetime, there are matters that require his attention, and there is every reason to believe that peace will soon be curtailed. And in these circumstances, he will have no time for anything save his work.''

"And you, are you going to Brussels?"

He nodded. "My regiment has been summoned, but I would have gone even had the summons not come.''

"Then you will see him?"

"I will.''

"And will you take a letter to him for me, please?''

"If you wish.''

His tone was still cool. She wondered gloomily if his attitude reflected that of Philip. There was a question trembling on her tongue. She had already revealed far too much—but she had to know. "Has he . . . spoken to you . . . of all that took place here?''

"He has mentioned it,'' he said crisply.

"What . . . what does he think of . . . of me?''

"As to that, I'd not be knowing, Lady Vanessa. Your name has not crossed his lips since first he told me of the reasons for his departure. And at that time, he limited himself to the facts of the incidents.''

"I see. I thank you for having told me. I will write the letter now, if you will wait—or will you be in town a day or two?"

"I will be here until the week's end."

"Will you come here again? Or may I send this letter to your lodgings?"

"I will come again," he said. He paused, and then added, "But I do have a word of advice for you, Lady Vanessa."

"And what is that?"

"I suggest that you do not write to him. He is busy. He is tolerably happy, and as I have already explained, he has no intention of returning to this world. And whether or not a reconciliation could be effected, I cannot think that you would be very happy in the life that he has chosen."

She was silent a long moment. "I think," she said finally, "that you must have a very poor opinion of me, Sir Alastair. Believe me, it cannot be worse than my own. You seem to feel that it would be best if I did not try to communicate with him. Is that it?"

"Yes, I do," he said positively.

"I appreciate your frankness. I also admire you for your loyalty to Philip. I am sure you feel that you are speaking in his best interests."

"I am sure that I am."

"Well, that is that, then. I will not employ you as my courier, Sir Alastair, and you, of course, will forget all that I have told you."

He looked immeasurably relieved. "I think that you are being very wise," he commented. "And as for the rest, Lady Vanessa, 'tis already forgotten."

"Thank you." She forced a smile. "You are a very good friend to Philip. I appreciate that. But I have monopolized you far too long. Please . . . eat, drink, and be merry. After all, this is a very happy occasion." She moved away from him quickly, and sending a glance around the room, saw Phoebe, who was standing with three elderly ladies, smiling and nodding, as they evidently gave her their felicitations. Moving toward her, she waited until they had gone. Then, standing close to her, she murmured, "Phoebe, darling, do you really want me to go to Brussels with you?"

She was answered as much by the hopeful look she found mirrored in her sister-in-law's eyes as by her, "Oh, yes, dearest Vanessa, and Johnny wants it also. Though of course he would never think of pressing you to leave London in the middle of the Season, and . . . and nor would I, of course, dear."

"That does not matter," Vanessa assured her. "I only refused because I thought that you and Johnny might want to be alone."

"I hoped it might be that," Phoebe murmured. "Johnny thinks that he . . . he might need to be away on some occasions, and he does not want me to be lonely—it being a strange city and all. Will you come, then? I should like it above all things."

"Of course I will come, dearest," Vanessa said. "I will be delighted to accompany you."

10

They were all going to Brussels!

Lady Elizabeth, informed of Vanessa's decision, had originally objected to the plan, reminding her pointedly that she had promised to help her launch her two newest protégés with a series of teas and musicales. However, seeing that her niece's mind was made up, she ceased to argue, saying with some sympathy, "Very well, child, I understand, but of course, you cannot go without a proper chaperon."

She was impervious to Vanessa's protests that she had turned twenty-two and that Phoebe, as a married woman, could act in that capacity. Her aunt was adamant. "Phoebe will have much on her mind. There's no arguing with me, Vanessa. Either I go or you will remain here!"

With Lady Elizabeth in that mood, Vanessa could only agree. Actually, she finally had to admit that it had been a very good notion. There was no denying that her aunt had a great talent for organization. With much the same methods that she employed in arranging a concert, she arranged the voyage, remembering many important matters that the three younger members of her family had overlooked. It was due to Lady Elizabeth that they had their horses, their post chaise, and their curricle on board. She also made the arrangements for the servants, finding comfortable cabins for the coachman, the three abigails, Johnny's valet, the housekeeper, and the cook, determinedly refusing to hire what she contemptuously called "native servants," saying caustically, "Their habits are different from ours. Their cooks might have learned to make sauces in France, but are they able to keep a kitchen clean? I am not at all sure of that!''

It was impossible to argue with her, impossible to tell her that their tenure in Brussels might be curtailed because of Wellington's military maneuvers. She merely begged them to trust her, and since that was tantamount to a command, her niece and nephew, intent on their separate concerns, did not even attempt a rebuttal.

Standing near the prow of the crowded little packet bringing them from Dover to Ostend, Vanessa felt extremely depressed. Dover had vanished into an increasing mist, one which shrouded the distance as well. All that remained in view was the dark, tumbling sea. A wind was rising, and under its impetus the wet sails snapped and flapped. Other, less definable sounds entered her ears. Staring into the whiteness that had blotted out the sky, she had the uncomfortable feeling that they were sailing into nowhere. Her thoughts were chaotic. The last few days had been incredibly hectic; she had not had the time to think. She had been totally concerned with preparations for the voyage and for their eventual sojourn in Brussels. However, now that she was finally embarked on that same voyage, she was being attacked by a gnatlike swarm of second thoughts. These took the form of doubts, many edged with despair, as she reluctantly recalled her conversation with Sir Alastair.

In the beginning, his attempt to discourage her, actively to keep her from Philip, had been a goad rather than the deterrent he had obviously intended it must be. She had made her decision and it had been necessary to act quickly, because Phoebe and her brother were leaving within a fortnight's time. She had had very little opportunity to consider the wisdom of her move. She had, instead, clung desperately to the idea that she was killing two birds with one stone. Phoebe wanted her to come, and contrary to her expectations, so had Johnny. She winced, recalling a private conversation with him.

" 'Twill be good for her to have you and Aunt Elizabeth with her," he had said a shade grimly. "Boney's on the move and out for blood, with all the mad French behind him!"

"I wonder why?" she had mused.

"Pour la gloire!" he had said sarcastically.

"I should think they would have had enough of glory, with those thousands and thousands of their young men dead in the Russian campaign, not to mention the Peninsula, Egypt, and Italy!"

"They will remember only that he once brought most of Europe to its collective knees and that the tricolor fluttered on many a foreign flagpole. Already he's assembled an army of one hundred and fifty thousand men—with Marshal Ney going over to him as easily as he once pledged his allegiance to Louis XVIII. Napoleon is a name that still inspires the French and frightens the rest of the world. And his ambitions remain the same. But I hardly need explain to you what has happened or what he is. You have read the newspaper accounts too." He had put an arm around her. "I am very pleased that you will be with Phoebe, my dear. We are not anticipating a move until midsummer, but one never knows what will happen. While we cool our heels in the Low Countries and wait for a favorable moment to cross France's borders, Napoleon might employ a different strategy. He is a master of surprises, as you know."

Johnny was pleased that she was coming with them, but would Philip be pleased? Something Sir Alastair had said during that most uncomfortable conversation returned to plague her, which, of course, it ought never to have done. "He is well and tolerably happy," he had said.

Naturally, she wanted Philip to be well and happy, but had Sir Alastair implied that his happiness was predicated on the fact that he had recovered from that uncomfortable indisposition called "love"? He might even have found another love. Had that been what Sir Alastair was hinting? Certainly it would not be surprising, given Philip's undeniable charm and his handsome appearance, not to mention his title and his wealth. Any woman would have been glad to have his love. Tears started to her eyes. That love had been within her grasp and she had forfeited it. 'Twas no one's fault but her own that she had lost it, and judging from everything Sir Alastair had told her and much that he had not told her, she would never be able to retrieve it! In fact, she was bound on a fool's errand!

In that second, a gust of wind and an unexpected dip of the small vessel resulted in her losing her balance. She fell heavily upon the sea-drenched deck, and to her horror, started sliding in the direction of the railing. Futilely she tried to scramble to her feet, but she could not seem to manage it. Then she felt herself roughly jerked to her feet. A hoarse voice was in her ear. "Go below, will yer! 'Aven't no business up 'ere. Females!"

"I am sorry," Vanessa shouted. Relieved at not tumbling into those moiling waters, but feeling bruised both mentally and physically, she was able to make her way into the common cabin, only to find a number of the passengers being vilely sick.

Feeling an unfortunately companionable queasiness, she staggered out, managing to reach the tiny cabin she shared with her aunt. That redoubtable lady took one look at her and ordered her to her bunk.

"Lord, Lord," she muttered as she produced a basin, "in my day we were made of sterner stuff. I remember my first journey to France. 'Twas when poor Marie Antoinette was still queen . . ."

Interesting as those recollections must have been, Vanessa failed to listen to them. The subsequent intelligence that the captain had yielded to the battering of the contrary winds and changed his course from Ostend to Calais made little impression on her, and nor did her aunt's bracing assurances that she would be feeling more the thing once they docked. Until they set foot in that busy and noisy French port, Vanessa had been positive that she would die and be buried at sea. It was a feeling she later found she had shared with Phoebe, who, loving wife that she was, had much resented her husband's

blithe insistence that a return to health and strength awaited
her on the quay. Unfortunately, the trip was also much
lengthened by their detour. They would need to go overland
to Dunkirk, a distance of some twenty-five miles. Their next
stop would be Bruges, and then Ghent, which was not far
from Brussels.

However, save for a voyage up the still waters of a canal,
they would be traveling on the comfortably solid earth. While
that news proved infinitely cheering to Vanessa, it made no
impression on Phoebe, who continued feeling poorly. Lady
Elizabeth's insistence that she eat a hearty meal at the inn to
which they had repaired before the journey to Dunkirk in the
afternoon proved to have most unfortunate results—to the
point that they were eventually forced to abandon plans for
that contemplated departure. To do her justice, Phoebe had
valiantly made the effort, but the swaying of the coach had
reminded her all too strongly of her late experiences on
shipboard.

Lady Elizabeth's patience having finally worn thin, and
Lord Greysham being of no use at all in a sickroom, it
became Vanessa's duty to sit with the sufferer, alternately
applying cold cloths to her fevered brow and producing a
basin for her more pressing needs.

"You are too good to me, my love," Phoebe said in the
intervals when she could talk. "But why do you not let my
abigail or yours relieve you?"

"Shhhh, my dear," was Vanessa's usual response. She,
too, had wished the maids might assume her duties, but
unfortunately, they were all laid low with similar complaints.
She could wish that her sister-in-law were not so grateful to
her. It made her feel singularly unworthy, for if the truth
were to be told, she was fast learning that she did not have
the temperament to be a nurse, and furthermore, she loathed
being in a sickroom. It was fortunate that Phoebe could not
read a mind that was overloaded with frustration and, though
she hated to admit it, even to herself, resentment. She had not
anticipated such delays, and during the ensuing twenty-four
hours she would have given much if she could have gone

ahead without the encumbrance of her family. Naturally she was heartily ashamed of herself for these feelings. She could blame them on "love," which had warped her disposition and turned her into a person she did not admire in the least!

By their third day in Calais, Phoebe was well enough to endure the five and a half hours of travel that it would take to reach Dunkirk, a city that, they learned upon arrival, was vastly overcrowded. Accommodations were almost impossible to procure, and after three more frustrating hours, they were directed to a mean little inn where they did obtain what was euphemistically called a "suite of rooms." By this time they were all too weary to protest quarters which smelled strongly of camphor and other, less felicitous essences. The exigencies attendant upon making a surly landlord understand their wants as well as directing them to the road to Bruges drove all other considerations from Vanessa's mind as she and her aunt attempted to use their elegant French to combat a dialect which seemed to be low Dutch combined with a few English phrases inserted where they would do the least good. They were near to despair when Lord Greysham had the inspired notion of addressing the landlord in German, which brought smiles of pleasure from him and joy all around.

If the rooms were uncomfortable, the beds lumpy, and the sheets gray, they were cheered by the sight of the road to Bruges, which lay along the shore, so near to the sea that the waves bubbled up against the legs of their horses. The only member of their little group who was not moved by the beauty of golden sand combined with the azure of a placid ocean was James, their coachman.

"An' 'ow'll we know hit won't carry us out there to the fishes?" he demanded belligerently.

"You are talking nonsense, my man," Lady Elizabeth retorted. "You'll not be swimming these cattle."

An argument was obviously in the offing, but evidently the thought of disappearing beneath a wave and being devoured by some great leviathan of a fish was less awesome than contending with her ladyship when she was in one of her determined moods.

"Yes, Lady Elizabeth," James capitulated with a meekness belied by the set of his jaw and the expression in his small eyes. However, once they were on their way, the contrast between the hard-paved roads over which they had traveled from Calais, which had left them badly shaken and half-deafened by the clatter that sixteen hooves plus four wheels could make upon a pavement, and the soft sand convinced even the resentful James that it was not only a pleasant way to travel but also a welcome relief.

Bruges, unfortunately, was a sorry contrast to the combination of vivid skies and rolling waters they had passed. It was a small dismal town that seemed to be populated mainly by masses of Prussian soldiers, who eyed Phoebe and Vanessa with open admiration. Their remarks could, even without Lord Greysham's angry reactions, be easily construed as offensive.

Fortunately, their stay was brief. In little more than two hours they were on shipboard again and going down a canal to Ghent, a voyage that must needs take an entire day, they had been told. Yet, despite *this* delay, it was particularly pleasant to see the sights on shore, the old houses with their ornate crenellated facades and the verdant farmlands lying below protective dikes. It was easy to see how the Low Countries came by their name, Vanessa realized. They were so singularly flat.

In common with her aunt, she was amazed at the price of the journey. With all their luggage, their servants, their carriages and horses, and with the addition of a delicious dinner served on board the vessel, it came to a mere three pounds, ten shillings!

"Let us have some more welcome surprises of that nature," was Lady Elizabeth's comment. She added, "I do hope that opera in Brussels will be equal to our own."

"I hardly think they will be staging operas at this time," Lord Greysham commented dampeningly.

As it happened, a stay of only forty-eight hours in that city proved him wrong. They soon discovered that there were not only regular opera performances in Brussels, but theater as well, and horse races, mills, gambling, bull and bear baitings, these in addition to routs and balls, the latter given by a score of English residents, not excluding the Duke of Wellington. There were fetes at the palace and festivals in the parks. If there were also cannon in the squares and on the ramparts, if soldiers thronged the streets or trained on parade grounds or whatever open space might accommodate their drills, still, to a man, the city seemed to have recovered from its brief if virulent attack of Bonaparte fever.

The hotels were full of visitors. Some of these, of course, were those English who had fled Paris in the wake of Napoleon's triumphant entry, but others let it be known that they were there for pleasure alone. Consequently, space was limited and rooms were dear. Fortunately, Lord Greysham, being highly esteemed by his grace, the Duke of Wellington, was granted quarters in a great barracks of a house, conveniently close to the center of town. It was very old and it had evidently been unoccupied for a long time, intelligence that surprised its prospective tenants, especially since the custodian who showed them through the mansion had been at considerable pains to point out its assets. These included sculptured and painted ceilings, magnificent if dusty chandeliers, fine Venetian-glass mirrors, paneled doors, wonderfully carved furniture, and the gold leaf in the counsel table in the upper hall, imported from France during the reign of Louis XIV.

Upon moving into this establishment, they found that their guide had failed to point out the fact that it was exceptionally drafty. Some of the furniture had been attacked by termites and was extremely unsteady, and it was well that the volumes in a huge library proved to be printed in either the German or Flemish languages, for as such they offered no temptation to the reader, who would be otherwise frustrated by the incursions made by bookworms.

Their guide had also failed to point out that the cellars were populated by rats. These, according to an affronted housekeeper, were particularly adept at spotting poison and eluding traps. Their cleverness extended to devouring whatever they could find in the larders.

Settling into what its new tenants privately called "the monstrosity" took a fortnight and a little over. In that time, Vanessa had little opportunity to concentrate on the reason that had brought her to the city. When, at last, she did have a few leisure hours, she found it quite impossible to convince herself that her impetuous decision had any root in reality.

Brussels was far bigger than she had anticipated, and to search for Philip in its crowded thoroughfares was to look for a needle in a mountainous haystack! It seemed highly improbable that she would ever see or meet him out walking, and tentative inquiries, surreptitiously put to various members of the armed forces, regarding the surgeons' corps, brought her only the information that these had not yet assembled. She considered visiting the hospitals, but common sense told her that he would not be working in any of them. With their initial meeting in mind, she had gone riding in the park with Phoebe and her brother, but while she had found many an interested masculine eye upon her, the dark brown pair she so assiduously sought was not in evidence.

Disappointment was a pain in her chest, an obstruction in her throat, and nightly tears on her pillow. It wrought on her temper and also on her logic. There were times when she wished devoutly that she had never spoken with Sir Alastair. It did not help to remind herself that she had initiated their conversation and, against his will, had relentlessly exacted the information concerning Philip's present location.

By the time another week had crept by, Vanessa was beginning to agree with the poet Gray that "when ignorance was bliss, 'twas folly to be wise." She had preferred wisdom, and inadvertently, wisdom had catapulted her into this city—now inhabited by them both, yet affording precious little likelihood of their ever meeting! In a sense, that was her fault too. In other circumstances he might have attended some of the balls and routs given by the British residents. It was her cruelty that had helped to drive him from the polite world!

"Oh!" Phoebe, seated with Vanessa in an open carriage, suddenly waved, and with that same hand covered her mouth and turned away.

"What is it?" Vanessa inquired curiously.

For some reason, Phoebe had blushed deeply. "Nothing, dearest, nothing at all," she said hastily. "I thought I saw someone I knew, but I find that I was mistaken."

"Oh?" Vanessa glanced in that same direction. "Who?"

"No one, Vanessa." Phoebe put a hand on her sister-in-law's arm. "I told you I was mistaken," she emphasized. "Gracious, look over there! Two of those Brunswickers in their horrid black uniforms. I do loathe the color, and to wear that huge skull and crossbones over their visors—can they actually believe it frightens the enemy?" She tapped Vanessa on the shoulder. "Quick, look at them. I think they are high-ranking officers, too. Perhaps one of them is the duke himself."

"I have seen the duke, and danced with him too—as have you. Furthermore, we have both remarked on the uniform," Vanessa reminded her dully. She had caught sight of what Phoebe must have seen, the tall blond young man who was strolling up the Rue Royale, and her heart had given a great leap, for, of course, it was Philip! There was no mistaking his lean body or, as he had turned his head in her direction, his deep brown eyes, such a contrast with his fair hair. However, the cry that might have, under other circumstances, sprung to her lips remained caught in her throat. Meeting Phoebe's compassionate gaze, she slid down in her corner, bringing her sunshade close against her head in the off-chance that Philip might happen to see her. She did not believe that likely, for he was smiling most attentively, most affectionately at the ravishingly lovely dark-haired girl who was clinging so possessively to his arm and who returned his smile with an extra quotient of adoration.

"Vanessa, dearest . . ." Phoebe caught her hand. "It might not be . . . I mean, she could be just a friend."

"I am quite sure she is his friend," Vanessa agreed dryly. "And 'he is well and happy,' " she added in a lower voice.

"What did you say, my dearest?"

"Sir Alastair told me that Philip was well and happy," Vanessa amplified. "I expect he thought he was being tactful or perhaps compassionate in not telling me anything else. I wish he might have told me everything."

"My love"—Phoebe put her arm around Vanessa's shoulders—"there may have been nothing to tell. Perhaps he did not mean anything more than what he told you. 'Tis only the construction you are putting on it."

"Perhaps," Vanessa said dubiously. As if he had been a magnet and her eyes changed into iron filings, she turned her head. She did not see Philip or his lovely companion, which, she reasoned dolefully, was probably just as well. She said, "Phoebe, dear, would you mind very much if we were to drive home?"

"Of course I would not mind, not in the least," Phoebe agreed. "But, Vanessa, I repeat, she might mean nothing to him, nothing at all."

"And she might mean everything," Vanessa countered. "She is very beautiful."

"She is certainly not your equal, my love. You are a rose and she is, at best, a sweetpea."

"And a rose has thorns, does it not? Philip learned that easily and early." Vanessa smiled mirthlessly. "Please do let us drive home."

Phoebe nodded, and leaning forward, gave the order to the coachman.

As much as she had wanted to come to Brussels, Vanessa was even more anxious to leave, but that, of course, was utterly impossible. Ostensibly she had come there for a reason, and the reason was Phoebe. She could not desert her. Though her sister-in-law was totally wrapped up in her husband, it was increasingly apparent that *something* was under way. Johnny was, of course, noncommittal, but there were rumors. Some of these came from places as unlikely as the opera house.

As usual, Lady Elizabeth had spent as many evenings as

possible in the box she had rented immediately upon arriving. Though she did not find the singers nearly as accomplished as those she had heard in England, she had discovered to her delight that one Michael Perry, a manager who had hired several of her protégés, was in Brussels. He had sighted her as she had stepped into her box and had rushed up to her during the interval with cries of joy. Since he always had a fund of useful and useless information at the tip of a busy tongue, she had heard, in addition to the *on-dit* concerning the unfortunate altercation between the conductor and a leading tenor, that an invasion of France was being contemplated by the allies.

"Why else, my dear Lady Elizabeth, would we be overrun by soldiers?" he had demanded rhetorically. "Uhlans, Pomeranians, Silesians, Brunswickers, I vow the air is too, too full of their wretched dialects, an utter, utter agony to the sensitive ear, do you not agree?"

Johnny, of course, had derided Perry's assertions, giving his aunt an opinion regarding opera singers *and* their effete managers that had infuriated her to the point that she would not speak to her nephew for two whole days.

Vanessa, finally consenting to attend a ball with her brother and Phoebe, had spoken with one Lieutenant Alan Woodforde, an officer in the Sixteenth Light Dragoons, who, while also denying Lady Elizabeth's operatic intelligence, had looked rather discomfited when Vanessa mentioned it. In answer to her observation regarding the large increase in the military population of the city in the short space of three weeks, he had said with an indulgent smile which she had quite longed to strike from his face, "I beg you'll not trouble your lovely head about that, my dear Lady Vanessa."

Lord Ordway, another acquaintance of Lady Elizabeth's, had come to Brussels mainly because it was the place to be, as he had said, with half the *ton* present, and he gave it as his opinion that Brussels was only a stopping-off place. "I have it on the very best authority that there will be an invasion of France—from Holland."

Someone equally knowledgeable had mentioned Ghent, but

most of those who claimed to be informed had, by the latter part of May, begun to echo Mr. Perry, who still insisted that he had received his information from an absolutely impeccable source. However, despite Mr. Perry and his predictions, the army remained in Brussels, and the officers at least acted as if they were in that city to gamble, to flirt, and above all, to dance!

Since, as her aunt had tartly informed her, a lady could not and should not remain in the dismals forever, Vanessa was enjoying an even greater social success than had been her lot in London. Now that she no longer searched the crowded streets for a possible glimpse of a blond head and dark compelling eyes, she found it easy to laugh and flirt with any one of a number of ardent young officers. If she had desired it, she might have spent twenty-three out of the twenty-four hours riding, attending routs, gaming, and dancing. The table in the hall was loaded with invitations, and enough bouquets arrived each morning to stock the flower market in the Grand Place. She also went to the opera and visiting with her aunt—rarely with her sister-in-law. Privately taxed as to the reasons for this by her aunt and her brother, she had merely looked at them in extreme surprise and replied that she had had no intention of deliberately avoiding Phoebe's company.

That, of course, was not true. Vanessa did not like being alone with Phoebe. All too often, a silence would fall between them and she would become aware of Phoebe's unspoken sympathy, something she could not reject out of hand because it remained unspoken. She longed to tell her sister-in-law that she did not miss Philip, not in the least, that Lieutenant Woodforde and Captain Hamilton were of equal importance to her. However, her very protest would have revealed that truth she was striving to conceal and which rose to torment her each time she found herself alone with Phoebe.

More than ever, she longed to return to England, not to London, but to the country—more specifically, to a small estate in Lincolnshire which was part of the family property. Once there, she had every intention of staying in residence forever and ever! Unfortunately, such a retreat was out of the question. Too many fleeing English crowded the roads and the canals. Furthermore, she had ostensibly come to be with Phoebe, and the time was fast approaching when she would need the support Vanessa had offered. She did have Lady Elizabeth, but her aunt had put too many sorrows behind her. Her view of life was long and would not easily adapt to the anxieties and fears that a soldier's lady must needs experience.

Though no one seemed to know just what Napoleon intended, the knowledge that the man who had once subdued nations was planning another coup kept the allies on edge. That was obvious to everyone who lived in Brussels. The very air was electric with excitement. Vanessa found it evident at the routs, the fetes, and the balls she attended. The young officers with whom she danced laughed too easily and too loudly, the while they clutched her too tightly. Their conversation bordered on the inane, but she had the sensation that they hardly heard themselves talking or herself answering. Yet, seemingly, the only thing on their mind was the joy of the moment.

By the beginning of June, it seemed as if all the youth in Brussels and a great many of its elders as well were concentrating their interest upon the Duchess of Richmond's ball, an event that promised to be the most glittering in a season crammed with events that more than merited that description. Everyone who was anyone would be present. The guest list was known to be replete with crowned heads and illustrious titles. Tickets were highly prized and the uninvited were in despair.

Lady Vanessa was among the ranks of the envied. More than that, she was known to belong to a household which cherished amongst its four members no fewer than four of those precious invitations! The ball would take place on the evening of June 15.

Some few minutes after the hour of nine on that night, Rose, Lady Elizabeth's abigail, stood back from her mistress and pronounced herself "onchantay" with her ladyship's purple silk gown. She added that it was "tray onfortuné" that her ladyship would not "tread a measure," which sentiment caused the countess to threaten instant dismissal if Rose did not stop this Frencified nonsense and remember that she hailed from Penzance in down-to-earth Cornwall!

As for herself, she continued caustically, she had better things to do than to waltz the hours away in the heat of a June night!

Phoebe, wearing her favorite blue silk, was told by her adoring husband that she looked like an angel. He also had compliments for his sister, magnificent in golden satin with a topaz necklace around her shapely throat and a shining topaz-and-gold tiara in her chestnut curls. Both ladies were lavish with their compliments for Lord Greysham in his bright red uniform jacket adorned with gold epaulets and shining gold buttons. Phoebe had displaced his valet in order to tie his scarlet sash, and his legs, his sister said, looked very shapely in his long tight trousers strapped under his narrow boots.

The servants stood in line to watch them go. Vanessa, looking over her shoulder, waved at them and, excited, they all waved back, Letty executing a waltz step.

It was a very warm night. The heat embraced them as they settled into the post chaise, but Lady Elizabeth, her eyes on the cloud-filled sky, said, "It appears that we might have rain tonight."

"Impossible, Aunt Elizabeth!" Vanessa exclaimed. "The duchess would never allow it."

They all laughed.

"The duchess!" Lady Elizabeth snorted as their merriment died down. "She has the devil of a temper, you know."

"We do know," Vanessa commented. "We have only to look at the duke. Until she arrived, he seemed in a tolerably good humor. Now he goes about as if he had been pecked by several hens!"

"Come, she must have a great deal on her mind," Phoebe said with her usual tolerance.

"Yes, where to place the orchestra and what flowers to set about," Lord Greysham commented dryly. "Not to mention the order of the dancing."

"I hope that there will be a great number of waltzes," Phoebe said. "I do like them more than any other dance." Her eyes lingered wistfully upon her husband's face.

"And so do I, my dearest," he replied. "Though I regret that I cannot hold you close enough."

Vanessa, catching their exchange of loving looks, felt her eyes smarting. In other circumstances she might have had her husband by her side in this carriage. Impatiently she banished this thought. It was time and past that she stopped dwelling on the man responsible for her presence in Brussels. At this juncture she could only be pleased that she had seen neither Philip nor Sir Alastair. However, she was surprised that the other had not put in an appearance. She had expected that he must come to see Lady Elizabeth, but he had not surfaced for all he had said that he would be in the city. She suspected that he must have learned that she was also there, and his disapproval of her presence must outweigh his regard for her aunt. Whatever reason had kept him away could only please her, and actually it was his own fault that she had come! If he had only told her the whole story, she never would have set foot on the boat that had borne her across the channel, and consequently she would have been spared the sight of Philip with that young girl.

She *was* young, too. Vanessa doubted that she was more than eighteen—four years younger than herself, ten years Philip's junior, unsophisticated, unspoiled, adoring, and judging from her expression that day, admiring. She was just what Philip needed. He had certainly had his fill of jealous women! Her lip curled as she thought of Lady Maria. If she did not resent her so much, she could actually be sorry for her current plight.

In one of her recent gossip-filled letters, Felicia had written that Sir Thomas Glazebrook had closed his London house and put it on the market! He had subsequently taken his wife back to Yorkshire, and a friend who lived in that same vicinity had told Felicia that Maria was miserably unhappy and heavily pregnant. "She is rarely seen in the village, and the *on-dit* is that Sir Thomas keeps her under lock and key. Of course, that is unnecessary, for evidently the word is out, and she is not invited by any of the local gentry.''

"My love," Phoebe broke into Vanessa's ruminations, "we have arrived."

"Oh." She flushed. She was nearest the door, which was open and the steps already there. Clutching the post boy's proffered arm, she hurried down them.

The palatial house that the Duke of Richmond had hired for the Season was a bright beacon in the darkness. It must have taken considerable maneuvering for James to get them so close to the entrance, she realized, for the way was filled with post chaises, coaches, and curricles. Many other guests had arrived on horseback or on foot. There were many soldiers. She recognized the black uniforms of the Brunswick corps. The Duke of Brunswick would be present, and also the Prince of Orange and the Duke of Wellington. She saw an officer in the dark green of Orange's Nassau regiment, who was very young. They were all so young, and it was impossible not to wonder when all those brightly clad, laughing young men would be marching off to battle, but she need not think about that tonight. Tonight was a time for pleasure, for music, for dancing, and for midnight suppers and champagne. Even her aunt had agreed to remain until sunrise!

The ballroom was huge and brilliantly lighted. It seemed to have more than the usual supply of mirrors, and certainly there must be thousands of candles in three huge chandeliers. As usual, she was immediately surrounded by a large group of young officers, all eagerly demanding dances. She did not see Alan Woodforde. That failed to surprise her, for he had told her he might be late and he had begged her to save some dances for him. Accordingly, she left two spokes on her little ivory fan empty. She smiled ruefully. If it had been known that she had saved them for him, all speculation would have ceased and bets would have been placed as to when their engagement would be announced.

Only Alan would know the truth, for he had already offered for her and she had gently refused him. He had been momentarily downcast but had rallied and begged that they might remain friends. She had readily agreed, and she had gone on seeing him. She did like him, but she knew that she would never love again. That was behind her. Once she left Brussels, there would be no more dancing. Tonight, however, was not a time to think either of the future or of the past. Tonight she would make every effort to enjoy herself.

A hectic gaiety prevailed in that immense room. It seemed to Vanessa that everyone was moving too quickly, laughing and chattering too loudly. There was an urgency even about the music, and were the musicians really playing in three-quarter time? It seemed much faster, especially when she was on the floor and whirled so quickly that she was half-dizzy. Yet she had no difficulty in following her partners. There were a great many of them. She had even been claimed by the Duke of Wellington. He danced well—he was known for that. Tonight, however, he seemed extremely preoccupied. He missed a step and apologized profusely, but she had the impression that he was speaking at her rather than to her. His place was taken by the Duke of Richmond, who was his usual gloomy self and did not speak at all. Then, during a lull in the music, while she and her partner, one Lieutenant Ralph Sheridan of the King's Light Dragoons, waited for the next waltz to begin, she saw the tall form and bright hair of Sir Alastair. He was in the uniform of the Highlanders' regiment and he was standing with a small dark girl who also was familiar.

Vanessa's throat began to throb as she recognized the pretty child who had been walking with Philip on that never-to-be-forgotten day. And now his friend Sir Alastair was about to waltz with Philip's bride? Was she his bride, or merely his fiancée? That was not important. If she were here, then Philip, too, must have received one of those prized invitations. She sent a lightning glance around the room, but of course she did not see him. He would not be dancing, anyway. He would be watching. He must be present, and Sir Alastair must have known about the girl when they had talked in London. Of course he had known. She had already arrived at that particular conclusion.

The music was commencing. She let her partner lead her
onto the floor and hoped devoutly that she would not be seen
by Sir Alastair. That, fortunately, was unlikely. The floor
was even more crowded than it had been when she had come
in. She did not see him, and, she thought, it would have little
mattered if she had. She need not, after all, have come to
Brussels for Philip: she was here because of her brother and
her sister-in-law. She could not help glancing in the mirrors
as they danced past them. Would she glimpse Philip's reflec-
tion? No, she did not see him, and nor did she see Sir
Alastair—nor Phoebe and Johnny, for that matter. The couples in the mirrors were strangers to her. Anger rose in her
mind. It was occasioned by the tears that had blurred her
eyes. Where was Philip? With whom was he dancing while
his fiancée was in the arms of Sir Alastair?

Vanessa came off the floor and was claimed by another
partner for a country dance. She did not see either Sir Alastair
or Philip among the group that went through the patterns of
the dance. This time she kept her eyes averted from the
mirrors. She did not want to catch so much as a glimpse of
them or of the lovely girl that Philip would marry or had
already married. It was getting late, but it was not late
enough. How many hours would intervene before they could
go home?

Finally the country dance came to an end and she was led
off the floor, only to return for a cotillion. It was past
midnight when she looked down at her fan and found the
spokes empty. Alan, however, had not yet arrived. She was
heartily glad of that. Her feet were aching. She wanted
nothing more than to be able to sit down and watch. Purposefully she moved toward the chairs at the far end of the room.
Most of them were occupied by weary chaperons. The smat-
tering of sulky faces one usually expected to find at any ball
was not in evidence. It was a night when even the most
ill-favored damsel might triumph. Vanessa found a chair in
the second row and was about to take it when someone said
in surprise, "But you are not dancing, then, Lady Vanessa?"

She tensed, hardly daring to turn around and face the

speaker, but she must, of course, and he was there, his dark eyes fastening on her face as she looked up at him. Breathlessly she said, "Good evening, Sir Philip." Stupidly she added, "I thought you must be here."

He was understandably surprised by that observation. That was evident in both look and voice as he answered, "Did you?"

"Yes." She nodded. His dark eyes had appropriated her gaze and were holding it captive. As usual, she felt as if her soul were being drawn out of her body. Still, she was able to say, "I saw your fiancée . . ." She paused, appalled at what she had just uttered, but it was impossible to summon those words back. They seemed to have taken form and hung in the air between the two of them. "I mean—" she began.

"What can you mean?" he broke in. "I have no fiancée.'

She had a brief feeling of wild joy before a logical explanation forced itself into her mind. "I am sorry. I assumed—but you are wed, then?"

"No, not wed, either," he said in surprise. "Why would you think so?"

"Sir Alastair told me . . ." she began.

He frowned. "He could not have—"

"No," she interrupted. "I did not mean that he said you were married. But—"

"Ah, here you are, Lady Vanessa." Lieutenant Woodforde stepped to her side. "And have you saved me the dances you promised?"

She could not turn from Philip, not yet. "No, not this dance, Alan," she improvised. " 'Tis given to . . . to Sir Philip, here. The next will be yours."

"Ah, pray excuse me, then." He smiled and bowed. "I will be back to claim it soon, though."

She was alone with Philip once more, and feeling extraordinarily foolish. She attempted a light laugh, but of course it was not successful. She did manage to say, "You see, I have no manners. 'Tis the gentleman who should ask the lady to dance. And—"

"You only anticipated me," he interrupted. Taking her in

his arms, he whirled her onto the floor. "I approached you with the hope that you might grant me a dance."

"You are kind to say so," she murmured.

"I am not being kind." His gaze remained intent. "I was being entirely honest."

"Both, then," she said insistently.

He was silent a moment as they executed a complicated turn. Then, inevitably, he said, "Why would you assume that I was married, Lady Vanessa?"

" 'Twas foolish of me to reach that conclusion, I know. You see, I saw you shortly after I arrived in Brussels. You were with a small, dark young girl—very pretty. I thought . . ." She paused as she heard a discordant note amidst the orchestra. It sounded like a bugle . . . and was that a drumroll . . . and did she hear bagpipes? "What was that?" she asked.

"What?" he demanded, and then frowned, his head cocked, as he too listened. "That sound. I am not sure." He paused mid-step. Vanessa also came to a sudden stop, staring about her. Other couples had also ceased to dance. However, still others continued, and the music of the small orchestra remained uninterrupted. Then, as she glanced about the floor she saw a man in uniform hastily making his way to the Duke of Wellington. He had been dancing with the Duchess of Richmond. The man—a messenger, obviously—was carrying an envelope that he presented to Wellington. The duke took it hastily and ripped it open, extracting the paper and perusing it.

A sudden fear filled Vanessa. It was augmented by the sounds of those distant drums, bugles, and pipes, a military band, its martial music forming a discordant accompaniment to the gay strains of the waltz. The duke had finished reading the missive. He turned and said something to the duchess, and those words, overheard by those standing nearby, sped from mouth to mouth with the swiftness that bad news always travels.

"The French . . . the French," someone wailed.

"Fourteen miles!" a woman shrieked. "Fourteen miles

away, only fourteen miles out of Brussels. We'll all be slaughtered!''

"And the Prussians, defeated, wiped out!" was another cry that went the rounds.

Some of the women burst into tears, and the young men in uniform, grave of countenance, moved toward their various commanding officers. Vanessa caught sight of Phoebe and Johnny. Her sister-in-law had clutched her husband's arm. Her mouth was turned down, her eyes enormous. Her face reminded Vanessa of a Greek tragedy mask she had once seen in the British Museum. In another moment they had vanished amidst the crowds. And still the martial music sounded in her ears, louder now because the orchestra had finally stopped playing.

Vanessa stared up at Philip and experienced a great surge of relief because he was not in uniform and did not have to join her commander. In that same moment, she saw Sir Alastair shouldering his way through the masses of people who still remained on the dance floor. With him was the girl who was neither wife nor fiancée to Philip. She was looking at Sir Alastair as Phoebe had gazed at Johnny, and she was clinging tightly to his arm, as tightly as she had clung to Philip that long-ago day in the street.

Sir Alastair had reached them. He did not seem to notice her. His anxious gaze was on Philip. He said tightly, "The French have struck . . . you will care for Mathilde?''

"Ah, no, you do not go!" The girl caught at his sleeve. "My Alastair, you do not go, please, not yet."

"I must, my love," Sir Alastair told her gently. His mouth was grim as he added, "You have married a soldier, you know."

"I will take you home, Mathilde," Philip said. He added, "My dear Lady McLean, may I introduce Lady Ventriss?"

"Lady McLean, Sir Alastair, my good wishes and my prayers for your safety," Vanessa murmured.

Sir Alastair kissed her hand. "I thank you, Lady Vanessa. Mathilde . . ." He embraced her and would have turned away.

"*Ah, non!*" she cried again. "I will go with you to the door, yes?"

"You must not lose sight of Philip," he warned. "You'd best stay."

"No," Philip said quickly. "I will accompany you and Mathilde." He looked down at the girl. "I must get her home before the streets become too congested." He turned to Vanessa again. "I pray you will excuse me."

Was there a shade of regret in his tone? No, undoubtedly that was wishful thinking. Vanessa said steadily, "Of course, I quite understand. We will all need to be leaving soon, I'm thinking."

With obvious anxiety, Philip stared at Vanessa. "You will be able to get home easily, I hope."

"Very easily," she assured him quickly. "James, our coachman, is here, and by great good fortune, he is even close to the door. I will bid you good night, Sir Philip." She turned to Sir Alastair. "And may God watch over you and protect you."

"I thank you, Lady Vanessa," Sir Alastair responded. With his arm around his wife, he moved away.

"Fare you well, Vanessa." Philip's compelling gaze lingered on her face for another moment.

"And you, Philip," she murmured.

He turned away then, and hurried after Sir Alastair and his lady.

She watched them as they started to walk quickly across the ballroom. She watched them until they were lost in the crowds that were also hurrying toward the doors. The huge room was emptying with remarkable swiftness. Nearly all of the bright young men in uniform had gone.

"Vanessa, Vanessa, ah, thank God I have found you." Phoebe ran toward her. She added breathlessly, "Come, my dear, Johnny wishes to say his farewells."

"Yes, of course, dearest. Have you seen Aunt Elizabeth?"

"She is with him." Phoebe pointed vaguely.

As they, too, hurried across that vast floor, Vanessa saw that the musicians were finally packing up their instruments, but outside in the distance, the bugles, the pipes, and the drums still resounded in her ears, providing the accompaniment for armies that would soon be on the march to meet and defeat—or be defeated by—the eagle that had escaped his keepers.

11

Boom, boom, boom.

The distant sound of the cannon reverberated through the city, vying with the more immediate crash of thunder. The clouds had begun gathering at six in the evening, and by seven the sky, usually still light at that hour, was black and the servants had already drawn the curtains and lighted candles in the parlor and dining room.

The cannonading must stop soon, Vanessa thought as she lifted a corner of the drapery and stared out into the darkness. It had been going on since two in the afternoon, but the armies would not be able to move by night. She shuddered. That was not precisely accurate. They had moved by night at Napoleon's command, and from the bits and pieces of news they had heard during this long, long day, which, for them all, had commenced with the sound of that martial music vying with the waltz, the Prussian army had been destroyed and the French were on the road from the village of Charleroi, which was perilously close to Brussels. Still, even armed with this depressing intelligence and primed by old stories of the atrocities committed by the French in the villages and towns they had conquered, Vanessa was not frightened for herself.

Phoebe, she was glad to see, was bearing up extremely well. In fact, her sister-in-law possessed reserves of strength she had never anticipated. In spite of the fact that she had had little or possibly no sleep since they had returned from the

ball at three that morning, she had followed Johnny's hurried
instructions regarding the possible evacuation of the city.
With Lady Elizabeth and Vanessa, Phoebe had calmly
superintended the packing of their garments and the deploy-
ment of such goods as they must carry with them. Vanessa
had also happened upon her as she gently comforted her
terrified abigail and an equally frightened parlormaid hired in
the town upon their arrival.

Phoebe had further amazed Lady Elizabeth and Vanessa by
saying determinedly, "I will not leave, you must understand.
When Johnny comes back, he will expect me to be here
waiting for him. I could not disappoint him."

Lady Elizabeth had regarded her in silence before saying
just as decisively, "Then I am of the opinion that none of us
must disappoint him. Do you not agree, Vanessa?"

She had agreed, and she had been relieved as well. In the
midst of her concern over Phoebe and the shock that the
French attack had inspired, not to mention the dread name of
Napoleon, was the memory of the moment when she had
been, however briefly, in Philip's arms, Philip, who was
neither married nor engaged and who had looked at her
impersonally until he had offered his final and necessarily
brief farewell. Could she extract any hope from the way he
had looked at her or from the deepening of his voice as he
had called her, not *Lady* Vanessa, but simply Vanessa? Had
she only imagined a softening of that dark gaze, which, she
thought, had lingered on her face a moment before he had
hurried away?

What had happened to him? That was a ridiculous question.
Naturally, he would be with the corps of surgeons awaiting
the wagons bringing in the wounded from the battlefield.
Judging from all she had heard and read about Napoleon's
fierce fighting forces—never more fierce than now, at what
might prove to be his last stand against the allies—Philip and
his fellow physicians would have their hands full. She forebore
to think of those casualties in numbers. She knew only that
there must be many.

She stared out of the window. It had grown even darker,

and of course she dared not venture out onto the streets, much less a mile or so into the woods where Lady Caroline Capel, a friend of her aunt's, was living.

Her ladyship and her large family were ensconced in the Château de Waldeheuse, a charming mansion, if rather lonely. Vanessa did not know Lady Caroline well. However, she had visited her twice in the company of Lady Elizabeth, who had been a dear friend of her late father, the Earl of Uxbridge. Her brother, the current Lord Uxbridge, was one of Wellington's friends and the leader of the Household Brigade, which meant that he was currently in the very thick of the fighting.

Through that family connection, Lady Caroline always had news before anyone else was in receipt of it. Furthermore, she was expecting another addition to the family and had spoken about needing a nurse and a physician. She must be acquainted with several physicians in the city, and possibly one of them might know where Philip was stationed. However, that was an extremely complicated way of obtaining the requisite information and, at present, not feasible. It might be better to go to one of the city hospitals. The physicians there might know where the surgeons' corps was to be found— but that, too, was a long chance.

And if she were to discover where he was, what difference would that make? She could hardly seek him out in the midst of his labors! It was ridiculous even to contemplate such a course of action. Even if she were to find him, he would hardly welcome the sight of her, unless . . .

She hastily dismissed the wild idea that had suddenly occurred to her. She could not administer to the wounded. Not only were most nurses men, but the women who sometimes served in that capacity were generally camp followers. And judging by her experiences in tending Phoebe on board ship, she would be of precious little use in a sickroom. That course of action was one she could not possibly entertain. It was preposterous!

As it happened, Lady Elizabeth spoke to Lady Caroline on the morning of the next day and learned that she, at least, had no intention of leaving Brussels.

"The roads are too congested, and since we've little knowledge of the army's movements, I contend that we are safer here," she had said frankly.

By the morning of June 18, Lady Caroline's "little" knowledge had expanded to include the name of Quatre Bras, a tiny village where a great battle had been waged. However, few of those remaining in the city were cognizant of what had taken place. Rumors were rife, and these were augmented by the great number of wounded that swelled and eventually filled the hospitals. At length they lay on the wagons that had carted them from the battlefield. Those soldiers who could speak of what they had witnessed provided only imperfect descriptions. Some, seeing their comrades routed or slain, talked of a French victory. Others insisted that they had seen the French banners lying in the mud. No one knew for certain, but those wounded stragglers who arrived in Brussels by twos and threes and tens and twenties during the day and on into the night spoke of a new conflict near a hamlet called Waterloo.

There was an altercation in the street that stretched outside the parlor windows. A huge, lumbering traveling coach had been stopped by a wagon bringing in another load of wounded soldiers.

Phoebe and Vanessa stood watching as the two drivers confronted each other. The occupants of the coach were leaning out and evidently adding their voices to the altercation. Even at this distance it was easy to see that their faces were distorted by fear. They were fleeing from the city, and their selfishness was manifest as they gesticulated at the wagon, evidently screaming at its driver to let them pass. The men in the wagon lay quietly. They were beyond fear, Vanessa thought, and was doubly glad that she and her family were not among those who crowded the roads to Ghent and other, presumably safer cities. She turned away from the window and Phoebe followed her.

"So many, many casualties," she whispered.

"Yes." Vanessa nodded. "But that is to be expected when there's a battle."

"Of course," Phoebe agreed. She looked as if she wanted to say something else, but evidently changing her mind, she sat down at a small table where there was a silver tea service and two porcelain cups. As Vanessa joined her, she poured tea into both cups.

Vanessa, sipping the liquid, said, "It's good tea."

"Very," Phoebe agreed. She raised the cup to her lips but put it down again at a sudden burst of cannon fire, and sat staring blankly into space.

Vanessa put a hand on her arm. "I do not *feel* that anything has happened to Johnny," she said gently.

Phoebe shifted her gaze to her face. "Nor do I. But *would* we?"

"Johnny has always been extraordinarily lucky. He got into such dreadful scrapes when we were little, but nothing ever happened to him. And of course, he went through all that fighting in Spain and Portugal."

"I know that, but there is a great deal I do not know. It's odd, I love him so much—but we have rarely mentioned our childhood."

"You knew him when we were little," Vanessa reminded her.

"Only as a great rough boy who always pulled my curls." Phoebe laughed and then sobered. "Tell me about his scrapes. Do you mind?"

She did not mind, but it was hard to assemble her thoughts of that distant past. The sight of the wagons rolling in and the wounded men limping behind them had filled her with a mixture of horror and pity. At the same time, it had brought her a vision of Philip. He would be working unceasingly, as would all the surgeons. She longed to be at his side. If she had acted upon her earlier impulse . . . But she had not, she had been afraid. But there was no use thinking about all that. She turned to Phoebe. "I can remember one time when he would climb—"

"Listen to the guns," Phoebe interrupted distractedly. "I am sorry." She put a conciliating hand on Vanessa's arm. "I did not mean to interrupt."

"No matter, my dear." Vanessa stifled a sigh and dredged up memories for her pallid sister-in-law. As she spoke, the clock struck twice. It was two in the afternoon. The cannon boomed in her ears. How long would they continue to belch forth their fire? How long did battles last?

Toward evening, the distant boom of the cannon ceased, and so did the sporadic bursts of rifle fire. Vanessa, who had been resting in her chamber, came down to join Phoebe and Lady Elizabeth for one more cup of that ubiquitous tea. "It is so quiet," she observed as she slipped into a chair beside her aunt.

"Yes, very," Phoebe agreed. "I wonder—"

"Do not wonder!" Lady Elizabeth advised.

"No, I should not, I expect," Phoebe answered apologetically.

"Oh!" Vanessa sprang up and moved to a window, holding aside the drapery and staring into the gathering darkness. "It is dreadful to have no news, to know nothing, to just sit here and wait and wait and wait! Oh, God, I wish I were a man."

"Enough!" Lady Elizabeth exclaimed. "Let me hear no more of that nonsense. We women have our place."

Vanessa whirled on her. "And what place is that place? We are useless."

"Hush." Lady Elizabeth glared at her. "These outbursts are unlike you, Vanessa, and let me add that they certainly do not become you!"

"I will relieve you of the necessity of enduring them, then!" Vanessa went swiftly from the room. Tears threatened. They were of no use. She furiously blinked them back and went into the vast drawing room. They had all been avoiding it because its tall windows faced the square and the wagons. It had been necessary to shut the windows against the stench that was borne on the wind. However, she had gone to them that afternoon after leaving Phoebe and had stood watching women working with the few orderlies who had come to tend the wounded. Those females were not useless. They fetched and carried, they bandaged, they soothed, they comforted.

Seemingly they were impervious to the smells, the sights, the heat, the flies. She had wished she could have joined them, or had she merely wanted to search for Philip until she found him, until she could be with him? It was difficult to sort out her feelings, feelings she should not have been entertaining. She ought not to wish that he were with her, when he was needed so desperately. He would not want her near him. She would be of no more importance to him than a fly on the wall. Once more her feelings of frustration arose to plague her. She had no place in his world or in his life. He was a dedicated man and she was a useless ornament of society—that was how he must regard her. If only she might show him that she was different, but that was impossible. It was too late, too late.

A sound broke into her thoughts, the fall of the knocker on the front door. And who would be arriving at this hour? She started out of the room, and as she did, she heard the knocker descend again, not loudly, a mere tap in fact. She wondered where the butler was and remembered that he, a man from Brussels, had fled the city, accompanied by their timorous parlormaid. She quickened her steps, arriving in the hall at the same time that Phoebe also hurried in, with Lady Elizabeth behind her.

"Be careful," the older woman cautioned as Phoebe ran to the door. "We are not to open to strangers." She paused with a frown as Phoebe pulled wide the door, flinging it back with such force that it slammed against the wall. Wordlessly she opened wide her arms to the man who came staggering inside, his scarlet uniform muddied and torn, his face white, his eyes wide and staring.

"Johnny!" Vanessa started forward, and stopped as she saw his arms go around his wife.

"My love, my love," Phoebe was murmuring over and over again. "You are safe—you're alive and you are safe."

"Safe? Am I?" He spoke wonderingly, and then suddenly

he clutched her and broke into tears. "So many gone, Phoebe," he sobbed. "So many . . . so many . . . so many."

Lady Elizabeth moved forward and touched Vanessa on the shoulder. She nodded, and together they left the hall.

Late on the morning of June 19, Vanessa awakened with a feeling of deep depression. It had been a strange, tumultuous night, with bonfires in the streets and sounds of wild rejoicing.

The French had been routed and vanquished. The allies were victorious. The Duke of Wellington, the Iron Duke, had triumphed in that last conflict—the battle of Waterloo.

At what price?

Once he had regained his equilibrium, Johnny, fortified by cakes and brandy, had sat below in the dining room, talking of strategies and confrontations. He had wanted to talk, had refused to go to bed. Yet Vanessa had had the impression that he was unmindful of his audience, unmindful of anything save his experience during the last three days. He had spoken of death and destruction, of comrades cut down before his eyes, of French ferocity and German blunders, of uncounted losses.

The sound of his dull, uninflected tones was yet in her ears. The look in his eyes still haunted her. So might one who had returned from hell have looked, she thought. She hoped that it had helped him to speak of these horrors, but she could not be sure of that, for when he had reached the end of his account, he had said confusedly, "Why am I here? I should not be here. Woodforde was beside me when the shot was fired . . . why did it strike him and not me? My horse stumbled and nearly went down. That must be the reason it missed me. My horse stumbled, Vanessa, do you understand?" He had sounded apologetic, as if he were begging her to forgive him because Alan Woodforde, to whom she had denied a dance three nights ago, was lying amongst the dead on the blood-soaked ground of the battlefield.

"Why, why, why?" her brother had repeated, until Phoebe had put her arms around him and gently urged him to his feet.

He, who was usually so strong and decisive, had gone with her as docilely as a needful child.

The sound of sobbing startled Vanessa. She looked around her and saw Letty staring out of the window. "What's amiss?" she asked gently.

The abigail turned a frightened face toward her. "Oh, milady, did I wake you? I never meant to start blubberin' like this."

"You didn't awaken me." Vanessa slipped out of bed and came to her. "What is the matter?" she asked again.

"It . . . it's 'im. I 'ad a dream . . . an' I know there's somethin' wrong. We dream true, we does. The folk in our family, I means. My grandma, she be a Scotswoman an' she 'as the sight. Told me as 'ow my ma was goin' to die, an' she did. Told me lots o' other things, too. Told me I 'ad the sight. An' I seen 'im, all bloody-like."

"Who, my dear?"

" 'Im, my Tom wot's a dragoon." Letty turned a woebegone countenance toward Vanessa. Yet, at the same time, her expression was oddly defiant. "I met 'im 'ere. We walked out together, we did. 'E's a good man for all 'e's a soljer; they say as 'ow soljers 'as their way wi' a girl, but 'e didn't wi' me. 'E only kissed me afore 'e went off to fight. An' we was plighted, we was. 'You 'aven't got nothin' to fear for me, Letty,' 'e says. I'll come back to you, see if I don't.' " More tears fell. "An' last night, I dreamed I seen 'im in the street in one o' them wagons an' the blood were a-runnin' down the side o' 'is face." She stared at Vanessa. "Milady, I knows 'e's there. I got to go to 'im. Only, I . . . I knows you won't let me."

"Child . . ." Vanessa stroked Letty's tumbled hair back from her tear-swollen face. "Of course you must go. But you must not go alone."

"There's nobody'll go wi' me," Letty moaned. "Cook's scared outta 'er wits, an' Rose . . . they wouldn't go out on the streets for nobody, they tells me."

"I'll go with you," Vanessa said decisively.

"You, milady?" The girl looked at her in horror. "You

cannot go out there. Not wi' all them soljers wanderin' about. There's some which isn't sick.''

"I can and will go with you," Vanessa said staunchly. "And believe me, I know what you must be feeling. Help me to dress, please, and when it's possible, we'll leave. Is my aunt up yet?"

"She be gone already, milady."

"Where?"

"She's gone to see Lady Caroline."

"And my sister-in-law, is she stirring yet?"

" 'Aven't seen 'ide nor 'air o' 'er, not this mornin', nor 'is lordship neither."

"I see. Then we will leave now, as soon as I am dressed, Letty, my dear."

"Oh, milady, how can I ever thank you?" the girl sobbed.

"Hush, now," Vanessa said soothingly. "We must hurry and be away before my aunt returns."

A half-hour later, Vanessa, wearing a light muslin gown but with a hooded cloak wrapped about her, came into the square that lay before her house. Her teeth were tightly clenched as she made her way along a narrow path bordered on either side by the bodies of the wounded and, she feared, the dying. She had believed the view from her windows had primed her for what she must needs see, but she was not prepared for the gaping wounds, for the agony she saw written large on the pale faces of men, some of whom looked to be no more than boys of fifteen or sixteen. Their ranks were still being swelled by new arrivals. Officers, sagging in their saddles, rode past, and masses of footsoldiers stumbled after them. Beside her, Letty, staring about her in horror, began to sob.

"Do not weep!" Vanessa commanded curtly.

The girl stared at her openmouthed. Then she seemed to understand, and with an almost palpable effort she straightened her shoulders and wiped her eyes. "I'm that sorry, milady," she murmured.

"Water, water, gi' me water . . . ." a man mumbled.

Vanessa looked about her. There was no telling which of

them had asked for water. With the strong June sun beating down upon them, they were all in need of it. She glanced around the square, hoping to see some of the orderlies she had glimpsed from her window the previous day. She saw a few, but there were not enough to fill the pressing needs of this vast assembly, surely. That there were other wounded men in the main square of the city, she did not doubt. Perhaps the orderlies were with them. And would these poor unfortunates continue to lie here in desperate need of water in this all-pervading heat and with the flies buzzing about them? She could not let that happen.

Turning to Letty, she said crisply, "We'll need to fetch water. We can go to the public fountains, but we will need jugs or even buckets—some manner of container. I think . . ." She was suddenly filled with a sense of helplessness. Where would she find what she sought? And where could she seek someone to aid her? She could not minister to them alone. Letty might assist her, but there had to be others. She could recruit some of the servants, but Letty had told her they would not leave the house. Of course, she could insist, but if they were unwilling, they would be useless. However, if she were to speak to an orderly, perhaps . . . She glanced around her and tensed, seeing a small, slender boy in a faded red suit, garb that plucked a chord of memory.

He was moving among the wounded men, peering down at one and then another. Why? What did he have in mind? Had he come to rob them? There were such human scavengers upon the battlefield. Johnny had mentioned them last night. No, she did not believe him to be one of them, and why did she think she knew him? In that moment, he looked up, and Vanessa, seeing huge black eyes in a thin dark face, a Gypsy-like countenance, knew where she had seen him before.

"Gabriel," she whispered.

There was a throb at the base of her throat. If Gabriel were about, Philip, too, had to be nearby. Impulsively Vanessa started toward him, wishing that he were not so far away. Unfortunately, in that same moment he put an even greater distance between them, as he turned and walked swiftly toward a group of buildings at the end of the square.

"Gabriel," she called, but of course he would not be able to hear her amidst the moans and cries of some of the wounded men. "Gabriel!" she shrieked, and rushed after him.

"Milady!" Letty cried.

Vanessa came to a stop, and glancing over her shoulder at the girl, called, "Letty, dear, best follow me." Looking in the direction the boy had taken, she found him already some distance ahead. He did not have to step as carefully as she did. He was small enough to dart among the wounded men without touching them. She had to find some sort of pathway through them. It was not easy to pass them by. They called out to her, and one of them caught at her cloak.

"Help me," he pleaded.

"I will be back," she promised breathlessly. "I am going for help now." She looked into his face. He was one of the younger soldiers, a mere lad, a private in the dragoons. There was a rude bandage on his shoulder and a bloodstained rag around his head. "I will be back," she repeated.

Those words became almost a litany as she threaded her way across the square. Then she came to a startled stop, because Gabriel, having reached the buildings, suddenly turned a corner and was lost to view.

Vanessa quickened her steps, and finally coming to the place where he had vanished, found a narrow alley and, at the end of it, a flash of scarlet in a doorway. She ran after him and came into a long dark hall. To her consternation, Gabriel was nowhere to be seen. She became aware of a heavy odor of disinfectant and guessed that she was in some manner of hospital. Would she find Philip here? She stared about her, but it was impossible to see very much after the brightness she had just quitted.

"Milady . . ." Letty's quavering tone touched off a series of echoes.

Glancing quickly back, Vanessa saw the girl's dark shape framed in the bright aperture. "Letty, dear," she called.

"Wait outside for me, unless you'd like to see if you can find your friend."

"I'd best wait for you, milady," the girl said nervously.

"Very well. When I come back, I'll help you find him."

"Th-thank you, milady."

Turning back, Vanessa stared about her, wondering where Gabriel could have gone. She could see better now that her eyes were finally adjusted to the gloom. Moving on down the hall, she found a door. It was half-open. Had he gone in there? She hesitated a second. Then, pulling it open, she found herself on the threshold of a small chamber with a high ceiling and plaster walls seamed with cracks. Directly in front of her was another door, also partially open. Had Gabriel gone in there? Impulsively she stepped forward, then stopped, aware that she had stepped into a pool of water. Glancing down, she gasped in shock, seeing that the water was dark red and that her light kid slipper and a bit of the hem of her dress were stained. Inadvertently she cried out and moved back, feeling very queasy. She managed to steady herself, thankful that she was not prone to swoons.

In that moment she heard footsteps hurrying across the floor of the inner room, and the door was jerked open. "What's this?" a harsh voice demanded. "Who cried out?" A second later, he said in accents of disbelief, "You!"

Vanessa looked up and saw a tall man, his face glistening with sweat. His shirt was plastered to his body, and in one hand he was holding a thin knife, also stained with blood. A shudder coursed through her, but she quelled it, saying as calmly as she might, "Philip, I am glad I found you. I thought you must be here, since I saw Gabriel. I need your advice, please."

"My advice?" He stared at her incredulously, his face registering disbelief and a growing anger.

She understood his anger. He had heard her cry out and believed himself to be confronting a hysterical woman. She said hastily, "Out there in the square, water is needed, and a shade over their heads. Those poor men cannot continue to lie there in that relentless heat. I cannot provide them with shade, but I can and will bring water to them. I can wash their wounds as well. I need only to know where I can get someone to help me carry the containers that I must also have. And I will need a cup, too."

"Do not think of this!" he remonstrated. "You cannot deal with those men. They do not require your pity or your tears."

"I do not intend to give them either," she retorted. "I asked you if you know where I might find pitchers or buckets, something to hold water, for God's sake."

"You have had no experience in helping—"

"Have the camp followers, the whores that bind the wounds of soldiers?" she interrupted. "Have they had more experience than I?"

"They are not fine ladies," he said contemptuously. "They are not afraid of blood. They would never act on a whim and abandon them—"

"Philip," she broke in again, "I cried out because I had stepped into blood and 'twas not expected." She glanced at her shoe. "But I do not believe that is what has angered you. You are still hurt, and rightly so. However, this is not the time to plague you with descriptions of how I have suffered, how on the very night before the duel . . ." She paused and swallowed, feeling the sting of tears in her eyes. "Forgive me, I have promised that I will say nothing of that. But will you let your prejudices against me stand in the way of another willing and able pair of hands to help those hapless men out there, those thirsty men who crave the water you cannot take the time—nor should you—to provide?"

"They will not be out there much longer. You are not the only one who has offered to help them. Private citizens have come forward and have said they'll take them into their homes. It remains only to find the means to carry them there."

"Then let some of them come to us! We have rooms to spare!"

He still regarded her dubiously. "Have you consulted your family on this matter?"

"You must know that I have not, but I'll not need to consult them. My aunt will not raise any obstacles, nor will my brother or my sister-in-law, I can assure you. But at this present moment my main concern is with the needs of those men out there. Tell me where I can find pitchers and jugs and where I may draw water. I would return to my house and fetch them, but I would be wasting time, as I am wasting time now in this futile argument. Oh, Philip, do not be a fool. Help me so that I may help them, I beg you!" She stretched out her two hands and held them palms upward. "Please."

He was silent a moment, staring at her. He looked very weary, she thought compassionately. His eyes were bloodshot and his eyelids puffy. His face was thinner and drawn. She wondered when he had last slept, but that was not her concern, and judging from his attitude, he was not her concern now—nor, she thought desolately, would he be ever again. The hope she had experienced on the night of the ball could be forgotten, must be forgotten at this moment. She could not concentrate on personal matters, not when the men in the square needed her instant attention.

The silence between them was lengthening. Would he refuse her after all? If he did, she would search for others who might help her.

Philip said suddenly, "You have heard my arguments. Let them stand as warnings, too, if you are determined on this course."

Vanessa realized that she had made a crack in that chill facade. Deep inside of her, something rejoiced, but she said only, "I am warned. Where can I find the containers?"

"There are some upstairs. They are heavy, though. And you'll not know where to find them. I think I will have to go with you and fetch them. We are badly understaffed, you see. Little provision was made for this." There was a slight break in his cool voice, and a vulnerability in his eyes, but in another second it had vanished and he added crisply, "Come, then, we must hurry."

"No," she protested quickly. "It is not necessary that you

come with me. You are needed here. Let little Gabriel accompany me. He's with you, is he not?''

There was another pause as he stared at her. Then, with a curt nod, he turned away, moving into the other room. ''Gabriel,'' he called.

Vanessa heard the lad's piping voice and then Philip's low tones. How spent and weary he sounded, she thought, wishing that she could help him, work beside him, but she did not dare offer.

It was another few minutes before Philip returned. He brought Gabriel with him. ''He has agreed to show you where to find what you need.'' He favored her with a long doubtful stare. ''However, I cannot help but think—''

''Philip,'' she interrupted crisply, ''I am sure you have concerns far more pressing than to speak with me any longer.'' She glanced down at the boy and found a replica of Philip's doubts in his dark eyes. Unmindful of his obvious lack of trust, she added,''Come, Gabriel, I know you are a 'tiger,' but remember that Gabriel is an angel as well.''

She was rewarded by Philip's slight but genuine laugh and received an even greater reward as he tapped the boy on the shoulder, saying, ''Go along with the lady. I am depending on you to give her anything she requires.''

''Thank you, Philip,'' she said softly, and went quickly out of the room.

Four hours later, Lady Elizabeth, standing in the main hall of their house, facing a weary Vanessa, was fearful in her wrath and more caustic in her speech than her niece had ever known her to be. She seemed to have grown at least two feet as she glared at Vanessa.

''Can you imagine?'' she intoned. ''Can you possibly imagine what you have put us through? We—''

''Aunt Elizabeth,'' Vanessa interrupted, ''if you will please let me explain—''

As if she had not spoken, Lady Elizabeth continued, ''We returned to find you missing and no one amongst the servants any the wiser! Your brother, who is bone-tired and ought to be in bed still, is out *searching* for you, and Phoebe is frantic—and you come up here and tell me blithely that you have been to the public square, the *public square*, if you please, administering to those . . . those . . .''

"Soldiers," Vanessa supplied in a faint voice. It was an effort to stand there and receive her aunt's condemnation, when her head was aching so abominably and when her gown and cloak were soaked with sweat and plastered to a body aching in every limb from the effort of stooping over one man and then the next, and the next, giving them the water they had gulped so gratefully. Their gratitude had come near to breaking her heart, especially when she was doing so very little for them. Nor could she be sure they would have the care they needed, the care she had promised them. Even with Letty and little Gabriel also administering to them, it had taken four hours just to treat some fifty-three out of that hapless group. Her heart had ached when, out of sheer weariness, she was forced to stop. The memory of their stoic acceptance of pain, their halting words of gratitude, had served to cement her resolution.

"Soldiers," she repeated. "More than soldiers, Aunt Elizabeth, heroes, who have won the day for us. 'Twas not the duke and his officers alone. They could have done nothing without the troopers, the footsoldiers, and they lie there so patiently, so uncomplainingly, and they are so g-grateful for the slightest attention. A drop of water to wet their parched throats, a kind word, a promise we were not even sure we could fulfill—that was all we could provide. We could not bind their wounds, nor could we shelter them from the pitiless sun." She dashed a hand over her tearing eyes. "Aunt Elizabeth, Philip has told me that some people are taking them in. We must do so as well. We have room enough, room to spare. Please, Aunt Elizabeth, we must."

Lady Elizabeth did not answer immediately. She favored Vanessa with a sharp, suspicion-laden look before she said curtly, "I see. You've spoken to Philip. And you think that this is the way to impress him?"

Vanessa stared at her in an anger mixed with horror.

"No!" She stamped her foot. "No, no, no, 'tis not for Philip. It is for them, for *us*, because we owe it to those who fought so bravely. But for them, the French would be in this city. They would be raping and pillaging and . . . Good God, has nothing I have been saying made any impression on you? Do you think me naught but a scheming, lovesick—"

"My dear . . ." Lady Elizabeth's tone was softer now. "Calm down. You are overwrought, and no wonder, out there in that heat most of the afternoon. You must rest."

"No, I do not want to rest. I want you to give your permission. I want Johnny's permission to use whatever space we have to shelter these poor sick men."

"You have it."

Vanessa turned to find her brother standing in the doorway. He was pale and gaunt. He looked exhausted, but he spoke strongly. "You are right, Vanessa. Without them, we never could have succeeded in routing the French." He fixed his eyes on Lady Elizabeth. "We must make room for them."

"Yes"—Phoebe hurried down the stairs—"we must make arrangements. How many can we accommodate, do you think, Vanessa?"

Lady Elizabeth answered for her. "I would imagine that we could have four or five to a room. More if we move out the furniture from the second drawing room."

Vanessa said softly, "I do thank you."

"And now"—her aunt regarded her anxiously—"you must rest, my dear."

"No," Vanessa said determinedly. "We must make arrangements. 'Twill soon be dark. Perhaps we can move some of them in here tonight. They must not lie out there all the night through."

"You cannot think of that now, Vanessa," Lady Elizabeth protested. "You must not tire yourself."

"Tire myself?" she repeated incredulously. "They are more weary than I shall ever be!"

Vanessa had cause to remember those words as the days flowed into weeks, and she, with Phoebe, Letty, and even the

superior Rose, tended the twenty soldiers they were able to
harbor in two bedrooms, the second drawing room, and the
dining hall. It was a time of anguish as wounds festered and,
in some cases, gangrene set in before the handful of surgeons
could attend to the victims. There were moments when she
almost felt as if Death, wrapped in its shadowy cloak, waited
in the hall. Sleep became a matter of snatched moments in a
cot set in the larger drawing room, with an ear alerted for a
cry or a groan from boys of seventeen and eighteen, racked
by pain or by the terrors envisioned in nightmares.

She was also on hand to read to them or to write to distant
sweethearts or wives. She rarely saw Philip. He was wanted
in a hundred different places but, oddly enough, she did not
think of him. She had no time for dwelling on the past, and
the future, too, ceased to have any meaning for her. It was
only her present duties that mattered—though occasionally
the bleakness of her days was relieved by an unexpected
moment of joy, such as when a boy sunk in fever suddenly
rallied and recovered, or the morning Letty came to tell her
that Tom, recuperating in a house outside of town, had gotten
a message to her, telling her that his wound was not serious
and he would be with her soon. Mainly, however, day melded
into night and the sun rose on another day, and most of the
events had very little meaning for her save when Phoebe
came to bid her farewell and surprised her by explaining that
she and Johnny were bound for France.

"France?" she had repeated in surprise. "When?"

"We will be starting tomorrow." Phoebe had looked at her
with surprise. "But, Vanessa, my love, you cannot wonder at
that? We've talked of nothing else since the Duke of Wellington summoned him."

"The duke . . ." she had repeated vaguely. "I do not
remember."

"But you were delighted, you told us." Phoebe had looked
worried. "I do believe you ought to be getting more rest, my
dear."

"I do rest," she had responded, and had been annoyed
because the conversation was taking her away from more

pressing duties. Subsequently she had bade them Godspeed and forgotten them in tending her patients. She had also ignored Lady Elizabeth's entreaties that she take a few days away from her charges and rest.

"Is Philip resting?" she had demanded. "And the other women who tend the soldiers—are they resting? I cannot rest. They depend on me."

"You'll not be of much use to anyone if you become ill," her aunt had warned.

"I'll not become ill. I am extremely strong and healthy. And, Aunt Elizabeth, I am sure you must agree that I have enjoyed a lifetime of rest!"

On a night some two weeks after the departure of her brother and sister-in-law, Vanessa sat in a small room off the hall, one containing only a single cot. Its occupant was one Robert Brown, a youthful private separated from the others because he had been fever-struck and had cried out loudly, disturbing them.

She was writing a letter to his sweetheart, a girl named Barbara. As, at his slow halting dictation, she wrote about his hopes of seeing his love again and his regret at having lost an arm, Vanessa's heart ached. The fever had weakened him and it was believed that he might not see his Barbara again, which was why she had come to look in on him before going to bed.

"There you are, Robbie," she said, finishing the letter and sanding it.

"You're that kind, milady." The boy gazed at her wonderingly, as if he could not quite believe in her presence. His attitude reflected that of many whom she had tended. It had left her even more ashamed of a life spent in what seemed now to be an endless round of pleasure.

She did not deserve their gratitude, they who had given lives and limbs to preserve herself and others, equally undeserving. She thought of Philip and her eyes filled with tears as she remembered the foolish fears that had driven such a wedge between them, that had separated them forever—for what could a man of his integrity, his stature, want with her

who had been so cruelly doubting and who, despite the fact
that she had known him long enough to appreciate him, had
failed to stand by him when he most needed it?

Equally heinous had been her desire that he forsake his
profession, she who had had more than an inkling of what it
meant to him. She had actually preferred that he become a
useless member of the *ton*, a so-called "ornament" to society.

"I did not know," she whispered defensively.

She knew now, knew his dedication, his sympathy, his
kindness, as well as his nearly miraculous way with the sick.
She had heard from all sides about the cures he effected when
all hope had been lost. His very presence seemed to imbue
his patients with strength—and she would have come between
them! No, not in the long run. Their marriage would not have
lasted, she was sure of it. It would not have deserved to last.
If only she had met him now . . . if only everything that had
happened had not happened. She could think of only one
moment when she had acted as she should—and that was the
night she had wanted to stop the duel, the night that some
sense of the truth had touched her. She wished she might tell
him about that. He might not think so hardly of her then. Yet,
she had been turned from her purpose, and afterward . . .
She ran trembling fingers through her hair. She must come to
terms with the fact that she had forfeited his respect forever!

Yet, in the last few days, on the brief occasions when he
had been able to visit the men, he had seemed more like his
old self where she was concerned. Yes, he had been kinder,
but . . . She frowned. He might have been influenced by
Lady Elizabeth, who contended that she was working too
hard. That was why yesterday—had it been yesterday
evening?—he had said, "You must not deprive yourself of
rest, you know." His concerned gaze had lingered on her
face.

Vanessa ground her teeth. She had been angry at her aunt
for suggesting that she was some sort of fragile flower. She
had been well on the way to proving that she could stand up
to strain as well as, say, those camp followers he had praised.
She swallowed a lump in her throat. There were not many

patients in the house now. Many men had been sent back to England. Soon the others would go too and Philip's visits would cease and she would have no choice but to return to her former idle life.

Her aunt had spoken of joining Johnny and Phoebe in the house they had hired in Paris. They had plenty of room, they had written, and in that same letter they had included a glowing description of the city. Despite their defeat and the second banishing of Napoleon, to the Isle of St. Helena this time, the Parisians were welcoming. The Duke of Wellington was in fine fettle and much esteemed by his former foes. Many friends had come over from England, and life appeared to be a continuous round of pleasure.

"You must come, Vanessa," Phoebe had scrawled in a postscript.

Vanessa shook her head vigorously. She did not want to go. She had no desire to visit the modistes or attend fashionable soirees. She had had enough of that. Philip's dedication had inspired her. She wanted to work with him—at his side. She wished that she dared tell him that; but might he not believe it to be a mere ploy to win him back—a vain hope that!

The boy on the bed muttered, "Milady   "

Brought swiftly back to the present, she leaned over him. "Yes, my dear. Do you want water?"

"No, milady. The letter, will it go soon?"

"By the next post," she promised. Folding the paper, she rose and looked at him regretfully. He was so young and handsome. His Barbara must love him dearly. Stifling a sigh, she said, "She ought to have it in less than a fortnight. And now, Robbie, you must sleep." She took the candle from the table, leaving him in darkness. She was glad of that. Her eyes were wet, and if he saw them, he would be frightened.

"Good night, milady, and may God bless you," he murmured, drowsily now. He would be asleep before she left the room, she knew. She needed sleep herself. She was feeling a trifle light-headed, had indeed felt that way most of this day.

As she stepped into the hall, the light from her candle

shone on a dark cloaked shape standing motionless a few feet from the door. Fear shot through her. The candle in her hand wavered, projecting that silent figure's shadow on the wall—that figure that seemed to be the very personification of Death!

"Not yet," she whispered. "I pray you'll not take him yet. Let him live a little longer, please." Her hand trembled and the flame threw a taller shadow on the wall—then the candle was plucked from her hand. A strong arm encircled her shoulders and a stern voice demanded, "Why are you up at such an hour?"

"Philip . . ." she murmured, reality returning with the sound of his voice. "I thought   I feared   "

"My poor dear, I fear you are beyond thought   he said concernedly.

"I am not," she disputed, annoyed with herself for the weakness that seemed to be invading her limbs "Why are you here so late? You need your sleep "

"That is what I have just asked you," he said.   And it is time that you stopped driving yourself in this manner. You are overtaxing your strength. Now, come, I will take you to your bed now."

"I can walk," she protested as ne came toward her, arms outstretched.

"I disagree with you."

"And so do I," Lady Elizabeth said sharply. "You can see she is exhausted, can you not? I could hardly believe it when I did not find her in the drawing room. I hope you can talk some sense into her. That's why I sent for you."

Disappointment enveloped Vanessa. Her aunt had sent for Philip and that was the only reason he was here. She tried to edge away from him. "I repeat, I am able to walk. I am very healthy, you know."

"I am afraid that I cannot agree with that particular diagnosis," he said gently. "And since I am the physician. I must insist that you allow me to put you to bed."

She was too weary, too dispirited to protest, even when, rather than bearing her to her makeshift bed in the drawing room, he carried her up the stairs to her own chamber and, a second later, at Lady Elizabeth's direction, deposited her on the bed. "Now, you must sleep, my darling," he said insistently.

He had called her "my darling," she thought dazedly. She wanted to ask him if . . . But as her head touched the soft pillow, she could not remember what she had wanted to say. She could not seem to think at all anymore.

The sun was bright. It filled the room as Vanessa, opening weighted eyelids, looked disappointedly about her. She had been dreaming, she realized, dreaming very vividly about Philip. She had dreamed that he had come to her in the night and scolded her, telling her that she had done too much and must rest. He had also put his arms around her and kissed her, and it had seemed to her as if he loved her as much as he had before the separation for which she could blame only herself. Tears sprang to her eyes. It was not the first time she had dreamed of Philip, of the days when they had been happily looking forward to an April wedding. She had come to hate these visions that filled her nights and in the morning dissolved like dew on the grass with the first rays of sunshine. But she could not lie here and mourn the fact that she had awakened to cold reality. And why was she in her own room? She ought to be downstairs, close to the men she had been tending!

She sat up, and her head swam unpleasantly. She swallowed air bubbles and was reminded of those hours on shipboard when she had been so wretchedly seasick. Oddly enough, she felt very weak now, but that was to be expected. She had not eaten very much yesterday. She had not felt like eating. She reached for the pulley. She would ring for Letty and ask her for some tea. But she could not ring for her. Letty would be with Tom. And fortunately, she no longer needed to depend upon her abigail. She could dress herself now, and she could also get her own tea when she went downstairs.

She slipped out of bed, and again felt weak, weak enough to clutch the bedpost to keep from falling. She stood there a moment until the room, which seemed to be circling around her, righted itself. Then she made her way to the basin, and lifting the ewer, poured water in it. She felt a little better once she had washed her face and the upper part of her body. She would have relished a long warm bath, but she did not want to put the servants to the trouble of bringing up the water cans, when they too were occupied with those soldiers who still remained below. Going to her armoire, she selected an old round gown which was easy to put on—and without the buttons that were so hard to slip into their buttonholes.

Even after she was in her shift and gown and stood combing her hair, Vanessa still felt uncommonly weak. Her mirror showed her a distorted image—the glass had never been good. It seemed to her that she looked paler than usual. She really was not feeling her best, but despite that, she must go down to see poor Robbie and the others. There were a great many people dependent on her still. She bit down a sigh as she thought of Robbie. She would not need to spend many more nights at his side. She had a vague memory of coming out of his little room and seeing Philip and thinking that he was Death, when in reality he was a giver of life, was life itself, she thought proudly. He had worked so hard in these last weeks, not sparing himself at all. And last night he had been very kind to her, speaking to her so warmly, just as he had been wont to speak all those months ago. She could not dwell on that now. She was needed downstairs.

Coming out into the hall, she was amazed at how quiet it was. Even upstairs they could hear the plaints of the soldiers as they were recovering, and later, when they improved in health, their laughter and their chatter. She heard nothing at all.

Reaching the stairs and starting down them, she stopped as another wave of dizziness washed over her. She remembered her aunt scolding her, saying that she was overtired. Obviously she was and that was why she felt so weak. However, there would be plenty of time to rest once the soldiers were gone. Aunt Elizabeth wanted to go to Paris, but she would not go with her. She wanted to do something useful—she was not sure what, but she could not go back to her old life. It was important to . . . She stumbled and clutched the balustrade tighter. She was really very shaky. In fact, she felt the need to sit down, and did so, wondering what had come over her.

"M-milady!"

Vanessa started, and looking down, she saw Letty regarding her in openmouthed amazement. She flushed, and reaching for the balustrade, pulled herself up. "I felt a little weak, you see," she said apologetically.

"Oh, milady, you ought not to be down 'ere. They'll be that angry. You was dead asleep, so I thought . . . Oh, dear me!" She hurried out of the hall.

Vanessa stared after her. She was surprised and confused. She had overslept—that was obvious from the position of the sun in the heavens—but Letty's reaction had certainly been peculiar. Reaching the bottom of the stairs, she hurried into the small room where she had left her patient the previous evening and stopped short a step from the threshold, looking about her in dismay. Tears came into her eyes. His bed was gone. In its place stood the table that had been there before, and the chairs beside it. There was nothing in the chamber that indicated that Robbie had ever been there. He had died during the night and they had quickly put the room to rights. She remembered seeing that dark cloaked form in the hall—it had been Philip, but she had mistaken it for Death, and Death had been waiting beside him. More tears fell. He had been her special patient. Why had they not called her? She would have to write to poor Barbara. The letter, she suddenly thought. Had they sent his letter, his last letter to her? What had she done with it—had she left it on the hall table? She could not remember. She had been so tired. She hurried out of the room and started toward that table.

"Vanessa!"

She turned swiftly, and much to her surprise, found Philip striding toward her. He rarely visited them in the morning! He was looking angry, too. She flushed, remembering that she had overslept, but that did not matter—what mattered was Robbie's letter.

"The letter," she said distractedly. "I do not know what I did with it. I . . ." She paused, realizing that he would not know what she meant. She was having trouble collecting her thoughts this morning. "You see . . ." she began.

He strode to her side and put an arm around her. "What are you doing down here?" he demanded sternly.

"Robbie's dead, and the letter . . . the letter I wrote for him, I do not know where I put it. You must find it and send it . . . or I must."

"Robbie?" he said blankly.

"He's not in his room. That means he's dead, does it not? And it's all set to rights again. Barbara will want to have his last letter. I told him it would go out in the next post, but I do not know what I did with it. I had no notion that . . . that he would die during the night. Oh, please, you must help me find the letter!"

"What's amiss?" Lady Elizabeth hurried into the hall.

Seeing her, Vanessa was shocked. Her aunt seemed to have aged overnight. She was very pale and there were deep circles under her eyes, and surely there were lines she had never seen before. "Oh, Aunt Elizabeth . . ." She would have gone to her, but Philip was holding her. He was holding her close against him, she realized.

"Vanessa, my dearest girl." Lady Elizabeth came to her and, astonishingly, there were tears in her eyes. "Oh, thank God, thank God. But you should never have left your bed. It is too soon."

"Too soon?" Vanessa echoed. "But I overslept."

"She overslept," Philip said fondly, his hand caressing her arm. "That is all she knows."

Vanessa looked up at Philip and then at Lady Elizabeth. She said slowly, "I think I understand. I have been ill?"

"Yes, my poor child, very ill." Lady Elizabeth frowned. "We told you you were doing too much."

"Far too much." Philip's arm tightened about her. "You gave us a devil of a fright, my dear."

She loved the feel of his arm around her, loved the way he was looking at her, and then she gasped as he suddenly lifted her, and holding her against him, strode into the drawing room and put her on a couch. "You are not to go leaping about the house," he said sternly. "Not yet."

His eyes were not stern. They were soft, and now he smiled at her as he had been wont to smile months ago. She just wanted to lie there and look at him, but she had to know what had happened. "Have I been ill a long time?"

"A week and five days," Lady Elizabeth said.

"That long!" she exclaimed. "What was the matter?"

"Exhaustion and a low fever," Philip said.

"I do not remember."

"No, you would not," Lady Elizabeth said, crossly now. "And it was all so unnecessary. If you'd paid attention to me . . . You nearly drove yourself into the grave, my girl. If you'd not had the constant care of the best physician in the world . . ." Her voice quavered. She swallowed and said gruffly, "Well, you are more the thing now, my child. And I will leave you to your doctor." She went swiftly out of the room.

"The constant care?" Vanessa repeated. "You took time away from them to tend me? You should not have done that."

He was regarding her gravely yet tenderly. "We will rather concentrate on what you should not have done." He sat on the edge of the couch. "You are not fashioned from iron, my dear."

"I wanted to help. The letter . . ."

"The letter? Oh, yes, Robbie's letter. It was found and posted. I think it must have reached the girl at the same time he arrived to give her its contents in person."

"I . . . do not understand, or rather, I do." She clapped her hands. "He did not die!"

"He did not die, my dearest. Thanks to the fine nursing he received, he recovered entirely from the effects of the fever."

"Oh . . ." Tears rolled down her cheeks now. "Oh, I am glad. I was so worried about him."

"It seems you were worried about everyone save yourself, my love. You do not seem to know the meaning of moderation."

"Do you?" she asked.

"I do, because I must," he said gravely.

"I do not believe you. I have never seen anyone more selfless, dedicated, or devoted. And when I remember that I would have willfully caused you to abandon your calling. Oh, Philip, I am so ashamed of myself. Can you ever forgive me?"

"You did not understand. Consequently, my dearest, there's nothing to forgive."

"There is everything to forgive!" she cried passionately. "My failure to believe, to give you the support you needed, when you needed it the most. Oh, God, how can I ask you to understand my unreasoning jealousy? How can I ever explain it to you?"

"My dear love, there's no need to explain it. You have explained everything—including your effort to go to me on the night of the duel."

She gave him a startled look. "I couldn't have. I never . . ."

"You'd not remember, my dearest. However, you were a most talkative patient, and in common with many who are fever-stricken, you spoke with great clarity at times. And in common with such patients, you unburdened your soul."

"I did not. I—"

"You did, my love, my dearest love. I know all there is to know . . . nearly all."

"Nearly all?" She knew she was blushing, and wanted to look away from him. "I . . . do not understand."

"I am yet puzzled as to why you would believe me either engaged or married."

"Oh, dear, I do not like to tell you," she sighed.

"But you must," he pursued.

"I saw you with her, Lady McLean, when I first arrived in Brussels. You looked so happy and she was clinging to your arm. I saw her dancing with Sir Alastair that night, also. I thought that she and you . . . my jealousy, again, do you see? And, I also thought 'twas no more than I deserved. To lose you, I mean."

"Good God." He stared at her in utter amazement. "Have you so small an opinion of yourself, that you could see that child and imagine . . . ? Can you think that anyone knowing you could so easily forget you? I will not say that I did not try, when I thought all was hopeless, but you were already a part of me, one I could not remove by any surgical means."

"And you, my dearest Philip, were a part of me," she whispered.

"Then these two parts must be joined, do you not agree?"

"Oh, yes, most definitely, I do agree, but—" Her next words were stiffled by a kiss.

Several ecstatic moments later, Philip said, "I am going to take you to your room now."

"No." She stirred against him. "I want to stay here with you."

"I will stay with you," he said firmly.

"But . . ." she protested.

"Enough," he scolded. "Have you not learned in your weeks of nursing that the orders of the physician are never to be countermanded by the staff?"

"I have that." She nodded and joyfully abandoned her arguments.

There were rows and rows of beds. Her back was aching, but at the thought of those who needed her, she went on, giving them a word of encouragement, a glass of water, anything she could provide to soothe them. And there was Letty with Tom! Sir Alastair suddenly strode beside her. That was odd! She thought he had retired to the Highlands with Mathilde after Waterloo.

Waterloo?

She did not like to think of Waterloo, but she was in the square now and Philip was frowning at her. She went toward him, but he receded, seeming to fade. And now she saw Maria, glaring at her.

"You cannot have him, Vanessa!" she shrilled. "He's mine!"

"You're wrong, Maria," she said gently. Poor Maria, she

looked so plain and dumpy now. Maria faded, too, and there was Felicia. When had Felicia come to Brussels? Would she be giving one of her balls? The Duchess of Richmond had given a ball . . . she would not welcome competition. She moved restlessly and felt arms clasp her, and it was Philip again.

"Vanessa," he was calling her. "Vanessa."

"Do not let me take you away from your work. They need you more than I. But no one could need you more than I, Philip. . . ." She was confused. There was Gabriel in his red livery, but he was grown taller and married and their head coachman.

"Vanessa, love," Philip said in a louder tone of voice.

She stirred and opened her eyes, staring about her. Brilliant sunshine filled the huge bedchamber. She tried to move her head, but her hair was caught. It had grown very long and her husband did not want her to cut it and now he was lying on it. "I was dreaming," she said.

He sat up, freeing her hair. "You certainly were . . . of Waterloo, again."

"How did you know?" Before he could answer, she added, "I must have been talking in my sleep."

"Very coherently," he agreed fondly. " 'Tis well you are a good and faithful wife. Just think if you were not—with the way you talk in your sleep, I would undoubtedly have grounds for a divorce! And how did you come to dream of Maria?"

"I do not know—save that she is coming to the hospital here, for her fifth lying-in. It's base of me, I know, but I am glad we'll not be present and 'twill be Alden who will see to her. She always looks at me so angrily."

"Poor Maria, I wish I could convince her not to eat so much." Philip shook his head. " 'Tis not good for her to be so heavy when she's so little, but she'll not heed my advice."

"Advice is not what she wants from you. Poor woman, I never saw anyone lose her looks so quickly."

"Yes, 'tis a pity," he agreed. "We'd best get up, my darling. It will soon be time to leave for the concert."

"You say that so casually," she giggled. "As if we did

not need to travel nearly two hundred miles for that concert. I hope you do not mind.''

''No, I shall be glad to see Phoebe and Johnny and the children, as well as to hear your aunt's latest protégé. Furthermore, I think one ought to go to London at least once every two years, if only to give your friends and the rest of the *ton* a glimpse of my most beautiful wife.''

''Who is most reluctant to leave her two lovely children, not to mention our new dispensary, your hospital, and Yorkshire in general.''

''Come, come, my angel, if you do not put in an appearance once in a while, they'll think I've mesmerized you.''

She put her arms around him, and pressing her lips against his ear, whispered, ''And have you not, my dearest?''

About the Author

Ellen Fitzgerald is a pseudonym for a well-known romance writer. A graduate of the University of Southern California with a B.A. in English and an M.A. in Drama, Ms. Fitzgerald has also attended Yale University and has had numerous plays produced throughout the country. In her spare time, she designs and sells jewelry. Ms. Fitzgerald lives in New York City.